Advance Praise for

THE FIFTH LASH

& Other Stories

"These new stories from Shivani (*Anatolia & Other Stories*), many set in Pakistan, parse the disconnect between public and private behavior, and the desires that must be muted in order for people to survive. In "Love in a Time of Communication," Javed, a young worker at General Tires in Karachi, tries to get his parents a phone line while dreaming of love for himself. Social mores come into play often, such as in "The Abscess of the World," which follows David, an American student, to Karachi to feed his fascination with Islamic law, while his Pakistani roommate at Princeton, Agha, looks to leave his past behind and work on Wall Street. In "The House on Bahadur Shah Zafar Road," the course of young Abid's life, full of A-levels study, dreams of Oxford, and first love, contrasts sharply with that of the family's young servant girl who has become pregnant. "The Censor" traces the constantly changing rules about what is or isn't permissible on the public airwaves; numbered paragraphs offer first-person accounts such as "The new rules of kissing are, it's allowed if it's done Indian-style.... But no American kissing." Shivani is a perceptive writer who puts his finger on the contradictions his characters navigate to survive daily life."

—*Publishers Weekly*

"This collection about the lives of Muslims all over the world—many of them practicing and pious—is bold, raw, raunchy, and funny. Geographic schizophrenia, ontological dyspepsia, matters of mangled identities, issues of class and gender and yes, sex, are connected with actual, lived Islam in a genuinely entertaining and informed manner. But these stories go further. They ask the reader to consider the possibility that when it comes to contemporary portraits of Muslims, fiction might actually be a much better medium than memoir, than non-fiction, than journalism, and even film. That confidence renders this a most original work."

> —Ali Eteraz, author of *Children of Dust: A Portrait of a Muslim as a Young Man*

"Anis Shivani's stories have both style and vigour. The Fifth Lash is an intriguing, intelligent, provocative collection by a tough, confident storyteller."

> —Aamer Hussein, author of *Turquoise*

THE FIFTH LASH

& Other Stories

Also by Anis Shivani

Anatolia & Other Stories (2009)

Against the Workshop: Provocations, Polemics, Controversies (2011)

My Tranquil War and Other Poems (2012)

THE FIFTH LASH

& Other Stories

Anis Shivani

ISBN 10: 1-936196-04-2
ISBN 13: 978-1-936196-04-3
LCCN: 2012933131

C&R Press
812 Westwood Ave.
Suite D
Chattanooga, TN 37405

www.crpress.org

Cover art: Tapu Javeri, *Ghulam*

For Mehnaaz

Who Set Me Free

CONTENTS

LOVE IN A TIME OF COMMUNICATION

J aved has three hours to kill before his appointment with the divisional engineer for phones. At eight this morning he arrived at the local telephone exchange, and for the first time in several visits succeeded in paying the registration clerk fifty rupees, after which he paid the peon at the front gate another twenty, which got him entrée into the main offices. Then he was able to pay the recording clerk fifty more rupees, and so on along the chain until at eleven he saw an assistant to the divisional engineer, who got him the coveted appointment with the divisional engineer himself.

It's been three years since he applied for a phone line. For himself, he doesn't mind so much not having a phone, but with elderly parents at home, he'd like them to be able to call him at work in case there's an emergency. They suffer from nothing worse than arthritis and stomach disorders, but one can never be too careful.

It's the last day of his one-week of vacation for the year. He's lucky to get any time off; people who don't work for multinational corporations can't dream of such privileges. He gets insurance at little cost for his motorcycle, which he doesn't mind driving the twenty miles to work. General Tires also offers insurance that lets him have his parents see doctors at private hospitals. Last year, when Javed needed a hundred thousand rupees to round out his only sister's dowry, the company helped him get a loan. It'll be a long time before he pays it off, but it saved him.

In the corridor outside the divisional engineer's office is a row of potted plants, which he's already seen watered twice. A maali goes around taking care of the flora inside the dark building, while the plants and trees in the courtyard and outside the building don't seem worth his attention.

Javed sits on an uncomfortable wooden stool, with nothing to rest his arms on. A white ceiling fan whirls slowly, causing no air to stir. Unlike other government buildings where the din of small children is a constant backdrop driving him insane, here business is conducted quietly. He wonders if dressing well—he has his red tie on, and his new black shoes—will make the divisional engineer expect a bigger bribe to grant a phone connection.

Across from Javed sits an unremarkable-looking young woman, a string tightly tying her head covering. It's not a burqa by any means, but a token veil of modesty for someone without a fanatical mind. Her sky blue kameez and white churidar pajama are cloaked in a loose black tunic, another concession to modesty. She has a long nose, what looks like a bruise on one cheek, and weepy eyes. In his constant state of sexual agitation, Javed would expect himself to give more than a cursory look to this woman, especially because she is alone, but recently he's promised himself to suppress predatory thoughts.

A woman named Feroza, who used to be the personal secretary of his former supervisor at the company, has been the bane of his existence lately. Educated at convent school, she spoke flawless English. Her parents were disengaged from her life, and she had no flock of irresponsible siblings or manipulative relatives to worry about. She wasn't a beauty by normal standards—the wart by her nose, and her unusually arched eyebrows, took care of that—but Javed found her most attractive.

They'd started congregating with the same group of people at the company cafeteria for lunch and tea, then progressed to visiting Clifton beach and the amusement parks on weekends. Feroza spoke of her desire to settle down with a respectable, educated man, one who would tolerate her own career interests, and Javed interpreted that as a strong signal of interest in him. But she was only testing—or teasing—him, because at the end of a long courtship, she announced flatly in the cafeteria, in front of other people, that she was going to be engaged to the physically handicapped son of a family friend. Javed hadn't spoken to her since, and hadn't flinched when news came through the grapevine that Feroza had resigned from the company.

Javed catches the woman across from him staring. He looks back. She seems about to begin a conversation with him when a fidgety older man, shrunk as a dried shrimp, shuffles up to her, and starts complaining in a high-pitched voice about how they're being given the runaround again, and about the futility of waiting for the divisional engineer.

"Do you need a phone urgently?" Javed asks the newcomer, keeping his gaze focused on the woman.

The man isn't sure for a moment if he should reply.

Then animation floods his face. "Oh yes, a phone is of the utmost necessity in these times. Without it, no personal or commercial business can be transacted. It's of the utmost necessity."

He wanders into a rambling narration assessing dependence on modern technology, both praising and denigrating it. Javed looks from time to time at the girl, who seems bored by her companion's disquisition. Is he her father? Perhaps an uncle.

"Manager sahib will see you now." The imperious announcement comes from a pagree-wearing chowkidar, with rounds of ammunition and a rifle attached to his beige tunic.

The young woman's chaperone stops speaking in mid-sentence and starts walking toward the open door of the office, but the chowkidar halts him with open palm, and points to Javed instead. "Him."

Javed is cursing the malignant forces ruling the world as he rides at breakneck speed along Shahrah-e-Faisal to get to Gulshan-e-Iqbal. Twice he has barely avoided ramming into the rears of minibuses, as the drivers of the monstrous vehicles have slammed their brakes without warning.

It's a hot Sunday morning, and he's headed to the home of Mr. Majeed, the man who turned out to be the uncle of the morose girl at the telephone exchange. Except he no longer thinks of her so dismissively. The fantasy has built up over the last two weeks of anticipation. In his mind, she's now a failed romantic of the first order, someone who would easily drop out of her master's program in English literature to take care of sick parents, someone who was once beautiful and sassy but now shows the cares of the world in the changes marking her face. Who was it that said you could tell a person's biography by the face? Mr. Majeed, vocal and self-centered at the telephone exchange, now seems to Javed a benevolent older person doing his part for the happiness of the younger generation.

Javed's parents say they're delighted he was able to get the phone connection so easily, although he suspects they're just saying that to make him feel good. The connection hasn't been turned on yet, but a technician is supposed to visit any day now to start wiring. He'll need a small bribe, but it'll be nothing compared to what divisional engineers expect from customers. The divisional engineer Javed met had engaged in chitchat, telling Javed about his cousin who also worked at General Tires, letting him in on some scandals that Javed hadn't been aware of in his own company. Then he signed Javed's dog-eared original application from years ago and pronounced, "Show this to the clerk at the front desk. You'll have your phone in a matter of days." He stood up to shake Javed's hand briskly.

As Javed went out of the office, so did the chowkidar, who'd been lurking in the background. The chowkidar told the waiting man and woman—Mr. Majeed and his niece Masooma—to come back another time, since the divisional engineer was through for the day. Mr. Majeed launched into a condemnation of government officers who were really the servants of the people, whose salaries came from hardworking folks like himself, but who acted as if they were lords and honest citizens serfs without rights. Javed could tell that Mr. Majeed was saying these things only because they were expected of him; to go away without uttering a complaint would have made him lose face. The lack of real anger in Mr. Majeed pleased Javed.

As they left the building, they fell into conversation, Masooma trailing politely behind. Before long Mr. Majeed was asking Javed to lunch at his home. Javed assumed this was about him and Masooma, and the girl would undoubtedly be present.

While Mr. Majeed was cranking up his old white Daihatsu, Javed probed Masooma's face, but couldn't read her reaction to the plans.

"How much did the divisional engineer want?" Mr. Majeed rolled down the window of his car to ask the final question.

"Nothing."

"Nothing?"

"Nothing."

A flicker of a smile crossed Masooma's lips as she nodded at him from the back of the car.

Since that triumphant moment, his days and nights have been full of speculation. His limbs feel strong as he maneuvers the motorcycle around potholes and fallen branches and burnt tires and donkey crap along the narrow streets of Gulshan that lead to Mr. Majeed's house.

He's greeted by Mr. Majeed's wife, Sabira, an unexpectedly modern woman with a fashionable bob, no dupatta, and revealing yellow shalwar kameez. Javed dares to imagine she isn't wearing a bra underneath, but is pinched by a feeling of disloyalty toward Mr. Majeed, his benefactor, and stops pursuing that line of thought.

Mr. Majeed turns out to have once been a prize-winning journalist for the leading Urdu newspaper, until clashes with his editors became too aggravating for both sides, and he quit in a blaze of glory. His colleagues from the paper recall him as one of the few who refused to fall into the trap of self-censorship, even when it came to news where the average person could easily distinguish the embellishments of the state. For the last fifteen years, Mr. Majeed has been an advertising freelancer, offering his services to foreign advertising agencies that need translators, valuing his mastery of local idioms and trends. Mr. Majeed complains about the dull life of an advertising "medium," as he calls himself, but Javed detects no real tone of disenfranchisement.

Masooma is not in evidence. Yet the elaborate preparation—he can smell kebabs and biryani from the kitchen—must be to bring the two together. A young man like himself, with a decent job and education, shouldn't have to be in this position. But General Tires is not the place to meet life partners. He's never heard of a couple of his class and standing who've met at work, then married. At most, short-lived affairs ensue. The best women, women you expect to come through during crises and failures, are hidden away, out of sight except for the precious few who know them. Maybe Masooma is such a person.

Mr. Majeed is in no hurry to get lunch started. His inspiration for journalism, he tells Javed, was the war of 1965, when both parties told blatant lies. "War propaganda is only the extreme form of propaganda. Everything is propaganda."

Mr. Majeed's trendy, secular wife joins them in the living room. Sabira seems to be a woman who can rapidly dispose of cooking or other onerous chores. She scratches her knees, occasionally correcting Mr. Majeed's recollection of figures and dates. No children are in evidence. It's getting late. Lunch hour is long past.

It's been difficult to get a day off, but Javed is able to swing it when his supervisor agrees to let him come in on Saturday to catch up. Javed is riding to the telephone exchange on another weekday morning.

General Tires has been abuzz with activity since it's been announced that the military will be contracting with the company for its needs, rather than importing directly from abroad. Newly minted American MBAs have been prowling the company headquarters, in search of inefficiencies and vulnerabilities. Javed has talked to a couple of them, in the cafeteria, where they hang around and talk loudly to complete strangers, as though they're at a party, not the workplace. They seem stupid and ignorant about local conditions.

A couple of months have gone by, and the technician who should have hooked up the phone line has never shown up. Javed's parents have said they don't care about the phone one way or the other, but it's become a matter of pride with Javed. At work, everyone—even those far lower on the seniority scale than him—has a phone. Feroza had two phone lines.

Mr. Majeed calls him once a week at work. He got a phone line at home by asking the head of one of the advertising companies he works for to facilitate it. It took only a week that way.

From Mr. Majeed, Javed learns that Masooma had been invited to Mr. Majeed's house for lunch that day, and she'd agreed, but backed out at the last minute. Masooma says she has to deal with an unresolved situation: a broken engagement, without the loose ends tied up. The match had been the idea of her mother, Mr. Majeed's sister, a woman with a history of bad decisions. Masooma's intended was once a versifier for the People's Party. That told you all you needed to know about him. He's been working on his doctorate in sociology at Karachi University for many years. After getting cold feet shortly before the wedding, he's again making advances toward Masooma. To Mr. Majeed's surprise, the jilted Masooma is listening. There's no question about it, she should dismiss the dishonorable man at once.

In this way, Javed has assumed something of a similar role as that of Mr. Majeed in relation to Masooma: interested older observer, wishing the best for her, hoping and praying, but knowing deep down that the case is lost, because young women, headstrong and fed on Western ideas, will do what they want. But Mr. Majeed has dropped enough tantalizing hints about Masooma to keep Javed interested. She's been a champion runner. She's made the quickest recovery from a serious case of TB Mr. Majeed has ever heard of, through force of will. His wife Sabira has convinced him that Masooma is an essayist of the highest caliber, able to break down the nuances of Iqbal's poetry like an accomplished metaphysician, although Mr. Majeed hasn't been able to make Masooma show him her writings.

The promise is hanging in the air that there'll be another attempt at a meeting soon. Javed imagines calling Masooma from home and talking to her for hours every night, once his parents have gone to sleep. They could recite poetry to each other. Tell one another their most secret dreams and fears. But then the visage of Masooma's jilting lover looms up—Javed imagines him looking unsavory like a hippie but also handsome like a nineteenth-century North Indian prince—and destroys his vision.

The traffic on the city streets is worse than usual. There's a new restlessness among the bus and cab and rickshaw drivers, as though they're assured of imminent destruction—nuclear annihilation or something of that order—and don't care if they kill pedestrians on their way to wherever they're flying. Rude curses flow from the mouths of well-dressed men and women, even the elderly.

He imagines Masooma clutching his back with her small hands while he rides the motorcycle at exhilarating speed. She's fearless behind him. Her beautiful red-hued hair flies in the wind, attracting passersby who envy the young couple. Her hair, when the odious covering is removed for good, as Javed will surely coax her into doing, turns out to be her most alluring feature. When they ride on the wide boulevards toward Clifton beach or Manora island, she sings mehndi songs in an affectionate voice, songs he vaguely knows because they saturate the air, but whose every word Masooma remembers.

In the middle of this sweet dream, Javed is nearly run over by a speeding minibus, whose driver shouts ethnic slurs at him, while the passengers in the bus appear happy at Javed's humiliation, malicious grins on their faces.

When he arrives at the telephone exchange, he's

confronted by a line stretching to the end of the street. Flies buzz over garbage piles, and women in burqas with unruly children try to keep them away from the filth. The clerk at the registration desk, instead of the usual pleading by the customer, followed by bargaining for the bribe, says apathetically, "Hundred rupees to go inside." Javed is so furious he shells out the cash without protest.

Inside the exchange, the rates for all the entry points have been doubled. He pays silently. When he makes it to the corridor outside the divisional engineer's office, he realizes he's left at home the slip of paper with instructions for the technician to hook up his connection. No matter, the divisional engineer will recall him.

He waits outside like before, almost expecting Masooma to appear with Mr. Majeed. The only other customers waiting are a pair of fat, bald brothers in their forties, who sing Punjabi wedding songs, challenging each other for exact memory of the words.

Javed plans on telling the divisional engineer about the goings-on at General Tires, how the foolish American technocrats are clueless about local business culture. Money is not always the greatest motivator for Pakistani businesspeople. But for the visitors, everything is quantifiable. Javed laughs, recalling the blank faces of the Americans, empty of any signs of wisdom or worry, and smoothes the knees of his pants. He hasn't ironed carefully enough.

"You can't see the divisional engineer." The chowkidar from before seems to spit in his face.

"I can't? Why can't I? I've been here for hours."

"Your original file has some problem. It was discarded. You'll have to start the process over again. Go down to registration and get a new application. Twenty rupees."

Javed isn't sure if the twenty rupees is the amount he's supposed to pay for the application downstairs, or if it's payment for the chowkidar's information.

"I must see the divisional engineer." Javed names him, as if it were a talisman.

The chowkidar smiles. "He's been transferred to the downtown exchange. A long-awaited promotion. We have a new divisional engineer now. He's foreign-trained. You won't be able to get anything past him. Fix your application."

The chowkidar turns around to disappear into the office.

Javed doesn't even get to his motorcycle, before deciding the phone isn't worth it. Had he not been trained well by his uncomplaining parents, he would have pitied the idiots standing in line to get their phones, suffering the heat and flies.

THE ABSCESS
OF THE WORLD

"Tea?" Maulana Haroon asked David, and without waiting for an answer, commanded an unseen factotum in the adjoining room, "Bring some tea!" It would be David's fifth or sixth cup of the day, but to say no to a host was unimaginable. He was glad he didn't have to pick from a baffling menu as in America. It was plain old milky tea each time, though the more adventurous added cinnamon sticks or cardamom pods.

"So you come seeking—shall we say—information of a certain kind?" asked Maulana. "The type you can't get from books?"

"That's correct."

Maulana had been prepped about David's motive in wanting to see him this afternoon at the Baghpati Madrassa in Korangi, an industrial area of Karachi. David had gone through layers of deputies and administrators and secretaries, quite like making an appointment with a Princeton professor popular in Washington, D.C. or on the talk show circuit. Each layer, however, had been progressively easier to penetrate. They'd have a good bit of time between Zuhr and Asr prayers to go over David's questions.

"Your Princeton professors have run out of things to tell you?"

Maulana cracked a laugh, and David smiled along, although it made him uncomfortable. He respected his teachers back home. It wasn't that they'd exhausted their fund of knowledge. That was hardly the case. But he did hunger for immediacy, to be able to localize bits of knowledge in their authentic context. Words on paper were fine, but he wanted to experience first-hand the sweat and tears of people whose lives gave the words meaning. You had to be a believer first, to penetrate the reality of a text, or at least get close enough to true believers.

"There's something to be said for the direct student-teacher relationship," David clarified.

He'd made it sound as if Princeton didn't have a distinguished tutoring system. What he'd meant was that he wanted a teacher to push him beyond the limits of his imagination—Maulana Haroon may not be the one, but someone had to do this before he turned twenty-two—unlike his Princeton professors who were gentle with him as though breaking in a homely virgin in the antebellum South.

"Indeed there is," Maulana nodded.

A nattily attired boy, about ten, sporting a Michael Jackson T-shirt and baggy Calvin Klein jeans, matched with a Beatles moptop, walked in with the tea. He had a front tooth missing, which made him look all the more endearing. He smiled shyly at David.

"Hello there," David said. "What's your name?"

"Iqbal," Maulana interjected. "My son. My only son.

He wants to go to America as soon as he passes the A levels."

"What's your favorite subject?" This was a ritual question in Pakistan. Even adults were always being asked what their favorite subject was, as though everyone were an autodidact, pursuing botany or calculus after the kids were seen off to school or the day's insurance sales quota was filled.

"Islamiyat," Iqbal said, hesitating

"The study of Islam. He feels obliged to say this, because I'm his father, and a well-known ustad, but it's not true. What's really your favorite subject?"

"I want to be a musician." Iqbal smiled goofily at David. "Have you ever met Michael Jackson?" Iqbal had only a soft accent. He probably watched a lot of American television on Star TV and other satellite channels. Perhaps he took private lessons from a tutor with the right accent, a much sought-after service in this country.

"Michael Jackson? No, but I did meet Madonna once. In a bookstore, signing her children's book. I'm not sure if it was a book with pictures or just words."

"Does everyone in America know how to sing and dance?"

"I wouldn't say so. I'm really bad."

"The young man is here on business," Maulana said gently. "We shouldn't keep him with this chitchat."

"That's all right, I don't mind."

Iqbal settled down next to Maulana, crossing his legs in the classic position, which David hadn't mastered despite practicing in front of the mirror at his hosts' house in Defense Housing Society. Maulana patted Iqbal's head. Iqbal became silent, invisible, unlike an American boy his age. David's theory professors talked up the androgynous ideal, but how would they react if they saw Pakistani middle-class girls rebuking servants in public and going toe-to-toe with men in political debate, or Pakistani boys holding hands and showing affection toward each other? In Pakistan, the gender-bending seemed unintentional, pervasive, integrated in normal behavior.

David could see the chirping sparrows lined up on the ancient trees in the courtyard. All day, the different species of birds kept up a competitive medley. The sputter of the rickshaw, the pleading of the vegetable seller, and the wail of the muezzin meant that there was never a moment of silence.

Maulana, also sitting cross-legged on his soft white cushion spread, had the comfortable bearing of someone used to authority from an early age. The books lining the shelves of his visiting room were the usual suspects: Tabari and Ibn Katheer and Maududi's tafseers of the Qur'an, the Sahih Bukhari and Muslim collections of hadith, and the well-known compilations of fiqh, particularly from the Mughal emperor Aurangzeb's time. The madrassas followed the Dars-e-Nizami, established in India in the eighteenth century, and closely adhering to the medieval curriculum. Instead of modern astronomy and chemistry, they studied the musings of ninth- and tenth-century Arab scholars, as though Baghdad were still the intellectual capital of the world.

The only unexpected items on the shelves were commentaries by Ibn Taymiyah, the thirteenth-century Wahhabi scholar, the puritan whose thought had set off wave after wave of fanatic repression on the Arabian peninsula. In South Asia, two schools of thought competed for dominance. The Barvelvis, closer to pantheism, were laid-back, mystical, personalized, concrete, emotional, indulgent, agnostic, and eclectic. The Deobandis, closer to Wahhabism, were doctrinaire, rational, abstract, intellectual, censorious, literalist, and jurisprudential. Maulana Haroon belonged to the more accommodating Barelvi school, which was why David wanted to see him. Barelvis didn't care as much about propagating theology as winning hearts and minds through communal ecstasy. The Taliban, the jihadis, the Islamic political parties, on the other hand, drew inspiration from the Deobandis.

Maulana's cell phone rang. "Excuse me," he said, holding up his pudgy finger, snapping open his Motorola, and engaging in a gentle conversation with his wife. "On to business then," Maulana said upon concluding.

David decided not to consult his notes for this interview. They distracted both him and the interviewee. "As I wrote in my letter a few months ago, I'm writing a senior thesis on the evolution of modern Islamic law. The Hanafi branch, and its stance on modern commercial technologies and financial instruments. Is Islam compatible with capitalism?"

"You should read Maxime Rodinson on that."

"Rodinson! If I wanted to read Rodinson, I'd have stayed at Princeton. What do you think I could get from him?"

"He speaks in a language you can easily understand. The Prophet of Islam was a merchant by profession. Early Islam was entrepreneurial. The later accretions, some of the rigid prohibitions of interest—these are not central to the dogma."

"I know, it's the issue of interest I want to get away from. It's been overdone. I'm more interested in economic development."

"If you talk to anyone in Pakistan about Islam and economics, they'll push you into the dilemma of riba," Maulana warned.

Riba was Islam's term for interest. Most scholars believed that interest in any form was prohibited. Classical scholars had maneuvered around the ban with any number of legal stratagems. Today's scholars were less forgiving. Reformists wondered how you could have a modern civilization without interest. These debates got repetitive. David's whole point in visiting Pakistan was to acquire a sense of what was at stake in Islam becoming more compatible with economic modernization.

"Rodinson, Watt, Gellner, Gibb—wherever you find a nugget of truth, you must seize it," Maulana continued.

"But what about this!" David indicated the thick gold-spined books lining the shelves, in Arabic, Persian, and Urdu.

"This too, this too. Whatever form of argument appeals to you, stay with it and pursue it till the end." Maulana whispered into Iqbal's ear to get something to eat. "You can explore things from a native point of view, but there must be a context, a purpose. You can write fifty books, as scholars do, but…"

"But what?"

"Nothing. I admire your courage. I'm impressed you're interested in Islam, an exotic religion, although I'm sure at Princeton there are people from all over the world. Still, how many Pakistanis would give up a summer to study Christianity in some obscure part of the world?"

"Pakistan is not obscure. It's the fifth or sixth largest country in the world."

"Also a dangerous spot. Very dangerous. You must be careful, not take any unnecessary risks. Look, read as much as you want, but pick a specific topic. Narrow down your thesis. Come to me if you have questions. Maulana Zakaria's urs is on the first Monday of next month. Try to come."

This was exactly as his Princeton professors advised him. The urs, or anniversary, was typical of the Barelvi tradition's emphasis on saints venerated almost as much as the Prophet himself. There was danger in Karachi, but he could handle it. The party of the Muhajirs, refugees who'd resettled from India after partition in 1947, was constantly clashing with the local Sindhis, who felt outcompeted in education and jobs by the more sophisticated Muhajirs. Several people got shot on the streets every day, acts of terrorism the Urdu tabloid press inflamed and glorified.

"There's so much junk out there," David complained. "Junk information, I mean. Schacht and the rest." Orientalist scholarship treated Islam as a deviant cult, an imitation of Judaism on the part of the wily Muhammad, not a respectable religion in itself. A lot of Orientalist effort over the nineteenth and twentieth centuries had gone into proving the fabricated nature of the Qur'an, the hadith, and other sources of Islamic authority.

"You must study even Schacht and Goldziher with a fine-toothed comb, to see the flaws in their logic. If this is truly what interests you."

What did interest him? His parents were both physicians. Before landing at Princeton, he could never have predicted the academic path he'd follow. He'd taken Arabic for three years, and had a good feel for it. He probably spoke it better than Maulana, because South Asians spoke Arabic with an appalling accent. He and his girlfriend Sandra planned to work for the State Department; the importance of the Islamic world would only grow for America. There was something beautiful and pristine about Islamic civilization, apparent as soon as one stood before a mural in Cordoba or a tomb in Isfahan. Islam was the purest of religions, with the fewest intermediaries. Just one God, and the believer. Very Kierkegaardian. There was pleasure in pursuing this ultimately democratic concept to see where it led.

A quiet new boy brought the food—vegetarian snacks any Princeton health freak would have appreciated.

David and Maulana agreed on the flexibility of Islamic law, the opportunity to exercise ijtihad, or free thought, based on principles of analogy and precedent, rather than adhering to blind and slavish imitation, taqlid.

Iqbal didn't appear for the rest of the conversation, but when David slipped on his sandals outside the doorway and set off on the dusty path toward his borrowed Volkswagen, he saw Iqbal waiting next to the car.

The idea to visit Pakistan for first-hand research had been Agha's. His roommate was an economics major headed for Wall Street, but he had sympathy for David's abstract pursuits. "It can't hurt to tell the world the truth about Pakistan," Agha proposed. "We're not all a bunch of radicals burning effigies of American presidents." David objected, "I'm not interested in Pakistan, only in Islam." Agha countered, "The truth will reveal itself this way." From lending David his suits and ties, to accompanying him at conferences in New Haven and Cambridge, Agha acted as David's concerned older brother. Sandra never liked Agha's "materialism," but David didn't agree that

Agha cared only about money. Agha's family was rolling in wealth; getting richer couldn't mean much. Agha was really drawn to the excitement of high finance, the glamour of New York, the new Rome; it wasn't for David, but he could understand its attraction.

Agha's family were iron and steel magnates, beneficiaries of the privatization instigated by the dictator Zia in the eighties. Agha had two older sisters, Masooma and Bilquis, both married, and two younger sisters, Jahan and Saima. Agha claimed that being the only male child had taught him all he needed to know about the irrational female psyche before he ever embarked on his first relationship. A member of the Ivy, Princeton's most elite eating club, Agha loved to flirt, but didn't accept women as intellectual equals. He recently brought to their suite the newest target of his faintly disguised abuse, Marie, a French girl who was a sophomore in comparative literature. Marie seemed to get off on Agha's treatment. David wanted to live and let live, but whenever he felt himself taking charge of women, the spectacle of Marie accepting Agha's domination unsettled him. Agha justified, "It's no big deal, buddy, it's what women *want*," but everything in David's education pushed him to reject that attitude.

Among Agha's relatives and friends, David has seen none of the eccentric characters—both patriarchal and matriarchal, and sexual in-betweens—that populated Latin American and South Asian magical realist novels and supposedly haunted the faculties of youngsters torn between modernity and tradition. Rather, Agha's people were upscale versions of Iqbal, Maulana Haroon's son, with that same enchanting and annoying habit of wanting to be something other than what they were. There was no room to develop eccentricity if one wanted to live an existence known only from afar—although among Agha's circle everyone had traveled to the West since they were young, some even being delivered in hospitals in America and Britain for the coveted citizenship.

Saima was the cutest. The youngest of Agha's sisters, she said she was eighteen, although David felt she couldn't be a day older than sixteen. Agha showed more respect for Saima than any other female. Saima wasn't the most intellectual of his sisters, only the fieriest. David arrived a week after Agha had made it back to get an early start on the heat and the mangoes, and a Citibank internship. Agha and Saima came to the airport to pick him up. She started pestering him with questions right away. *Why was America biased toward Israel? Wasn't it true the Jews controlled the media in America? Why didn't Westerners drive smaller cars, so they wouldn't have to dominate the Middle East for oil? How come India had such a good image in America, but not Pakistan, when Pakistan had always been an ally? How could America be taken seriously on human rights when its own black male population was in prison? If Pakistan and India and Bangladesh and Sri Lanka could have female heads of state, why not America?* David never figured out if Saima was serious. Was she parodying the yellow press? Or was this the extent of her understanding? David responded: "I'm a scholar, I need to be impartial, these are loaded questions requiring me to take sides." To which Saima retaliated: "I'm not asking you to take sides, I'm asking you to give up sides."

The heat of Saima's questions, and her casual sizzling glances, burnt David to the core. He wanted to believe that Saima was a special case, but knew she wasn't. Everyone in Pakistan had an aptitude for politics, and not just Pakistani politics, but Indian politics, Chinese politics, African politics, European politics, and above all, American politics. *Guiding Light* and *The Bold and the Beautiful* could never compete with American presidential shenanigans for Pakistanis. At Princeton, not even members of the Republican and Democratic clubs got so worked up over politics, as did tiny Saima with her black hair and black eyes, and black looks at David's ignorance. If he were impassioned like this at the State Department, he would burn out in no time. A sixteen-year-old girl, who'd probably never had a boyfriend, was causing such a reaction in him! He'd imagined that once he started having regular sex with Sandra, his fantasies about random girls would evaporate, but that never happened.

Saima gave him pointed instructions: *Meet girls his own age, travel inland, always carry plenty of cash on himself, make friends with the cops,* and *accept the state of utilities.* Agha countered with his own set of instructions, namely, *Don't give money to beggars, don't ever ride in a rickshaw, don't talk religion with strangers, don't drop the Princeton name,* and *don't tell them you're a Jew.* It was easy to see why Agha adored Saima. She might be more positive, but she was an adventurer in the dark like David and Agha. Agha's list was filled with *Don'ts,* but he had an expansive vision. No incident involving Agha and Saima's *Do's* and *Don'ts* was likely to happen. At night, after conversation and eating ceased, it was hard to imagine he wasn't in an exclusive Princeton suburb. Agha's house seemed not only soundproof but event-proof.

Agha's oldest sister Masooma invited David to weddings all the time, but Agha would say that "David doesn't have time for that crap" and Saima would say that "those girls are beneath David's standard." David had no voice in these decisions. Agha wasn't personally interested in David's Islamic studies, and he couldn't bring himself to read the copious notes David took during visits with his favorite scholars. Agha's parents returned from Switzerland a couple of weeks after David arrived, but they were both so little in evidence that they might as well be vacationing in Europe still. David couldn't imagine his own oversolicitous physician parents leaving him and his sister so unsupervised even as adults. David's mother still called him every day, asking about classes and extracurricular activities and Sandra. Agha's parents could never be so dogged.

"Are you done with your project? Are you *halfway* there?" Saima bugged David one evening, after his grueling interview with a reformist scholar who put him on the defensive for being a Jew. Messy politics was interfering with pure legal theory, making adaptation, cross-cultural fertilization, tolerance, and universal civilization more complicated.

"Not yet."

"Hurry up, because I want you to meet my friends. Maybe you can set them straight about things I can't get through their heads."

He was sure he could hold his own. He wasn't doing too badly for his first extended visit to a third world country. He hadn't collapsed with guilt at the sight of grinning beggars with chopped off limbs. The noise level was frightening, but he was adapting. The old city, with its labyrinths of impassable streets where shrunken vendors peddled contraband Rolexes and Penguin classics, spoke of a common past. He maneuvered the Volkswagen amidst oblivious burqa-clad women and runaway infants, honking donkey carts and garish minibuses, and bicyclists with stacks of tiffin boxes winding their way like New

York messenger boys. Looking at the grand municipal buildings from the Raj, it felt as though the British had only left yesterday, for all the excitement about the approaching fiftieth anniversary of independence. Was it so wrong of him to wonder if Agha and Saima were strangers in their own country?

"Wake up, *Bible Boy!*" Saima had called him that ever since he launched into an exposition of exile in the Old Testament and the Qur'an. He'd stopped correcting her with, "That's Torah Boy."

"I'm here."

"I hope you don't daydream in your Princeton classes."

"Which is where you'll be following in Agha's footsteps."

"I have no desire to be at Princeton or any American university."

David didn't quibble. But where else would she study? Locally? She'd be a pariah in her family. Education abroad was a given. At the very least, she'd study art or music at some provincial British or American university.

"The friends you want me to meet, are they from Grammar School?" This was the Phillips Exeter and Andover of Karachi rolled into one, the main feeder school for the Ivies.

"I don't associate with those snooty kids."

Was Agha snooty? No, he wasn't. Agha thought *The Simpsons* was as good as *Great Expectations*. David felt confident Agha's sexual hijinks wouldn't persist long. After a couple of years on Wall Street, he'd hook up with some decent Maine girl, a vegetarian and lifelong subscriber to *Mother Jones*, and the couple would spend weekends at soup kitchens.

Masooma came with her chauffeur and servant in tow, carrying ghararas and shararas from Empress Boutique, wanting Saima's opinion on what to wear for their cousin Arora's wedding festivities, which would last about a month.

Under threatening rain clouds—the monsoons hadn't come yet—Saima took David to the suburb called P.E.C.H.S. This was a housing development built after partition for the civil service, but it had been taken over by the commercial elite. In Block Six of P.E.C.H.S., the commercial area was a major center for furniture and appliances. Saima's cousin Arora must already have visited here with her fiancé, picking out refrigerators and air conditioners and couches and beds. The smell of furniture varnish saturated the Volkswagen, even with the windows rolled up. He was tempted by peanuts, roasted on portable burners on carts and dispensed in paper funnels for a few rupees. But he had to leave plenty of room for the snacks surely awaiting them.

He'd compiled his notes for the week, making up for lost time with Saima's friends. She wouldn't tell him who they were visiting, saying only that she didn't want him to go back to America thinking that Pakistanis were all alike. He told Saima the trip to Pakistan had already paid off. His thesis was coming together. He would argue that specific political formations in each Islamic country determined the contours of Islamic commercial law; it was true in the Middle Ages and the early modern era, and it was true today. He realized he was skating over the stickiest problems of Islamic jurisprudence. The political context only explained irregularities in a particular systems of law; there was always a consistent worldview that was decisive. But his argument was also valid, as far as it went. The wide range of local interpretations contradicted any simplistic category as "Islamic commercial law." This still wasn't a manageable essay: it was a book, or many books. He would have to pick on a small angle—the workings of mudarabas and musharakas, forms of Islamic partnership—to illustrate his point.

He remained uncomfortable with the feeling of permanent lethargy, the drowsy sense that things had always been this way and would always be this way. In his unguarded moments it hit him hard. It came across in the way the chowkidar at Agha's house looked at David in the morning when he left, ready to take on the world. It was a stoicism born of weariness. The maalis, the dhobis, the cops, the clerks, the dukanwalas, the waderas, the mill-owners all looked at him as if nothing in his language, his style of perception, could alter their beliefs one iota. Even the dogs and cats were immovable in their haughty solitude. It was always four in the afternoon in Karachi, the temperature a hundred degrees in the shade, the sherbet seller or gola-gandawala broken by the heat—too many people, not enough jobs, too much mismanagement. The sparrows chanted their lament in the mornings, and the crows followed suit in the evenings. The footfalls of the British could still be heard, the Mughals were recent news, America was the omnipresent master, and it would all end in nuclear holocaust with India anyway.

There was no chowkidar to greet them at the house where Saima made him stop. The bougainvillea were uncared for, and the car a seventies Toyota with a flat tire.

"Khala, it's me," Saima yelled.

They went in when there was no answer. The front door opened into a room full of Oriental carpets in various states of display—rolled, unrolled, stacked high against the wall, spread over chairs and couches. Khala didn't necessarily mean Saima's aunt—it was a term of respect for any older woman. An antique hookah stood in a corner of the room, purely for ornamental reasons.

"Your Princeton education won't help here," Saima said.

"Thanks for warning me."

The problem with Asians was that they were inscrutable. David had read Edward Said's *Orientalism*, and was aware of being politically incorrect but he couldn't help it. No American teenage girl could be such a successful enigma.

Saima led him to a musty library. The Western canon was alphabetically arranged on the shelves covering the walls. Shakespeare's plays were duly followed by Smollett, Sterne, and Swift. A smaller Islamic canon was here as well, in Urdu, Persian, and Arabic. The books looked like they hadn't been used in years. Their comprehensiveness and order were a reproach to the idle visitor.

They settled into squeaking wicker chairs, arranged in front of a massive empty desk.

A servant of indeterminate age, demure in dark clothes, brought them tea and pastries. "Khala is out."

"So who are we here to see?" David was still scanning the book titles. "A well-read person, obviously."

"Uncle Salam. My great-uncle, from my father's side. There was a falling-out between the branches of the family long ago. My father's father and Uncle Salam came to blows at a procession honoring Jinnah. Uncle Salam wanted India to remain undivided. It's been a bad fifty years for him. He's ninety, so be gentle."

"Is the old man going to say something to make me second guess my success in Pakistan?"

"Ha, funny American."

David felt like a child ignorant of what the adults were planning.

"Children, children," a muffled voice came from the doorway. Uncle Salam looked like a tweedy professor from England, who had returned to Pakistan to live out his last years without the indignity of nursing homes, and who was still able to arrange the messed-up lives of brainy grandchildren with explosive bons mots. He had mottled pink skin, his head was bald and freckly, he wore reading glasses at the tip of his nose, and he had hair coming out of his ears, which his general handsomeness prevented from looking repulsive.

Saima helped him into a chair. David imagined his back creaked. He had joint problems, but little flab.

"You must forgive my hearing. It's the faculty I seem to be losing first. Ah well, there's no music worth hearing these days anyway."

"This is Agha's roommate David."

Saima seemed to have become transformed into an adult version of herself, as though she'd been married for twenty years, and was reliving happy memories.

"Princeton, huh?" Uncle Salam fixed his stare on David, making him wilt. "More exclusive than Harvard, and it gave the world the League of Nations. About as useful as Mountbatten's dictates."

"This is old hat," said Saima, "the debate is settled, India and Pakistan must accept each other as political realities." Saima's father might have said the same words to Uncle Salam, but it would have earned him a box on the ears and ejection from the house.

Uncle Salam ignored Saima. "So, what's your agenda in Pakistan?"

"My agenda is pretty simple."

"He's writing a paper—senior thesis, really—on Islamic law," Saima clarified. "He's poking his nose into stuff we gave up on hundreds of years ago."

"A thousand," corrected Uncle Salam.

There followed a discussion about the intricacies of mudarabas, musharakas, and other Islamic financial instruments, and the ethical dimensions of Islamic commercial law, a broader perspective than the simple ban on interest. Uncle Salam was an artful interviewer. The outpouring came from David, although he imagined Uncle Salam was an equal participant. Uncle Salam's mind was on something else.

"My concentration isn't what it used to be, since I gave up my pipe."

"I understand," David said, "my Dad smokes too. And he's a doctor."

"How can a doctor in America smoke?" Saima gasped. "I thought you guys were fanatical about these things?"

"My Dad's unorthodox."

"It's not right what we did to the Bengalis," Uncle Salam said in a non sequitur.

"Excuse me?" David was baffled.

"It follows from the logic of partition." Uncle Salam looked warily at Saima. "I know, I know, the debate is settled."

There was an uncomfortable pause. The crows' moaning could be heard outside. The baleful sound ought to be accompanied by Princeton's fall leave shedding, a riot of colors to counter the grim chorus.

"Uncle Salam would like your help," Saima said.

Uncle Salam coughed. "You see, David, my friend, it's like this. My brother started a veritable dynasty—although the latest strain, Masooma and Bilquis, might not cooperate and produce the necessary offspring. Anyway, after a while you realize that immortality is not obtainable. I want to tell you about *my* legacy, the part Saima keeps track of, even if her father doesn't care. I have a grandchild your age, Imrana, our youngest. An artist by temperament. She started with calligraphy, moved on to pottery. A couple of years ago, a foreign buyer came to the shop that carried her wares—an American. He came every week and paid exorbitant sums for Imrana's work, making the shop owner put pressure on Imrana to work faster. Soon he wanted to meet Imrana, to interview her for an art magazine. I think you can figure out the rest. The American was good-looking, but he was twenty-three years older than Imrana. They got married in an Islamic ceremony, at a mosque on the outskirts of the city, without anyone in the family knowing. Imrana's father and mother are both incompetent, so I've been the de facto parent, but Imrana never told me. Now she's in America, and we have no communication with her."

"I'm sorry to hear that."

"It's a pretty disgusting story," Saima said. "I knew Imrana well. My Dad would kill me if he knew how much time I spent consoling her, straightening out her emotional messes. This wasn't the first guy she'd had a crush on. It was her destiny, what happened in the end. Not that this means we shouldn't intervene."

"Was age the only problem?" David wondered what he was meant to do, as sordid as the story was. He could see the American dumping Imrana, once he got tired of her, for a newer, more exotic model—perhaps from Turkey or

Iran or Kazakhstan, countries so helplessly jealous of the West that even their exoticism was non-threatening.

"If only that were the case," Uncle Salam replied. "He's done something to her, I can tell. Before she stopped writing to us, she'd started railing against Islam, how it mistreats women, how the whole tradition is backward. Don't get me wrong. I have no love for the mullahs who claim their morality is the only true one. Moderation is the best course. It prevents disorder from happening in the first place. But it's one thing to decry the objectionable parts of religion, the distortions that have crept in over time, and another to question the very foundations of spirituality. People want to believe in *something*. It's best they believe in some harmless relic of the Prophet or worship at the mazar of some saint, rather than drool over the modernist architecture of a Hitler or the bureaucrats' dangerous fantasies in Islamabad. And to question the spirituality of people who raised you, who gave you their love, that's just crossing the line."

"We can't have that," Saima echoed.

David was surprised that Saima was supporting a diatribe against the ingratitude of the young. "How can I help you?"

"I thought about filing a case for kidnapping, but imagine going with that plea to the folks at the American embassy. They'd laugh it off. By definition, Americans don't kidnap, isn't that right? It's only Pakistanis who kidnap Americans! Did my Imrana kidnap this man, this—"

"Yes, what's his name?" David asked.

"He calls himself Raja Ghazanfar Asghar, but his real name is Gifford Bell III," Uncle Salam said.

"That sounds familiar," David said.

"It should," Uncle Salam said. "The guy teaches at Princeton."

Saima smiled knowingly. "He's an alum, and now he's gone back to Princeton. Artist-in-residence, although judging by his art—the gloomiest tapestries you ever saw!—I don't know about Princeton's taste."

"David, we'd like you to locate Imrana and talk to her," said Uncle Salam. "Just let us know she's all right, and this Gifford Raja guy hasn't brainwashed her. Is she physically all right?"

He could see himself worming his way into Gifford Bell's affections. Maybe get invited to his home. Have an intimate therapy session with Imrana, when her husband was upstairs to tuck in a child. All this was plausible. He'd dared to visit Pakistan. He'd collared scholars notoriously difficult to locate. Finding Imrana was the least he could do to show he was grateful. Agha would consider it a betrayal that David had a secret alliance with Uncle Salam, the black sheep of the family, but David accepted that risk.

"Do it, David," Saima commanded.

David nodded. "I will. I'll see to it as soon as I get back to Princeton." During his stay in Pakistan, Princeton had felt remote, an unreal part of his life, a fantasy he'd dreamed up, without texture and tone to lend it substance. Now, after a couple of blissful months free of history, Princeton loomed large again. He would have to press hard to finish his thesis by March 20, even if he sharpened his argument as a result of this trip. He felt now that the problems of the Islamic world went beyond resolving arcane contradictions within the structure of the law. They went beyond even settling differences between the abstraction of law and the grittiness of reality. The problem of Pakistan was really the perpetually lethargic days, when thought was at a standstill, expired in an overflowing gutter.

"David, Uncle Salam knew Jinnah personally. He could tell you stories you'd never believe of the founder of the country. You could write a novel based on what Uncle Salam could tell you in a single afternoon. Well, if you'd been a creative writer."

"Jinnah drank, I know," David said. "The mullahs were scandalized. He wore Savile Row suits. So? All the nationalist founders of the twentieth century indulged in such tastes."

"He was a stylist, an artist of the impossible." Saima's maturity stretched into the inconceivable. "His suave arrogance, his flawless harassment of Nehru and the British viceroys. He was quite the man."

"Gifford Bell thinks of himself in the same vein," David said.

Saima and Uncle Salam became quiet.

"You shouldn't have said that," Saima reproached him.

"I'm sorry."

"It's neither here nor there," Uncle Salam said. "Just get some information. That's all we're asking. You're obviously good at that."

They ate Persian food, juicy lamb and chicken kebabs with fluffy rice, lettuce and carrots on the side. Uncle Salam didn't mention Imrana again, except when he meaningfully laid his hand on David's shoulder as he was leaving.

He did finally make it to one of Masooma's invitations, their cousin Arora's wedding. Agha pressed him to go, because he wanted David to meet a girl he was interested in, a Wellesley economics student, Afshan, also headed for Wall Street. Agha refrained from aiming his usual insulting epithets toward girls he liked. For a change, he talked about Afshan the way David liked to praise and compliment Sandra. Afshan was a prodigy, with glowing recommendations from Paul Krugman at MIT, where Afshan had cross-registered for an international economics seminar. Afshan had done great work for Wellesley's South Asian club, inviting such luminaries as the Pakistani ambassador, an Oxford-educated female like the prime minister, to talk about the stubbornness of both Indian and Pakistani politicians as they fought over Kashmir, dispelling by her very presence the stereotype of Pakistanis as backward fanatics. Afshan worked for the Muslim students club as well, where she moderated forums on religious practices, showing that fasting and praying didn't interfere with economic competition. Afshan herself didn't regularly fast or pray, as was true of the Pakistani elite in general.

"What about Marie?" David wondered, as Agha sat in front, complaining about the Volkswagen's lame air conditioner.

"Marie? Oh, she doesn't factor into the equation, don't you see?"

David had believed Agha genuinely loved Marie, as hard as he was on her.

"Don't you care about her?" David thought also of Beulah, the girl from Tennessee related to the Gores, Mindy, the Oregon pianist, and Charlene, the Minnesota girl who had self-published an eco-terrorist manifesto.

"I care about her, of course I do." Agha's tone suggested he saw no problem seeing Afshan, at the same time as he trifled with Marie and other girls.

"Well, whatever, but don't tell me I didn't warn you."

"Warn me about what?"

"You can't mess with girls that way. Girls aren't as strong as guys in dealing with loss. Romantic loss especially." David pictured Marie overdosing on some killer drug in the suite he shared with Agha, the scandal forever ruining David's own name, and alienating him from Sandra, who would never believe any of his explanations.

Agha stifled laughter. He remained amused all the way to Arora's house, which was at the far end of Clifton, a final promontory jutting into the sea.

"Does this remind you of the Bushes' vacation home in Kennebunkport?" David wondered.

"This one is a grand affair in comparison, don't you think?"

The enormous solid stone house seemed in no danger of being swept out to sea, unlike the fragile wooden structure on the windy coast of Maine.

Trains of beautiful women with long dark hair and glamorous lehengas disembarked from chauffeur-driven German and British luxury cars. These were the wives and sisters of industrialists and financiers, merchants and politicians, retired generals and feudal landlords, whose collective will was holding off the full onset of modernity. *This won't last, this stalling of time*, David muttered to himself.

As though reading his thoughts, Agha said, "Don't worry, buddy, the common people don't resent the ostentation. The chowkidars and nawkar-chakar puttering around, they want to be like the sahibs. It's like in America. Envy keeps everything buzzing along."

David merged into the party of the rich and beautiful. Soft jazzy music recalling the seventies harmonized with the gentle slopes of the endless lawn. Turbaned waiters with crisp moustaches and clean hands plied guests with drinks. David wanted to be part of the fantasy. His eyes caught Arora, surrounded by a bevy of girlfriends eager to be at her side. Arora was the most beautiful girl he'd ever seen. Her features were perfect. She must bathe in milk and honey. Her cheekbones, nose, chin, neck, teeth were all some artist's arrogant summation of classic beauty. Yet Arora seemed transparent—not fragile, but open to flattery, receptive to the new.

Who was the lucky man Arora would spend her life with? Some dull industrialist or wadera? No man really deserved such fresh beauty.

"Wake up, dude. You're staring at her." Agha was at his side.

"I'm sorry." David stood rooted to his spot. He didn't want to take his eyes off Arora and company. "No wonder all the fuss about her."

"Quite a looker, isn't she?" Agha whispered. Then louder, "Listen, I want you to meet Afshan." Next to Agha was a short girl with indistinct features. Not Agha's usual flamboyant type.

"Nice to meet you." David extended his hand, working hard to contain his surprise.

"Nice to meet you too," said Afshan. "I've heard so much about you."

The three of them talked about mutual friends. This conversation tactic had irked David when he came to Princeton, everyone's social standing tracked by virtue of prep school friends in common. But now David was grateful for the conversational shortcut. It would help him get his bearings. Having glimpsed Arora, he felt like he was being let into the real attraction of Pakistani society for the first time, which again complicated his well-laid plans for describing the country to his scholarly interlocutors' satisfaction back at Princeton. Afshan and Agha and David did have quite a few friends in common; the world of the Ivies was small.

Over the course of the evening, David understood why Agha liked Afshan. She was steady, managerial, efficient, without being bossy or contrived. She called a spade a spade, and wasn't afraid to bring logical contradictions out into the open, without being arrogant. She was the exemplary wife for a busy New York financier. She would never be a drag on Agha. David figured if they split up, she would go her own way, without harassing Agha. So after all, Agha was afraid of women who wanted to be dominated? Or was it just Afshan's familiarity as a fellow Pakistani, rather than the exotic appeal of Marie and Beulah and Mindy and Charlene, that drew Agha?

"David, I know your girlfriend Sandra," Afshan said.

"Oh, you do?" It was turning dark. The soft music from invisible speakers stuck behind trees and rocks sounded more lustful. Today was Arora's official engagement ceremony, although the real engagement had taken place a year ago; there were no unfamiliar rituals as in mehndi or the weirder mayoon. The bridegroom had not yet shown up. Why was Afshan bringing up her acquaintance with Sandra?

"We met at a conference on the Middle East at Mount Holyoke. She's very attractive."

"I guess she is." David didn't feel like talking about Sandra.

He hadn't seen Saima all evening, but now here she was. "David. Afshan." Looking over at Arora's huddle, Saima said, "You'll be pleased to know that Arora's husband was once accepted to Princeton as an undergrad. He chose to go to LSE instead."

"Good choice?" David asked.

"You tell me."

"I missed seeing you this evening," David whispered. Saima looked at him strangely, as though pitying his delusions.

How could this girl be sixteen, or even eighteen? Such self-confidence and maturity only came after years of making mistakes, in college and in your twenties, in colorful cities like New York and London, as one sped through relationships and tossed out most experiences as being worthless.

Then David lost sight of Saima, and kept wandering around the lawn to find her. She was only sixteen, but that didn't stop his heart from pounding. He didn't remember similar emotions when consummating his relationship with Sandra. He wanted to get drunk, Agha to accompany him, and to tell Princeton to go to hell.

The crowd gravitated toward a canopy in the center, the chatter descending to an awed hush. The engagement ceremony was in progress. But he didn't care to see, and joined a group of wizened old men with baggy trousers and wrinkled cotton shirts, off by themselves in a corner, puffing away at cigarettes, cigars, and pipes. The cloud of smoke hurt his lungs, but he stayed.

"You're American?" asked one of the men.

"My posture gives me away so easily?"

"The accent. Patrician New England."

"I'm not patrician by any means. I'm not even a WASP." Again he was surprised by how much Pakistanis knew about American social relations.

He listened to the men complain about their wives' spending habits, the rule of the feudal lords, the disenfranchisement of taxpaying industrialists, the abysmal state of English-medium teaching in private schools, and the exclusion of Turkey from the European Union, all these topics mingling with each other like run-on sentences, reflecting the resentments of the idle rich.

Later, in Agha's company, a shy, diminutive man in his early thirties—with Uncle Salam's displaced look, that same impression of being alone in the middle of company—joined them at the table, while Agha's old Grammar School friends devoured chicken tikkas and boti kebabs.

"David, I'd like you to meet the man of the hour, Habib," Agha said.

This was Arora's husband-to-be. He was a Pakistani Prufrock, without the peach to look for on the beach (or was that Ezra Pound's character?), without even his flannel trousers rolled up. Habib looked like he'd just finished a full day's work at the bank, which is where he in fact worked: Citibank's currency trading section. At one time, he'd had plans to do his MBA abroad, but didn't want to go to America or Europe alone: "too much temptation for a guy my age," he said. He scratched his thinning hair, then rubbed his knee as though crushing an insect that had crawled inside. His nose and jaw were attractive; for the rest, he looked like someone who kept minutes at a secret conference of bankers. David gathered that Habib belonged to the solid middle class. He didn't have the throwaway confidence of the rich, like the rest of Agha's circle.

"Where did you meet Arora?" David couldn't help asking.

"We were introduced through a family friend. At a wedding, not long ago."

David wondered if a formal matchmaker had been involved. He seethed at the injustice. "I see. That's really nice."

They started talking about what David was doing in Pakistan. Habib had heard of Maulana Haroon.

"We're grateful to you for pursuing such obscure work," Habib said. "Our own people aren't interested in scholarship. But it's part of the cultural heritage, indispensable."

Later still, Agha showed David around the house. David wanted to go to the roof to feel the salty Arabian Sea lash against his exposed skin, the chilly froth of the ocean an antidote to his turbulence. Agha accompanied him to a set of grand stairs winding upward like origami, before retreating to the crowd on the lawn.

The thick air on the roof, the lingering humidity, and the faintness of the stars made comparison to the Bush residence in Maine laughable. *I'm in Karachi, I'll never see these people again, and that's fine with me*, David affirmed to himself.

No one had made an issue of his religion yet—except for that one scholar, and that was only because David brought it up to emphasize the commonality of the Abrahamic tradition. So Agha had been wrong about that. He had yet to ride in a rickshaw, but he would fix that soon when he went to the old city. He had been to a wedding now, although he hadn't talked to any beautiful girls.

Saima was behind him, touching him on the back. "I asked Agha where you were."

David was afraid to meet her eyes. He wanted to kiss her, even if it would be a capital offense, a betrayal of Agha's trust in him. Would he be kissing Saima or Arora or some idealization of Sandra, the Sandra who never was nor ever could be?

"I'd like to kiss you. I really would."

"David, I've never kissed *anyone*."

"You haven't?" That was hard to believe. Saima's classmates at Grammar School acted like savvy American high schoolers.

"I believe in waiting for the right person."

"What about the right time and place? Does that count?" David admired his own chutzpah. How pathetic was this? He was pleading with a teenager to let him kiss her, despite having an official girlfriend, Sandra, who had already guided him through sex as though she were his well-remunerated consultant.

Saima laughed. "Ha, funny American. You can hold my hand though."

They looked at the stormy sea, holding dark monsters, indescribable creatures of the night. Even when the surface looked placid, the ocean was never calm.

"You'll pursue what Uncle Salam asked you to, won't you? For his peace of mind. That's what counts. He's an old man, ninety. We must respect his needs."

"Of course I will."

Years later, he would read in the *New York Times* that Maulana Haroon had been picked up at a hotel in Karachi by the FBI in connection with a terrorism investigation, and that his only son had been shot fatally in the confrontation. A picture of Maulana's pregnant wife in shock—he'd never seen her on his visits to Maulana years ago—graced the front page. She looked beautiful even in the midst of tragedy. Maulana Haroon could not have been involved in terrorism in any form. It must be a colossal misunderstanding. David recalled the wistful look on Iqbal's face as he stood in the courtyard, next to the orange Volkswagen Agha had loaned him. Iqbal would have been nineteen when he was killed. David had mailed to Maulana Haroon a copy of his completed thesis, which won an award from Princeton's Near Eastern Studies department, but never heard back. He'd dropped his pursuit of Islamic studies shortly after graduation, coinciding with his breakup with Sandra. David's interest in Islamic law now seemed to him like a hallucination. He blamed Princeton, multiculturalism, lack of college counseling. His line of Swedish-style furniture, distributed widely in New England, kept him too busy to worry about the past, except sometimes during holidays, when the ghosts of history came back to haunt him. Alone among his friends, he'd gone into a low-tech business. Agha had become a superstar financial analyst, a vice president at twenty-seven, and a regular at New York parties thrown by the likes of the Agha Khan and Sir James Goldsmith's offspring. It had been difficult to remain intimate with Agha once David left Pakistan, although they remained cordial roommates. David had found it impossible to keep his feelings for Saima in check, and so he left Pakistan earlier than scheduled, disgusted with himself. From Agha, he learned that Saima never went to college abroad, keeping her promise, and ended up working for an NGO pursuing dual-track diplomacy with the Indians.

A latter-day reprise of Uncle Salam's original philosophy, he supposed. Uncle Salam had died at ninety-five, as soon as the new century began, but not before David accomplished one of the few things he was proud of in his life. Not only had he hunted down Gifford Bell the kidnapping artist and his brainwashed Pakistani bride, but insinuated himself into their household and infected Imrana with enough guilt to turn things around. Shortly before Uncle Salam died, Imrana visited him in Karachi. For years, she'd stopped making crafts because she was overwhelmed by the purity of Gifford's art. But in this morning's Arts section in the *Times*, there was a notice of an exhibition by one Imrana, first name only, at the Allenby Gallery.

WOULD THAT BE A NONSTOP FLIGHT?

Mr. Saeed likes his tea strong and dark, unlike my own father, who takes it diluted with milk, which already comes mixed with water, at least where my family buys it. Mr. Saeed talks often about his wife, Jehanara, and his two daughters, Mariam and Zubeida, both in their early twenties, wondering if my experience and outlook are similar to theirs. I'm his twenty-eight-year-old right-hand woman, Shakira, which makes me old enough for lonely old men to approach me as if I were a receptacle for all their woes, particularly the trifles, since I can't be taken seriously as someone with her own prospects still in sight. I'm an old woman, on many counts, in these parts.

On the other hand, men think my crossing the age of desirability—between eighteen and twenty-two, I should think—also makes me perpetually itchy for intimacy, of any kind, wanted or unwanted, hot or cold, lasting or fleeting.

This presumption used to bother me when I first started working for Mr. Saeed at Instant Travel Agency, next to Metropole Hotel and close to the American consulate. Our travel agency is a popular first stop for young married couples hoping to convert their newly acquired tourist visas into green cards within a few years—the man already boosted enough by the visa officer to flirt with me in front of his wife—as it is for portly businessmen who spend weeks in Amsterdam and Lisbon failing to sell fabric and crafts, and who think I'm emotionally available to make their financial troubles more tolerable.

This quick familiarity is ironic, because the only man I've been intimate with turned out to be a fraud, and didn't hang around for a repeat experience of the quick—shall I say, lightning-fast—intercourse he deigned to perform with me. His name was Murad, I knew him as a statistics tutor at the IBA, the Institute for Business Administration, and he claimed to possess a five-year multiple visa for America, which he was going to utilize as soon as he finished his MBA. It turned out he was on the run from the long arm of the law, having embezzled millions of rupees from the textile factory he worked for, and having undergone a complete identity makeover. So when I say I slept with Murad, I actually don't know who I slept with.

Mr. Saeed has lately been more agitated than usual because his wife has been threatening to join her parents in New Jersey—they're getting old, and her sister there is too much of a nincompoop to know how to take care of them, and besides, what harm is it if at their age she spends only half a year with Mr. Saeed?—and his daughters want to start a boutique, which in Mr. Saeed's opinion will definitely disqualify both of them for the attentions of respectable suitors, if they still have any chance left.

"Wednesday evening, then." Mr. Saeed distractedly signs off the latest batch of invoices. "My wife's looking forward to it. And so are my daughters."

It's settled then. I'm to visit Mr. Saeed's home, at his insistence, for the first time. I decide to wear my bright blue dress—a gift from my cousin in Nebraska—which I've only worn once, at the same cousin's engagement a couple of years ago.

"Do hotels in Peshawar really cost that much?" Mr. Saeed is talking about his nephew, Amjad, the newest employee of Instant Travel Agency, who's been sent upcountry to look into the possibility of opening a branch in the Northwest Frontier province.

I have a suspicion Amjad is overstating his expense account, but I keep quiet.

Over the last few weeks, a greater note of anxiety has crept into Mr. Saeed's interactions. Unlike in the past, when he was glad to unburden himself given the slightest opportunity, I now have to wheedle information out of him. His wife's plans to emigrate to America are becoming more concrete. A visa appointment is scheduled soon. Meanwhile, his daughters have decided to do an MBA together, at the IBA, to acquire the business acumen to invest in a boutique. Already, while Mr. Saeed prevaricates, some of the richer relatives have offered startup money. This much Mr. Saeed can handle. But the killer is that Mr. Saeed himself has been offered an opportunity, by his aging uncle in Baltimore, to take over a thirty-year-old travel agency. Instant Travel Agency has a mysterious owner who has never been seen around the offices, although Mr. Saeed, who has unlimited authority, is said to be compensated as handsomely as an owner.

Mr. Saeed, for the first time, is becoming tongue-tied.

It's amusing, I suppose. It gives me an excuse not to think about my own pressing dilemmas: how to take care of my parents when they become really old, on a salary that's barely enough to keep myself in good shape; how to ward off the fear of losing my looks and being alone the rest of my life, becoming an oddity in a society that values only connections and togetherness and community.

"Mr. Saeed, do you think I'm getting ugly?" Had I paused to think of asking this question, my nerve would have failed me.

"Why, of course not, Miss Humayun." Mr. Saeed uses my last name, as he does when he wants to appear wise. "If either of my daughters were half as pretty, no doubt, by now—"

"Your daughters *are* pretty," I console him. "You've shown me pictures."

"Indeed, I have." I'm surprised when Mr. Saeed doesn't pull out pictures of his family from his thick black wallet. He must be worried about having to move to Baltimore, when he's afraid to visit Peshawar on his own. I'm working on a theory that the travel business attracts some of the most egregious homebodies.

"If everyone leaves for America, who'll take care of things here?" I wouldn't have expected Mariam, the more giggly and flippant of the two girls, to have had the ability to turn dead serious at a moment's notice.

"Not everyone is leaving," Zubeida protests. "Out of a population of ten crores, if a handful leave, who cares? Only the smart ones have the gumption. The more educated ones."

"And the stupid ones remain here?" says Mariam. "Then who'll build the country?"

"We aren't about to build the country," Zubeida says. "We're about to start a boutique."

Mr. Saeed seems distant. His apartment, in one of the older high-rises facing Clifton beach, dating to the early seventies, gives the impression of darkness. His wife Jehanara is fond of replicas of Mughal paintings, and every wall has one or two. The dinner is lamb kebab and chicken biryani, heavy food, although lightened by fresh lassi. Jehanara has adopted a world-weary tone throughout, as though she got over Mr. Saeed's shenanigans long ago, and now only inhabits the marital state because any disruption would shatter Mr. Saeed's heart. The daughters are smarter than I expected, but the reason why they aren't married is also obvious: they're both chubby, especially around the hips. This wasn't apparent from the pictures Mr. Saeed has been showing me. Jehanara has none of this chunkiness. She's slim as a sixteen-year-old virgin on a vegetarian diet. Jehanara eats more than anyone at the table, though, and is refreshingly free of the Pakistani housewife's habit of lingering around unfed until the guests and family have all eaten. She speaks with her mouth full most of the time.

Could it be that Mr. Saeed has only been with Jehanara, just the one woman, in his whole life? I can't imagine him being unfaithful. He looks sedated in the fold, cozily entrapped within his familial realm. In his youth, Mr. Saeed was probably handsome and charming. He still has all his hair—and he's never tried to flirt with me, shooting racy double entendres my way, unlike other men.

"I hear in America men don't care if you've been married before," Jehanara says. "They consider it a good thing, if you're experienced. You could be a divorcée, a widow, young or old, and you don't have to be pretty. They're interested in how well you can take care of them. Which our women already know how to do."

"Everywhere men care for the same thing, respect," Mr. Saeed deflects.

"Respect for themselves?" Jehanara asks.

"Abba, don't go to America," Mariam pleads with her father. "At least wait until we finish our MBAs."

"You should ask Shakira about her MBA experience," Mr. Saeed says, "if it was all it's cracked up to be."

I try to cue in on what I'm supposed to say. "It *can* be, if you put your heart and soul into it."

"My father and mother need me in New Jersey," Jehanara says. "My older sister—her husband, an engineer, died years ago—is a bit disorganized when it comes to practical things."

"It seems like there are a lot of decisions to be made," I prevaricate.

Dinner over, we watch a video of Nusrat Fateh Ali Khan performing his vocal hijinks. I always thought there was more show than knowledge to his range. He seems too eager to impress. Mariam and Zubeida show me their designs for lehengas and shararas, cutouts that take me a while to imagine as finished outfits. I'm not impressed with their fashion instincts, but shower inordinate praise on their work.

Everyone's attitude toward me seems different since word got around that I visited Mr. Saeed at his home. Now, it's as though I'm his daughter, since Mr. Saeed taking me for a paramour is beyond the bounds of speculation.

The nephew, Amjad, has finally returned from Peshawar, with news that there are no prospects whatever for expanding business there. The competition, he says, from desperate, wily Afghan refugees, is too stiff. I suspect his verdict has to do with not wanting to be exiled to the Frontier province.

Amjad takes to chatting with me in my office. I'm the only one, other than Mr. Saeed, with the privilege of having a small private office, because it's expected that the men, even those senior to me, won't have as much need for privacy. One day Amjad tells me he wouldn't mind if I dropped a good word about him to Mr. Saeed, since that might help with his proposal to Mariam.

"Why can't men find women outside their immediate families? There are millions and millions of women. But men can only marry their cousins?"

Amjad looks shocked I'd be so aggressive. "Sorry, no harm done."

"You *should* be sorry."

Mr. Saeed calls me into his office to tell me he's decided Amjad should have more responsibility, since Peshawar isn't going to work out.

"What about the expense account inflation?" It's the only concrete complaint I have against Amjad.

"Oh, that. Boys will be boys. He probably had some fun on the side. It's not as if he tried to bankrupt me."

"I guess."

"Look Shakira, family is family. You have to make certain allowances. Otherwise, everyone would die alone, and have no one to care when they're sick and miserable."

"Does this mean you'll be going to Baltimore?"

"I don't want to. But Jehanara is determined to be with her parents. And if she goes to New Jersey, then what will I do here?"

I knew this was coming. No one can resist such temptation.

"New Jersey is hundreds of miles from Baltimore," I say.

"Not that far. In America, freeway travel makes distances short."

"Will your uncle cut you in on a good deal?" I've become rash in my desperation. What's prompting me to be so concerned for him?

Mr. Saeed smiles. "Shakira, Shakira. Don't worry. Everything will be all right. The new manager, I'll make sure he's someone good."

I wasn't thinking about my own fate at Instant Travel Agency if Mr. Saeed leaves. Mr. Saeed must already have started looking for his own replacement, but hasn't even talked to me about it. Shouldn't I have been considered? I have as much experience as anyone else in the company. I hold myself personally responsible for at least a quarter of the business the company does. I have many loyal clients.

"Amjad wanted me to tell you he wouldn't mind if I put in a good word on his behalf. To help with his proposal to Mariam." This is rude and disloyal, in addition to being reckless, but I'm past caring.

"That's strictly a family matter."

Now he'll shut himself down completely. I've lost his good faith. I'm surprised I don't feel regret. Rebellion courses through my veins. Where was this defiance when I needed it ten years ago, when I might have tried to do something as daring as leave for America, leave my parents and be done with it?

"I'm sorry, Mr. Saeed, I'm so sorry."

He looks benevolently at me, but becomes distant again. "We all have to do what's in our best interest. No one can look out for your interest as well as you can."

By the end of the week, Amjad has become de facto manager. Soon, it's announced that Mr. Saeed will be taking care of family matters, and appearing at the office only once a week.

I feel weary climbing the six flights of stairs to our two-room apartment. The neighbors have grown seedier over the years, as the building gets older, as they get older and stop caring. Two black cats growl at me as I disturb their concentrated feeding on the landing outside our door. We're lucky to be in a block that doesn't have its electricity cut off as often as other neighborhoods. There isn't a single empty apartment in the building. It's not officially allowed, but renters charge upwards of a hundred thousand rupees as "goodwill" for the privilege of transferring the lease from their names.

My father has a bad cough. He refuses to get a test for tuberculosis at the government hospital, only a few doors away. My mother has turned fatalistic, and also started praying, which she never used to do. A woman in the neighborhood—who performed the hajj at age sixty and underwent a transformation from sin to enlightenment—

is developing a cult following, as she gathers women, including my mother, in her daily milads and zikrs.

The one good thing—or bad thing, depending on how you look at it—is that neither of my parents ever bothers me about when I'm getting married, nor do they object to my late hours, or question me about my comings and goings.

"Mithi Bai sent some sweet rice."

That's the woman with the cult following. My mother greets me every evening with news of food.

"I don't care for sweet rice."

"It doesn't hurt to try."

My father coughs painfully, as he comes out of the bathroom. His white kurta pajama is threadbare. "Your mother won't make an appointment to see a doctor about the pain in her knees."

"You won't make an appointment to check out your TB."

"I don't have TB. Just a cough. It comes and goes."

"It doesn't come and go. It stays all the time."

He looks at me as though I suffer from an overacute sense of hearing, then smiles broadly. "It'll please you to know I've joined the building committee, and plan to do something about the trash and filth."

I do the right thing and respond well to this news of activity. This is the only father I have, the only mother. If they had a son, life would be easier for them. It's not their fault if they've given up on a bright future.

"Is there a problem if we pull the curtains open in the daytime?"

There's a bit of daylight left. I head to the windows and throw the curtains wide open. The view of the fire escapes in the buildings facing ours isn't that of paradise, but it's something. I worry about unsupervised kids falling off those steep, winding stairs, but no such accident has happened. There's a flash of lightning in the sky, although no clouds are in evidence.

The lights go out, which hasn't happened in a while.

"I'll get the candles. We'll need them soon."

I take a quick reassuring look at my face in the mirror, then head down to the general store in the front of our building.

THE
FIFTH
LASH

The next lash almost finishes him off. He's taken the first four without falling, his eyes looking straight ahead. No more than a tiny squeak, like that of an underfed rat stepped on by a lion, has come from him. But with the next one, a lifetime's anger, frustration, sadness, and misery seem to break loose. When I hear this cry, I can only wonder what kind of reproach must have been uttered at the moment of final indignity by my patron and murshid, my benefactor and master, who dragged me out of the filth of fatalism to believe in the power of a single man to change all of history. What must it have been like to hear the last rebuke of the man who contained within himself the powers and failings of a hundred million people, who was the living personification of all that his nation had become in the course of its glories and failures?

The flogger wipes his brow, tired himself. He looks like a pehelwan who earned his keep performing Greco-

Roman wrestling when it used to be a popular sport in Pakistan. Perhaps he was a second-grade protégé of Aslam or Bholu pehelwan, his main preparation consisting of consuming large quantities of greasy parathas and tikkas, so that he might reach the mass and girth of the Pakistani version of sumo wrestlers, prestige being measured by poundage. He's expressionless, although I've seen other floggers take to the job with relish, smiling brightly at the crowd from time to time, giving the thumbs up signal, accepting a bottle of Vimto or some sweet paan as they gather strength to deliver their next lash with the full force of their being.

The flogged man's back will be marked permanently by the scars. A party of hardened Red Crescent—formerly Red Cross—men and women stands ready to revive the flogged man if necessary, so that the count of ten lashes may be finished. They'll take him straight to the vermin-infested, electricity-deprived Civil Hospital after it's done, there to live or die as his luck might have it.

I've witnessed too many of these floggings in the last couple of years to be able to lose sight of my own sorrows for the sake of the condemned man. I try not to be bothered by the looks of delirium among many in the hot, sweaty, troubled crowd jostling for the best possible view of the tamasha. There are women here, more than you would imagine, and the occasional child of a working-class person. Most of the spectators, except for state functionaries required to be here, are from the lower classes. The crowd must be ten thousand strong; as time goes by, public interest in these spectacles seems to be escalating rather than flagging. Now that foreign movies are banned—only tame local ones, low-budget romances from Lahore, can be shown——and peddlers of video porn are aggressively prosecuted, this has become one of our few mass entertainments.

Did the drivers on the road circling National Stadium hear the inhuman cry of this man? If they did, did they pause or did they keep driving? Why isn't everyone in the country watching this? There has been discussion in the Urdu papers that the floggings—and hangings—should be nationally televised. The Minister for Religious Affairs—although it seems now that every minister's undesignated portfolio is religious affairs— objects that those who wish to be educated by the beneficial aspects of the Islamic punishments ought to be able to find their way to the nearest flogging venue without the government having to bring it to their homes live. There's also the question of whether watching television is haram.

The back of the dark-skinned wisp of a man on the flogging apparatus bleeds profusely. The blood of any man, no matter how anemic looking, is always the richest red, as if God Almighty never wants to scrimp on this account. His dhoti—the strip of white cloth wrapped around his loins—has turned red. Five blocks of white stone—they make me think of the aimless pilings of stone around the ruins of Moenjodaro, by Moenjodarans five thousand years ago or turn-of-the-century British archeologists—form a makeshift support for the man to lean his torso against and bend over. There's nothing to tie his hands or legs with, no way to restrain him except his own recognition that life as he knows it has come to an end.

The flogged man, a former activist for the PPP, the Pakistan People's Party, is in violation of martial law rules forbidding political activity. He's alleged to have distributed a leaflet containing the sayings of Chairman

Bhutto to fellow workers at lunch hour at the Pakistan Steel Mill in Pipri—the one that Bhutto founded in 1973. Others are in line to be flogged for similar crimes— disturbance of law and order, theft of government supplies or distribution of contraband goods, failure to observe restrictions against public eating and drinking during Ramadan—and their names and occupations will be publicized in the papers tomorrow. I haven't yet been to public amputations for theft—the right hand for a left-handed man, the left for a right-handed man—which I've heard have already occurred in Quetta and Peshawar, though not yet in Karachi and Lahore.

A piercing yell goes up from a wild-looking young man close to me. "Kill him! Kill the haramzada. Fahhash! Qatil! Mardood!"

The whip lands again on the condemned man's back. The first few, when the flesh on his back was intact, echoed with the crack of rigidity. Now they seem to strike his marrow and create a squishy sound. He has regrouped after his fall, ready to close out his quota of lashes.

Others near the instigator in the crowd look around uncertainly.

"Chup kar!" The flogger yells for the rebel to be quiet, as he gears up for another one.

The determination of the flogger incites the crowd to take up the chant of the wild man. "Kill him! Kill him!"

The police with their lathis and tear gas become alert, tightening the cordon, pushing the crowd back, treating the raggedy civilians with contempt

The flogger is disconcerted. He speedily administers the final lashes, letting up a bit, after which the Red Crescent people place the flogged man's comatose body on the stretcher, taking him to the ambulance waiting in a corner of the field.

"Khatam, bas khatam." The flogger signals the end of the show to the deflated crowd. The remaining men charged with crimes against the regime will miss their turn today. They'll await their fate, having witnessed the pain from close quarters.

I'm glad to be a free man. I hate to admit weakness in the face of terror, but I'm at best a lowly protégé of limited gifts, not the stoic Hercules my master was, refusing until the last moment to bend to the tyrants. You may have loved him or hated him, but you have to admire his courage against assassins and usurpers.

I used to accompany Bhutto when he dropped in for a bit to watch cricket at National Stadium against England or the West Indies. Bhutto wasn't a fan of cricket, unlike Zia who makes cricket victories against India occasions for national celebration.

The rabble who come to view the floggings at the stadium aren't allowed into the VIP stands. The enclosures are empty, the chairs dusty, the shamianas flaccidly waving in the loo—the hot wind blowing in from the Sind desert that deadens mind and spirit.

The people of Pakistan, despite the flood of Afghan refugees pouring in and taking away precious menial jobs, approve of the new tamashas. America and Pakistan have banded together to wipe out the terror in Afghanistan—the Soviet infiltrators with their godless ways, their disrespect for tribal beliefs—and the alliance promises to last an eternity. The eighties are shaping up to be a long night of misery. The massive National Logistics Cell trucks promenading on Shahrah-e-Faisal—the avenue renamed from Drigh Road to honor the Saudis—stream in from the port and head to Peshawar on the Super Highway. Rumored to carry arms supplied by the CIA for the mujahideen, they're a testament to the durability of the shadowy fight.

Outside, I'm almost killed by a speeding minibus, driven as usual by a manic Pathan. When he comes to a screeching halt to pick up a pair of burqa-clad women, I ponder the gleam in the driver's eye, the greenish tint of teeth ruined by niswar. The conductor hangs outside the door of the minibus with one hand, his gray shalwar kameez a contrast to the gaudily painted vehicle, its scenes of rural splendor with deer and horses. In the land of the free dreamed up by Quaid-e-Azam Muhammad Ali Jinnah and followed up by Quaid-e-Awam Zulfiqar Ali Bhutto, recklessness no longer carries shame.

When I made the bargain with Zia's people to save my own flesh from the kind of torture I've witnessed at the stadium, I hope I did the right thing by pursuing self-preservation without betraying the leader and the party. Would Bhutto himself have wanted me to act otherwise? It was not the quality of information the Inter-Services Intelligence and the Federal Investigation Agency were after. It was the fact of my abject compliance. That, I'm both proud and ashamed to say, I gave them without stint.

Twenty years ago on these same boulevards, it was thrilling to watch the transformation of Pakistan, the women switching from saris to skirts and dresses, their lush hair sheared into Western perms. Ten years ago they went from copying Western outfits and hairstyles to introducing originality: you could see it in the way they were simultaneously modest and aggressive, innocent and knowing. Today, you don't see women anymore. If they're middle-class, they're afraid to go out in public, except for the unavoidable teaching or nursing jobs. If they're working-class, they're covered in burqa. Except for the truly rich and the truly poor, both beyond the constraints of veiled modesty, half this country has disappeared overnight. How did we get here, when ten short years ago women stood shoulder to shoulder with men at Bhutto's rallies, shouting that we needed roti, kapra, aur makan—bread, clothing, and shelter?

I don't know how the people of Pakistan let off steam anymore, or if they even have any need to. How can a hundred million people be bottled up so quickly and easily?

"Do I drink the blood of the people?" Bhutto said. "So what if I have a weakness for Johnnie Walker and Chivas Regal?"

It was 3 a.m. Bhutto hardly ever seemed to want to sleep, staying up late without his face and body looking tired, without his impeccable British suit—his outfit when not dealing with the awam—looking crumpled. But that night I saw hurt and disappointment in his eyes, his thinning white hair a mess.

Zia ul-Haq, the servile chief of army staff with fundamentalist leanings whom Bhutto had hand-picked and promoted to his present position by skipping over six senior generals, ran his fingers along his waxed moustache.

Bhutto's mimicry of Zia, both in front of him and behind his back, had ceased earlier that winter. He no longer called Zia his "bandar general," nor did Bhutto, in front of visiting heads of state and ambassadors, pull anymore on an imaginary string to bring his monkey general close to him, telling his astonished visitor, "See how my monkey obeys me? He can play any trick I tell him to! Show us your tricks!" And Zia would always fold his hands below his navel, bend and bow and show his hideous teeth as he smiled, all the while thanking the master, "So kind of you, sir, so kind of you, all these attentions, so many attentions."

Had the Sher-e-Punjab, Ghulam Mustafa Khar, been there, he would have picked up Bhutto's spirits by repeating one of the master's sayings without a trace of irony. And they would both have laughed riotously. But the Lion of Punjab had been promoted and purged one too many times, and had finally joined the freakiest part of the opposition, Pir Pagaro's faction, after having been with Bhutto since the heady days of 1968, when the scent of revolution was as persistent and undeniable in Karachi and Lahore as in Berkeley and London.

Khar had been married four times, and his current wife Tehmina, perhaps the prettiest of the bunch, was always rumored to be pregnant. Unlike Bhutto, the Lion of Punjab kept an iron grip on his women. Bhutto's own mistress, the Bengali beauty Husna, lived across the street from 70 Clifton. I never saw the master get angry with Husna, despite her flirtatious ways with men.

Whenever the master spoke in his own defense about not drinking the blood of the people—followed by his signal gesture of tearing open his shirt and screaming, "Is there anyone who dares to shoot me? Then shoot me! I'm ready to die for Pakistan"—the adoring masses in Karachi, Pindi, and Lahore gave him a raucous reception.

But we weren't at a rally, such as when Bhutto victoriously brought home ninety-three thousand POWs from India in 1973, or greeted his brother Qaddafi after the 1974 Islamic summit in Lahore. We weren't at a siasi jalsa where tens of thousands of Pakistan People's Party supporters had been bused in, the occasion yet another declaration of a thousand year war with India, or recitation of the address to Henry Kissinger about Pakistan's determination to build the bomb even if it meant we had to eat grass.

It was the night of January 6, 1977, and Bhutto had called in Zia to tell him his intention to hold elections in two months, a long-awaited step that filled him with dread and giddy joy in equal measure.

"Asghar," Bhutto called to me, in no mood for flippancy, "bring the files."

I knew the ones he was referring to. They were on the Louix XIV bureau in his bedroom, compiled by his most trusted internal security advisors.

Then Bhutto said to Zia, "We're going to have elections in sixty days. That ragtag bunch of opposition parties, led by traitors and idiots—let's see what they come up with."

Zia smiled obsequiously. "At your service, sir." The dark circles around his eyes looked their murkiest, and his hair, parted in the middle, more thickly pomaded than ever.

How we end up waiting on masters we dare not imagine when we start out! I'd been directly in the Bhuttos' service since I was fourteen. I was born in the same year as Bhutto, 1928, certainly not in one of Sind's powerful wadero families like the Bhuttos, the Khuhros, the Soomros, or the Jatois, but in a humble peasant household on the lands of Sir Shahnawaz Bhutto, Zulfiqar Ali's illustrious and handsome father, the much decorated freedom fighter who'd worked side by side with Jinnah. It was 1942, and as a tall, muscular young man with a presentable appearance and ready wit, I was picked from several others to accompany Sir Shahnawaz on hunts with the British visiting his lands. I understood from their conversations that world war would finally make it impossible for the British to hold on to India. And I learned from both Sir Shahnawaz and his British guests the manifold arts of deference—for it was never clear, in that ambiguous half-decade of war, who had the upper hand, the Indians or the British, which meant that both sides had to tread carefully.

Sir Shahnawaz was my first Bhutto benefactor. I was sent to school in Bombay, and then Hyderabad and Lahore after partition, always expected to return to the ancestral lands in Larkana, where the senior Bhutto would pat me on the head, and tell Zulfiqar Ali's mother, Lakhi Bai, "Among the humble of the earth, walk the truly proud." Lakhi Bai used to be a seductive Hindu dancer, before converting to Islam. She was Sir Shahnawaz's second wife, after an early wedding to an older woman, a marriage of formality that consolidated the lands between the families. Zulfiqar Ali himself would be "married" to Shireen, a twelve-year-old girl who brought tens of thousands of acres of land, and although he claimed to his second wife, the beautiful Iranian debutante Nusrat, that he never loved Shireen nor slept with her, I know that Shireen visited him at Al-Murtaza in Larkana, and I am also quite certain that Bhutto had a daughter with Shireen whose existence has never been officially confirmed.

I had the full run of the Bhuttos' library in Larkana. I also had the good fortune to sit in on many a meeting with the founders of Pakistan, guests of Sir Shahnawaz, as they deliberated on a constitution that was to elude us until Zulfiqar Ali's own miracle of constitution-making in 1973, and figured out how to balance the country strategically amidst the imperialist aims of India, China, the Soviet Union, and America. When Zulfiqar Ali returned after studying at Berkeley and Oxford, and became a barrister at the prestigious law firm of Dingomal in Karachi, defending his friends against criminal charges, I made the new capital of the new country my home, and gained the master's trust, as he quickly acquired a reputation as a man who was going places. At Karachi's Sind Club, Bhutto spoke often of Sind becoming the Indian subcontinent's California, evoking that distant land with affinities in climate and soil, but utterly alien attitudes. It was a sign of Bhutto's charisma that even when he compared Karachi to Los Angeles in those early days before Karachi had sprawling suburbs, I gave him my full trust.

My thoughts on this irksome night of Zia's solitary conference with Bhutto were taking me too far astray. I made my way to the bedroom, and knocked gently on the door.

Begum Nusrat Bhutto, still beautiful and graceful though approaching fifty, said politely, "Come in."

She knew it was me. Bhutto himself never knocked. Though she wasn't a night owl like Bhutto, she waited until Bhutto came to bed, even if it was at five or six in the morning. She lay sprawled on the bed, the white silk sheets unrumpled, going through picture albums of Pinkie and Sunny when they were little girls, and Mir and Shah, the two sons, also at a young age.

"My children grew up as beautiful as when they were young," she said. This habit of nostalgia was a new one for Begum Bhutto. Frankly, it disconcerted me.

"Yes, Begum Sahiba, they did."

"Is Zia still with Zulfi?"

I nodded.

"I've never seen a more repulsive man." She smiled enigmatically. If she was afraid of Zia—in a country that had typically been run by the military, even when a civilian administrator had been given the official reins, how could you not be afraid of the army chief of staff?—she began to let on that night. "If it's true that ugliness outside reflects ugliness inside…" She didn't finish the thought. "Look at this picture of Pinkie picking roses in the garden."

I studied the photo, taken at 70 Clifton shortly after the dashing Bhuttos, Zulfi and Nusratam, had built the sprawling mansion to match their growing social reputation in the Karachi of the fifties.

"Begum Sahiba, I came to get some files."

"Of course." The light went out of her eyes, the photo album sliding from her hands as she slumped back. "This has been a long night."

Having finished my task, I was leaving the room, when she said, "Asghar, I want you to remain the eyes and ears of this family. Listen to Zia carefully when he thinks you're not being attentive. Bring the information straight to me if he ever slips up."

"Yes, Begum Sahiba."

"And wire Pinkie to come home from Oxford for the elections. Tell her I said so. Zulfi needs her."

I'd have to check on that with Bhutto, but I didn't say this to Begum Bhutto.

The stack of top-secret files I had come to retrieve had been compiled by Bhutto's Federal Security Force chief, Masood Mahmood, and his internal security adviser, Rao Rashid. They identified the potential security challenges of the coming election campaign. There were reports by the chief ministers and governors of all four provinces, building on information from police inspectors and intelligence operatives. The election could easily degenerate into chaos, once the lid was off and the opposition parties smelled blood. We had to forestall them at every turn.

When I went back to the dining room, Zia was sitting in the same stiff posture, his eyes shining as if viewing the face of God. Bhutto was sitting untidily in his chair. He needed the Sher-e-Punjab to draw energy from and to give it back, or if not the Lion of Punjab, then the other dashing figures in his circle—J. A. Rahim and Hanif Ramay and Malik Meraj Khalid and Mubashir Hasan. The chief of army staff drained all the power from Bhutto.

"Sir!" I said loudly, to bring Bhutto back to alertness.

"It's all right, you can go to sleep now, Asghar." It was the first time in all my years with Bhutto that he'd wanted me to go to bed before he was ready to do so.

I dared not disobey, even though I wanted to stay until Zia left. Perhaps the discussions about security were too classified even for me, although usually I was kept around even when high officers of the Inter-Services Intelligence came to brief the leader.

The Landhi jail hadn't registered on my imagination, until I started going there every Thursday to pump information out of J. A. Rahim, my favorite among the PPP founders. The imagination is swamped by the fortress-like Kot Lakhpat prison in Lahore, where Bhutto underwent his farcical trial on the charge of ordering the

Federal Security Force to murder Ahmad Raza Kasuri's father, and by the even worse prison near Pindi, where he was hanged. I myself was detained for only a few days at Kot Lakhpat, although I also became familiar with less foreboding houses of detention in Punjab and Sind.

The British system of administration—judge, jury, and executioner, not to mention administrator and collection agent, all combined in one—remains intact in these parts, through the legacy of Jinnah and Ayub and Bhutto and Zia. Who's going to mess with the sacred office of the district commissioner? The jails are the same from the time of the Raj. Their façades rise in the middle of busy commercial streets, as do those of the foreboding thanas, the nightmare of every law-abiding citizen. Objective facts in your favor are easily twisted into damning evidence by hearsay. The jail in Pakistan is part of ordinary politics.

Rahim sahib was the one who, afraid of the slippery slope, refused to go along with Mubashir Hasan when the latter advocated including "Islam is our faith" as the party's motto, along with "democracy is our polity" and "socialism is our economy." When a bunch of us—myself, Khar, Jatoi, Pirzada—were picked from our homes one night in September 1979, and flown over to Bhutto's grave in Garhi Khuda Bakhsh, there to assemble helplessly and ponder the ruins of our dreams, Rahim sahib was the only one who didn't take part in the namaz-e-janaza Khar commanded us to offer. Rahim sahib never took kindly to Bhutto's superstitions. Bhutto visited the mazars of pirs, quoted Shah Abdul Latif Bhittai, Sind's patron saint, and ordered ta'wiz for Nusrat and Pinkie's endless maladies. When Pinkie completed her first fast at the ripe age of sixteen, and Bhutto invited his closest friends to celebrate, Rahim sahib was conspicuously absent.

I'm met in the visiting room of the jail by an Inter-Services Intelligence man, whom I only know by the pseudonym "Talib." He's round, bald, blotchy with red spots all over, and doesn't care a whit about his pudgy, grubby appearance. He lights a cigarette and offers me one. I haven't smoked since 1967, when the PPP was founded and I decided to do away with my addictions. The only time I've heard anything about Talib's private life is when he told me his niece had been accepted to an animal husbandry course in Surrey. Talib doesn't mind the traffic of wardens and prisoners and visitors in the busy waiting room. He doesn't bother to keep his voice low.

"Something's afoot." Worried, he blows smoke rings, face turned to the ceiling. When I don't take the bait, he adds, "Some conspiracy to overthrow the regime, some movement to bring the crowds out on the streets. Again. As if we haven't had enough crowds to last us until the next century. Do you know anything about it?"

"I'm paid to be an informant, not to be the visionary leader of the opposition. I can't take you where they haven't gone yet."

There's more bite in my talk than usual. I'm just back from the flogging scene. The uncontrolled emotion of the young man in the crowd, who wanted to kill the poor man on the flogging rack, has disturbed my equanimity. On the way over to Landhi, in the minibus that reeked of human sweat and excretion and reminded me of the odors at Kot Lakhpat jail, the Pathan conductor kept pestering me to give him details of the "phansi," even when I kept telling him it wasn't a hanging, it was only a flogging. Did the man's eyes pop out and did his stomach bulge, the conductor wanted to know.

"We make the rules now, you understand," says Talib. "If we say you have to do something, you do it. You're a human Kodak, taking instant shots of our great leaders' rotten skulls. Once we have the snapshot, we decide if we'll shit on it, or preserve it in the gallery of rogues in the presidential bunker."

I'm familiar with his type from my time at Bhutto's side. Whatever the regime, they're with it a hundred percent; the minute the enemy takes over, they switch loyalties, as though they've never believed anything else. They move from certainty to certainty without any hitch.

"I agreed to tell you if Rahim sahib said anything important. He's a quiet man. He wasn't always, but now he is."

Talib springs up. "Meet Ghulam Mustafa Khar, the Sher-e-Punjab!"

I'm shocked to be face-to-face with the former governor and chief minister of Punjab, the man second only to Bhutto in the charismatic pantheon around him. Khar looks as if he's just finished a disagreeable lunch with a difficult subordinate, nothing more serious.

It's the first time I've seen him since the night of the funeral prayer at Garhi Khuda Bakhsh. When I rise, he clasps me. I can't read his expression. Is he on the side of the party, or is he also an informant, or worse?

"How's the founder feeling today?" Talib asks Khar.

So Khar is also visiting Rahim sahib. As if Rahim sahib could be plotting a conspiracy from inside Landhi jail. Among the PPP brain trust, he's the one least likely to come up with an aggressive response. He was the one—despite his socialist formulations—always warning Bhutto and the rest of us that we weren't a party of "dogmatic fanatics," who flipped his lid when Bhutto, without consulting him, announced in 1976 his plan to nationalize the cotton-ginning and rice-husking mills, supposedly to banish the corrupt middlemen who prevented fair distribution of profits to the hari, the kisan, the mazdoor. Rahim sahib stewed in anger that the new round of nationalization would alienate the middle class from the party once and for all.

I'm convinced the martial law regime has lost its head. It sees conspiracies where none exist. Ever since Zia rejected Carter's offer of four hundred million dollars to help fight the Afghan jihad as "peanuts," he dares to say and do outrageous things. They now have the luxury to pursue ghosts and spirits, rather than real dangers.

"Be strong," Khar whispers to me, hugging me again.

"Enough with the sentimentality," Talib hisses. "You guys are lucky we're not the FSF."

He's got both of us there. Khar and I know well that it was the twenty thousand strong Federal Security Force, Bhutto's supposed guarantee against a military coup, his own protective People's Army recommended by Chou En-Lai, that dealt a deathblow to the PPP spirit. Late one night at his home, Rahim sahib, having insulted Bhutto in front of others one too many times, was visited by the FSF and seriously injured. The final blow came when Rahim sahib called Bhutto a "giant among pygmies" at Husna's home.

"You're on trial, so be careful," Talib warns me, as I'm ushered into Rahim sahib's cell. Talib makes it sound as if my deal with the regime could be off, and I might be in for rough times.

The cell has been recently freshened up. The stinking hole in the corner, where the PPP's founding brain is supposed to evacuate and drain, has also been spruced up. A fresh sheet is on the wooden charpoy. It's a step up from the metal frames used as beds in worse prisons.

Rahim sahib gets up from the charpoy and yells at me. "Ghaddar! So you're here too! You've joined the gang of hypocrites. Khar, Pirzada, Jatoi, Mumtaz, they've all been here this week. I'm telling you, I don't know anything about a conspiracy. I'm from the awami wing of the party, not the fascist wing."

"I know that, Rahim sahib." Surely the cell is bugged. Is that the point of these visits? If Rahim sahib knows that, and so do Khar and the others, and I too, then what's going on here?

Suddenly, the air goes out of him. He falls on the charpoy.

"Sit," he commands me.

I don't know where I should sit. I settle down on the dirty floor. Rahim sahib doesn't notice.

It's quiet. The buzz of the flies, hovering over the shit and stink, is what's missing today from the cell. It's a standard ten-by-twelve, with the tantalizing bars in the upper corner of one wall letting in a stream of sunshine, and just enough clamor from the outside—the shouts of the rehri-wallas, the screeches of speeding minibuses, and the wails of ambulances—to make you do anything to get out.

"Tell Rehana to make you some of your favorite kheer."

"Sir?" Rehana, Rahim sahib's pretty, loyal wife, is under house arrest in the Karachi suburb of Nazimabad. A double M.A., and a star pupil when she met Rahim sahib at his lectures at Punjab University, Rehana begum has been trying to hitch me with a succession of her nieces since the days I first got to know the couple. Rahim sahib is hallucinating.

He becomes alert. "I'll tell you a secret. It's not Khar and Pirzada and Jatoi, those morons full of hot air, they have to worry about. Come closer, and I'll whisper in your ear." I get up and bend over. "Zulfiqar," he says. "Al-Zulfiqar."

Now I get it. He's talking about Mir Murtaza Bhutto, who left Oxford after his father's arrest in 1977, and four years later reportedly heads a terrorist organization found to avenge Mr. Bhutto's hanging. He's rumored to have been in Syria, Egypt, Saudi Arabia, Libya, Afghanistan, Germany, plotting revenge.

"There'll be something big in the news soon. I'll tell you more." But when I push my face close, he has a change of mind, and boxes me on the ear, stinging hard. "Ghaddar, you've joined them. Bloody traitor."

"Sir, for what it's worth, I think what they're doing to you is wrong. You shouldn't be here. This place is for criminals. You should be teaching at some respectable place—under any regime, under any political system. Your mind shouldn't be wasted like this."

"So that's what you think? And what about the party? Who's going to take care of the party?"

"The party's over, sir." I believe it. The masses switch from one diversion to another. You can only hold their attention as long as you perform one monkey trick after another. When you put away the bandar-ki-topi and the dug-dugi, they move on, restless to find something to titillate them or someone to hurt. "The party's over, sir, good and done. Finished."

"You liar!"

I tell myself to beg the warden to get Rahim sahib psychiatric attention. Some of us, because we turned informants or did the martial law regime other favors, have had to pay less of a price than others. Rahim sahib, who didn't bend, has the least useful information among any in the inner circle to share with the regime. They already know everything anyway. This is all another tamasha, for the insiders' own benefit, put on with the consummate skill of actors.

I can't make up my mind about the seriousness of the information about the Al-Zulfiqar plot.

I wouldn't have called it a dismissal. A suspension, yes, buttressed with stronger words than necessary. All in all, a moment's slip of class, a lapse of judgment. If ever it was going to happen, it was bound to be because of a dustup with Pinkie, the most inflexible of the Bhutto offspring. Mir and Shah and Sanam, I could handle with aplomb. Something about Pinkie never rubbed me the right way. She was like Khar in that sense, the Sher-e-Punjab being unlike the other PPP founders, displaying something of the quality of an opportunistic latecomer. That came across especially when Khar, or Pinkie, seemed to argue with most conviction.

I hadn't thought it was a big issue when I disagreed with Pinkie's advice to Bhutto that morning in April 1977 at 70 Clifton. I'd done that whenever Bhutto asked questions of both of us. Her answers were of the sort a naïve undergraduate at a Western university might offer, having read John Stuart Mill for the first time. It was acceptable when she was a nineteen-year-old undergraduate at Radcliffe, part of Bhutto's entourage, the only woman among ninety-one men at the Simla negotiations with

Indira Gandhi in 1972. But to be twenty-five, having read her PPE degree at Oxford, and started a one-year course in international diplomacy, and to come up with no more than her old inanities?

"Tell me, should I call for fresh elections?" Bhutto asked her.

The opposition, the motley alliance of mostly fundamentalist and ethnic parties known as the PNA, the Pakistan National Alliance, had mounted mass protests alleging that Bhutto's PPP had rigged the March elections to win sixty percent of the vote and seventy-five percent of the seats in parliament. Everyone understood that we would have won comfortably in the 1977 elections anyway; but having more than a two-thirds majority in parliament was important to Bhutto if he was to amend the constitution to vest more powers in the person of the president—himself. There had been some rigging, but not as much as the opposition claimed. The PNA had called for a pahyya jam hartal that Friday, borrowing from an old tactic used against the Raj. They hoped that business and transportation, from Khyber to Khairpur, would shut down.

The night the election results came in, with absurdly large victories in Punjab, was the worst I'd ever seen Bhutto, worse than at the time of the debacle of East Pakistan. "What have these foolish people done, Asghar? What have they done?" Bhutto dismissed all his confidants, drinking whisky until the early hours of the morning. He recovered his determination soon, but understood he was facing a new kind of threat, one so obviously of his own making that he would be hard pressed to keep the traitors at bay. The awam would always be with him, but what about the restless among the military, the landlords, the capitalists?

So Bhutto's question to Pinkie involved his very future. "If you make concessions," Pinkie said in her British accent, more pronounced after Oxford, "they'll ask for more and more. Don't call for new elections. Let them come around to accepting the results."

"Ah, Pinkie," smiled Bhutto, "if only it were that easy."

He was right. Pinkie's great accomplishment in life to that point was being elected president of the Oxford Union debating society. The list of topics she'd told me they debated sounded juvenile. Was the British commonwealth a viable entity? Should drug addicts have their compulsions satisfied in prison? Did America have a more idealistic foreign policy, or did Britain? Begum Nusrat Bhutto bragged to every friend and acquaintance about Pinkie being president of the Oxford Union. She all but skipped like a happy sparrow, now that Pinkie had come back, pleading with Bhutto to take Pinkie on the campaign trail only after she had fattened her up. For there was no doubt, Pinkie had become anorexic, and was at pains to hide it from her parents and her sister Sunny. If only Pinkie would show doubt once in a while, but she never did—unlike Bhutto, who often doubted himself.

"Papa, the awam count on you to be steady under pressure. Don't give in, or they'll sense weakness and lose trust in you." Which was not even the point. The doubt was never about the awam, as Bhutto understood, and I did too.

I'd just about begun to lose my patience, when Bhutto noticed my agitation and said, "Asghar?"

"Sir, if I may, I think we have to bend to the new political reality. We made a mistake. The overeager party functionaries in Punjab made a huge blunder. Now we have to correct it. And the best way to do that is to go so far out of our way to be humble and apologetic that the wind is taken out of the opposition's sails." I delivered this with much greater force and panache than I normally did when asked my opinion by Bhutto. I may have been his trusted aide, involved with his personal business, but I wasn't one of his political advisers or secretaries, and decades of loyal service to the Bhutto family had taught me to always keep my station in mind. "Miss Bhutto is wrong," I concluded, unable to stop myself.

"Bravo!" Bhutto put aside the morning papers, *Dawn* and *Morning News* and *The Sun*, and clapped slowly. "Pinkie, this man would give you a run for your money at the Oxford Union."

Pinkie seethed with anger. Her skin, true to her name, turned rosy all over. "Papa, this is an outrage! The Bhuttos set their own destiny. Only their heart tells them what to do. They don't stick a finger in the air and take cues from the gutless and obedient."

Bhutto laughed uproariously. I didn't see the humor, and launched into an explanation of why Asghar Khan of Tehrik-e-Istiqlal, the most secular among the PNA alliance, was a force to reckon with, because he expressed the wish of the people to be free of tyranny, and how Maulana Mufti Mahmood and the other religious party leaders, reprehensible as their thoughts were for taking the country back to the seventh century, represented the genuine aspiration of the people for spiritual solace. I must have gone on for a while, because in the end Pinkie had to say, "Asghar, I think your time is up."

Bhutto only looked curiously at me during my tirade, fiddling with his long, graceful fingers, and lighting up the pipe he'd lately taken up. When I was finished, he said,

"Pinkie is like my friend Qaddafi. They get inspiration from beyond the heavens, the same source that motivated Bulleh Shah and Shahbaz Qalandar." I was sick of these frequent comparisons of Pinkie to luminaries beyond her ken. In truth, we're all incomparable—although Pinkie's name, Benazir, literally means without compare. "You and I, Asghar, are like—"

"Like what, Papa?" Pinkie interrupted.

Bhutto never finished the thought. Zia arrived just then, his knobby hands clasped in front of his private parts as if protecting them, bowing and scraping his way to the breakfast table where Bhutto presided majestically. Zia always offered me a big smile, exposing his shiny teeth, suggesting either compassion or cruelty, I never understood which.

Once, soon after his surprise appointment as chief of army staff over the heads of others, I happened to exchange more than pleasantries with Zia. Bhutto was in a private session with his advisers and couldn't be disturbed. Zia waited outside the conference room, and I joined him. He talked about the difficulty soldiers had in keeping their heads above water on their abysmal salaries. He wasn't complaining. He just didn't know how to take temptation away from the soldiers, if they saw corrupt civil servants getting ahead without penalty, sending off their kids to study in England and their wives to shop in Dubai.

"Asghar, the human soul is infinitely corruptible," Zia said. "Every power in the hands of the authorities needs to be exercised to keep its tendencies in check. We're inherently fallible."

"But that's what politics is for. The exchange of ideas in the marketplace, so the truth wins out."

Zia smiled tolerantly. "As often as not, politics leads to dissension. The unchecked ego can play havoc with the fragile minds of the people."

Zia talked about the daily lives of the soldiers in cantonments, and I had to accept that he knew about their struggles firsthand, that it wasn't just academic talk, like that of the latter-day socialists, student and union leaders, who'd jumped on the PPP bandwagon over the years.

The morning of the disagreement with Pinkie, I wondered if anything animated Pinkie's soul, or if the space was empty. I don't know what compelled me later that day to enter her private territory, her sacred room itself, and go through the drawers, peek under the bed. Was I searching for incriminating evidence, something to cause a rift between father and daughter? Was I adopting FSF tactics in my eagerness to please the boss? My ostensible excuse, that I was looking for some files I'd misplaced, didn't even sound convincing to me. Bhutto asked me to take a leave for a couple of weeks, go off to al-Murtaza to clear my head. I needed to be at his side at this critical juncture as he planned his next moves to outmaneuver the opposition, but I also understood the extent of Pinkie's wrath if Bhutto didn't make the symbolic gesture to put me in my place, so I left quietly by train that day.

In those two weeks the country went up in flames. Hundreds of people were dead in clashes between protesters and the FSF in the major cities. Everyone outside the PPP seemed to have only one thing on their mind: get rid of Bhutto, at any cost. As if that was going to cure the country of its problems. Bhutto asked Zia to declare martial law in Karachi, Hyderabad, and Lahore.

I had listened to Bhutto talk to his ministers day in

and day out for five years. How complex and intractable the country's problems were! Squeezed by America on the one hand and Russia on the other, the Indian and Afghan and Iranian and Chinese threats always hanging over our heads, little money in the treasury because of the incompetence of the state-run enterprises and the out-and-out thuggery of the business class, provincial politicians in the NWFP and Baluchistan threatening secession with every acknowledgment of their autonomy—it was all Bhutto could do to hold the country together. The opposition acted as though the country were an advanced democracy five short years since our first-ever elections. Khar was a spoiled child. Despite their greater wisdom, so were the PPP founders, except for Rahim sahib, in wanting Bhutto to go faster than the people had been prepared. Pinkie thought you could repeat certain words endlessly and they would become true. Begum Bhutto was unnaturally happy in the midst of this end-of-the-world turmoil.

My vacation in Larkana only drew me closer to the master. The rallies throughout May and June of 1977 became monotonous and taxing. I saw Bhutto wilt under pressure, more than he had during the 1971 civil war. The more Bhutto conceded, the more the opposition wanted. They smelled blood. This didn't mean that Pinkie was right about sticking to our guns. The problem was that Bhutto's rapid-fire concessions were coming haphazardly, bearing the stink of opportunism and desperation, their logic difficult to penetrate. Bhutto couldn't afford to look like he was one step behind the opposition.

We were at a large jalsa at Lahore's Minar-e-Pakistan when Bhutto dropped the bombshell. "Merey aziz bhaiyo, behno, hamwatano, kisano, talibo, mazdooro, assalamualaikum." He began by addressing the peasants, workers, students, as he'd always opened his speeches since 1967.

At this site, only a few months ago, he'd announced a new set of land reforms to reduce the size of landholdings even more than in the 1972 reforms; for land to pass on to landless peasants was more than a matter of signing legislation, but we had to start somewhere. In the towns and villages around Lahore, over the years we had held many open kutcheries—modern-day darbars—where Bhutto called on the landlords and peasants of the area to air their complaints in front of each other, the PPP's local administrators in attendance to take note. Bhutto was at his best one-on-one with the poor and hopeless, acting for all the world as if he was one of them.

Today, as he addressed the hundred thousand people assembled to hang on to his every word, he launched into a peroration on Pakistan's identity as an Islamic nation. He reminded the audience that his 1973 constitution declared Pakistan an Islamic Republic, and that he'd branded the Qadianis infidels, depriving them of their rights of citizenship under an Islamic state. Now he was going to outlaw alcohol, gambling, horse racing, nightclubs, discos, all forms of blight on the purity of Pakistan, and declare Friday, instead of Sunday, the weekly holiday. My mind became numb. This time Bhutto didn't tear open his shirt and invite assassins to shoot him.

Afterward, Bhutto asked Zia again and again at 70 Clifton, in the days leading up to the final collapse on July 5, 1977, if he'd gone far enough with his reforms.

"As far as you can go, sir," was Zia's enigmatic response. He was beginning to come into his own. I saw the man with new admiration and fear.

Pinkie, of course, was never at Bhutto's mass jalsas. She worried about sunstroke in the hundred and ten degree heat, and heart palpitations in the crush of the crowd. Begum Bhutto agreed.

Talib, the ISI man assigned to me, refuses tea, biscuits, and the leftover samosas from last night. I assume intelligence people are always suspicious of poisoning. Talib is accompanied by two men, one to take notes, the other a giant whose sole purpose must be to engage in hand-to-hand combat should it come to that. While Talib relaxes in my rattan chair, the wrestler pokes around in corners, without permission.

"I've never been inside your place." Talib blows smoke rings. I don't believe it for a second. "You must have had nice rooms at 70 Clifton? I hear Bhutto had you in charge of some of the most secret dossiers compiled by the FSF. You had one on Zia, didn't you?"

I confirm it. "The file said Zia was the most loyal of generals. He had his finger on the pulse of the jawans, with whom he behaved conservatively. The chances of Zia calling on the army to take over, even under turbulent conditions, were said to be nil."

"Ah, what can you do! Intelligence people have their blind spots." Talib was being friendly. Perhaps he had a soft corner for someone in my position, not a principal, but a conveyor of information from one stubborn party to another. "For some time after the 1971 debacle, I continued to believe Bhutto had saved the country's honor, salvaged what little could be kept of Pakistan. I honored him for bringing back the POWs, for pressuring Mujib not to put those hundred and ninety-five soldiers on war crimes trials, for regaining five thousand square miles of lost territory from India. Then I realized. The bastard brought about the East Pakistan tragedy in the first place. I have my problems with democracy, but Mujib had won fair and square. Bhutto would rather break up the country than live with the results. Personal ambition, Asghar, my dear fellow, personal ambition run amok."

"Is Zia less motivated by personal ambition?"

Talib is surprised by my boldness. "Zia's motivation is the greater good of Pakistan. Never forget that."

"What do you think of jailing and stoning women for adultery if they bring forth complaints of rape? What do you think of cutting off the hands of people for petty theft?"

"Is that the sum of his reforms? Why do you PPP fellows always latch on to the most sensational actions, the weakest links? Zia is a humble man who cares for the downtrodden. No one's hands have been cut off yet."

"You'd rather have the Mughal darbar, the Raj kutchery, the arbitrary exercise of compassion, than the rule of law." I'm letting off steam before my final betrayal.

Talib understands this and lets me go on in this vein. The other two show no restlessness. Talib signals the notetaker not to jot down the wild accusations I'm making about the martial law regime.

"We're suspicious of people who never get married," Talib says when I'm winding down with my anger at Zia.

He glances over my sparse apartment. I've removed any remnants of Marxist literature, even literary theory by obscure Romanians and Hungarians translated into bad English. The bookshelves are empty of Faiz, the socialist poet who always suffers first when a martial law regime comes to power.

"You don't have any perversions, do you?" Talib is hinting at homosexuality.

"If I did, you'd already know."

"Be that as it may." Talib smiles. "Getting down to business, what's the big news you have to share?"

On my own initiative, I've taken Rahim sahib's hints about something big happening through the Al-Zulfiqar organization, to pry more information out of the other party bigwigs as well as the lesser lights. And something is indeed up. The Bhutto family isn't down and out yet.

Pinkie is in detention at Sukkur jail, in very bad shape from what I hear, having lost a lot of weight. Begum Bhutto is said to suffer from lung cancer, although Zia won't give her permission to travel abroad. He says there is "nothing the matter with Begum Bhutto," but he'd be glad to authorize her travel abroad if "she wants to do some sightseeing." But Bhutto's sons Mir and Shahnawaz, who've married a pair of Afghan sisters, Fauzia and Rehana, are free to do as they wish, out of the range of Zia's enforcers, organizing terrorist actions from Europe. Not a week goes by that Mir and Shahnawaz don't appear on European television, claiming responsibility for some terrorist act.

So far, their actions have been insignificant, barely registering with the exhausted Pakistani public. But now they plan to hijack a PIA airliner from Lahore airport, take it to Kabul, and demand the release of scores of political prisoners. I've learned this not from Khar and the other top PPP officials, but from some of Mir and Shahnawaz's most loyal lower-level followers, especially in the PPP stronghold of Lyari. It's being talked about freely in the backrooms of paan shops and restaurants, as though it were a gang action of ten-year-old kids. I'm taken to meet one Abdul Karim Baloch, who confirms the plan and wants me to convey a message of loyalty to Pinkie, believing I'm still in touch with her and loyal to the old PPP structure. He wants to know how Pinkie wants the party apparatus to proceed once the regime backs down after the hijacking.

Why is this plan being discussed so openly? Surely, the martial law regime already knows. The dreaded FSF, such a big cause of Bhutto's alienation from the party's stalwarts, has been absorbed by the ISI. The old renegades in the secret police are now working for the new regime's military intelligence. The ISI may have a tradition of being plodding, but I can vouch that the FSF people are damn good, on to things long before they happen.

Part of my reason for telling the ISI everything I've learned about the plot is my strong suspicion that the regime already knows and I won't be shifting the course of events. But there are more complex reasons as well.

If Al-Zulfiqar succeeds, they say the next step will be something catastrophic, so big that Zia will have to release Pinkie and Begum Bhutto, and be forced into exile in Saudi Arabia or the Gulf. Pinkie is ten times the feudal Bhutto ever was: she'll embark on a vendetta of cleansing everyone who had anything to do with her father's "judicial murder," as she always refers to the travesty of the trial and execution. No one will be spared. If her father didn't attempt anything remotely like the East Pakistan genocide to deal with the 1977 PNA agitation, she might well take the country down such a path. Bhutto never had that remorseless streak of brutality. His own power was earned through charisma and sincerity, as mixed-up and cruel as he could be. When he acted forcefully in Baluchistan and the NWFP, calling out the army in the early seventies, it was to put down secessionary movements. How could he have allowed a replay of Bangladesh?

"Can we trust you, Asghar?" Talib says when I've recited the details of the plot as far as I've been able to follow, and given him the names and locations of key PPP activists the ISI hasn't got wind of yet. "Why are you doing this?"

"I want all this to stop. I want the cycle of violence and counter-violence to come to an end. Anything to bring this viciousness to a stop."

"Anything? A few floggings here and there to put the fear of Allah in people's hearts?"

I look defeated. "I only meant the goondas."

Talib smiles. So do his two companions. Benevolence is at last in the air, and it feels good after four years of terror.

"I'll see what I can do about your petition to travel abroad," Talib says as he leaves. "Thank you, my friend. You've been of invaluable service to the state. You won't regret your actions. I'll pass the word about your loyalty to my superiors all the way up the chain."

"My loyalty?"

"Loyalty. Come on, fellows."

The notetaker clicks off his pen, and inserts his notes in a sealed envelope, which he busily licks.

"Los Angeles or London?" Talib asks.

"Excuse me?" I realize he's talking about where I'd prefer to be exiled—if he's serious about it. "Los Angeles," I mutter. Could it be possible? Bhutto's sunny California, where he first imbibed his radical ideas, even if Rahim sahib thinks that he was the prime instigator of

Bhutto's radicalism! London is a beehive of PPP activists. Whenever Mir and Shahnawaz declare a terrorist victory, the BBC and the *Guardian* treat them as heroes. Can't they be arrested and prosecuted for killing innocent people? And they pale in comparison to what I fear from Pinkie.

I've turned informant twice, to save my own skin. I hope this will be enough. I look around at my bare room, as though I'm already a stranger to the misery. Somewhere in the city— perhaps in Baldia or Korangi—a tiny rebellion is surely being put down by the guns of the regime. Lives are being lost in vain. Some are fighting for Bhutto, some for Mufti Mahmood and the other mullahs. We no longer know what we're fighting for.

The last evening of our freedom, Bhutto's Bengali lover Husna paced like a tigress in her room at the annex to 70 Clifton. Begum Bhutto never acknowledged Husna's presence in the annex to me or anyone else.

Whenever the crisis of the moment became too tense, Husna would move into the annex from the house Bhutto had bought for her across the street, and there was nothing Begum Bhutto could do about it. The reason Bhutto had been so attracted to Husna, apart from her seductive dark looks, was her versatility in discussing politics with him for hours at a time and holding up her end well. Begum Bhutto would never be able to match that. At best, Begum Bhutto could offer desultory yes and no responses to the Quaid-e-Awam's serious inquiries.

While Husna pranced hotly at the annex, 70 Clifton was in an uproar. Zia was due to arrive any minute. If the deal with the PNA had been concluded the night before, canceling the results of the previous elections and calling for a fresh round to satisfy the opposition, why was my heart still so heavy? Where did the feeling of doom come from? Rao Rashid, Bhutto's most trusted intelligence and security aide, with his finger in every pie, had assured him that the opposition would soon fracture. Zulfiqar Ali Bhutto was the only national leader. I'd lately begun to mistrust Rao Rashid's perennial optimism.

Husna called me into her room at nine in the evening. She wore a silk slip, her heavy breasts exposed, her thighs shifting in the flimsy cover like pillars of solace. She caught me staring, and only became more daring. She wanted to make sure we got a replacement for one of Zulfi's favorite pairs of black wingtips, the next time we were in London.

I told Husna I hated being dragged away from Bhutto's side at crucial moments for such trivial distractions.

She patted me on the cheek. "Asghar, you're such a child."

Abruptly, she went into the bathroom. I could hear her crying. I no longer wanted any part of this insanity, so I walked next door to the living room at 70 Clifton.

What they said about Husna's preternatural calm wasn't true. When her husband, a leading intellectual, was killed by the Pakistan Army in 1971 in Dacca, while she was already living in Karachi to be near Bhutto, she was said not to have shed a tear. A lie.

Bhutto was in solitary conference with Zia. Zia turned out to be a chain-smoker. I hadn't known that. He'd never touched a cigarette when cooling his heels for a meeting with Bhutto. Tonight he was smoking away with abandon.

"Sir, the army will do its duty by the government, follow the constitution in all respects," I heard him claim in his squeaky, blatantly modest voice. "The jawans expect no less. You elevated me above six officers more senior than me. I'll forever be grateful for your generosity, sir."

Bhutto looked alarmed. He slipped a note to me with instructions to get one of his new suits ready for a press conference at 70 Clifton as soon as Zia was gone, and to make sure that the press secretary called the television, radio, and newspaper reporters to be on the scene by 11.30 p.m.

Bhutto had been telling Zia how he needed martial law retained in Karachi, Lahore, and Hyderabad, not to mention the army holding on to its tight grip in Baluchistan and the NWFP, all through the campaign and elections, possibly in November. But now Bhutto clamped up with Zia about his plans for new elections.

They talked about the Shah of Iran, Bhutto's fair-weather friend who'd pitched in with American planes and arms to help suppress the Baluch insurgency, but refused him three hundred million dollars to bail him out of the economic crisis the same year.

"The Shah exaggerates the fundamentalist threat to squeeze more aid out of the Americans," Zia said. "Iran's is a sophisticated civilization. The Shi'ite clerics have not an enlightened arrow in their quiver. The proud Persian civilization would never go for clerics who propagate senseless rebellion from the holy shrines."

"That's not what my intelligence reports," Bhutto said. "Khomeini is a real threat. He's a star in exile."

"The Shi'ite clerics are so rigid that if my daughter Zain violated some Islamic injunction, they wouldn't show her any mercy." Zain was Zia's twenty-year-old mentally retarded daughter, his youngest, whose every whim Zia catered to. He'd proudly shown me pictures of her, during an interminable wait for Bhutto. By all appearances, she looked completely normal.

"If anything happens to me, I expect Pinkie to continue my legacy," Bhutto said in an apparent non sequitur. "I have groomed her well. I don't expect to live more than ten years anyway. Ten years, maximum. My heart, my liver, they'll give out before then."

"Children are the pride of dutiful parents, sir." Zia rubbed his long hands as though performing wudu before prayer.

The black mark on Zia's forehead, acquired by diligent namazis after years of persistent head-banging while performing sajda, shone brighter than ever. Positioned like an ugly beacon on his head, it called forth medieval demons, the legendary churayls and bhoots of the rural imagination. I felt like grabbing a heavy brass ornament from the mantelpiece, one of those gifted by the Shah of Iran to his "brother" Bhutto, and smashing it with all my power on Zia's skull, killing him in front of the master, even if I had to spend the rest of my life in jail.

"Anyway, it's all over now," Bhutto said to Zia. "We've resolved all our differences, the opposition and I. You can go home and rest."

"The army, I can assure you, sir, will follow the constitution to the letter," Zia repeated. "It will never do anything to destabilize the country. The jawans are one hundred percent behind me, sir."

Bhutto had dragged out the accord with the PNA for four months after the disputed March 7 elections. At first he'd refused to negotiate. The opposition had no ideology of its own, save for one point: oust Bhutto at any price.

Secularists like Asghar Khan shamelessly cohabited with hotheaded mullahs like Shah Ahmad Noorani, united in their hatred of Bhutto, resentful of the sway he retained over the awam. Bhutto tried to have his friends in Saudi Arabia and the Emirates intervene on behalf of sanity and order. He gave the army a freer hand to quell protests. A month ago, he had announced a deal with the PNA to hold new elections, but then disappeared for yet another tour of the Middle East, leaving the opposition wondering about his intentions. Only the night before, he had finally agreed with Pirzada, Rao Rashid, and his other deputies that he would go along with each and every one of the opposition's demands. Until six in the morning, the PPP leaders had been drinking in celebration. Husna joined them toward the end, while Begum Bhutto was nowhere to be seen. Only Rahim sahib, back in Bhutto's good graces, had been grumpy. "You've left it till too late, I'm afraid," he admonished Bhutto. "The army is emboldened. Dangerous precedents have been set. They think the constitution is a piece of paper they can toy with."

Bhutto looked enraged. I thought of the time the FSF had paid Rahim sahib an unwelcome visit in the middle of the night. I shuddered to imagine what poor Rahim sahib, in his seventies, must have been through. I hoped I never fell on Bhutto's wrong side.

Pirzada tried to defuse the situation. "Rahim ji, as law minister I cannot allow any downer tonight. That would be a crime against the state punishable by five years' rigorous imprisonment."

Bhutto's advisers laughed, but Rahim sahib didn't find it funny. Neither did I.

Bhutto hadn't announced his intention to seal the deal to the PNA or the public as of the morning of July 4. He wanted to drag the desperate opposition over the coals some more, let them stew in their own juices, imagine worst-case scenarios. It was only the meeting with Zia that settled the case—something about Zia's manner must have alerted Bhutto that time was running out. It had to be now or never.

As soon as Zia left, Bhutto had the PNA leaders called, telling them he agreed to each of their demands.

The press conference began at 11.30 p.m. at 70 Clifton. "We've concluded a historic deal with the opposition," Bhutto said. "We'll have a public ceremony tomorrow to sign the accord. This is unprecedented in Pakistan's history. Politics is the art of give-and-take. If I play hardball, the other side is free to do so as well. The interest of the country, the legitimacy of the constitution, its preservation, comes first. I apologize to my brothers and sisters who've had to be dragged through the nightmare of the last four months. We hope the return of stability will attract much-needed investment to the country. Pakistan is open for business again. Let there be an end to the strikes, the riots. Let politics, the supreme human art, take center stage again. My thanks to the Shah of Iran, King Khalid of Saudi Arabia, and all those who lent their good offices to resolve these sticky matters."

Bhutto didn't stay around to answer the press's questions. No doubt some were thinking, How many times have we heard this before? Is this deal real? Pakistan had been caught in too much politics since 1967, when Bhutto started the first populist movement. Siyasat, siyasat, every step of the way. Bhutto loved it, it gave him life. Husna claimed to love it. I let it push aside any thoughts of a private life. But did the people love it too? Or were they like Begum Bhutto, tolerating it as a necessity, but not pleased?

At 2 a.m., 70 Clifton was surrounded by the army. Bhutto was transported in a military helicopter to the Murree rest house, and I went with him, part of the retinue of aides he was allowed to keep for three weeks, as Zia, the new ruler, at first allowed him comfortable conditions of detention. The soldiers who had come to wake me up from sleep were amused that the detained prime minister would want to take his loyal servants with him. The colonel who glanced briefly at the papers I collected from my file cabinets said, "You'll be needing these, I suppose, to mount your defense. Fine, take all the papers you want. Documentation is always good." I thanked him for his generosity.

JEALOUSY

When Shabbir first asked Mehreen to get pregnant, her response was to make even louder noises in the bathroom.

Having taken exceptional care with washing his penis and butt, so that the black hairs shone and sparkled—did he secretly grease the hair there, when she wasn't looking? Was there a special glistening agent for pubic and anal hair?—his extraordinary demand from the bed seemed to be his justification for the ritual on that particular night. Perhaps all the rubbing and massaging of the pelvic area was a form of stealthy masturbation. No married man wanted to openly masturbate, since it signified an irreplaceable loss in the marriage. If marriage wasn't for sex, what was it for?

"I can't hear you," she said, washing her feet and calves in the bathtub—Shabbir noted if there was dirt under her toenails, if her heels were stained—while she had the tap in the sink also running full blast.

"I said, we should probably have a baby," he repeated.

Marriage was for pregnancy, then, that was her answer. She'd been dreading it for three years. Already, they'd waited longer than the typical Pakistani couple. They were at the stage where other Pakistani couples would have felt free to ask why the "little prince" (they never said "princess") hadn't yet made his appearance in the world—as though Mehreen and Shabbir possessed some secret fertility drug to produce on order a bundle of joy for grandparents to adore.

It was typical of Shabbir to announce something of this magnitude through the barrier of the bathroom door. It was at moments like this—there were all too many of them—that his brash presence intruded into Mehreen's dream world, her real world, her other world. The rest of the time she thought she'd put Shabbir in his special box, labeled, "Dangerous, Fragile, Explosive Material: Handle with Care," and as long as she followed the hazmat instructions, there'd be no trouble for her.

But Shabbir had a way of smashing out of his box, boldly, nakedly, pubic hair and all, standing in front of her, demanding attention. She wished he was a child who could be pacified with a lollipop. She wished he would develop interests, hobbies, obsessions other than her. His sole preoccupation apart from work—for an engineering firm in Manhattan—was his growing collection of theological books in Arabic, which he couldn't read, but pretended to, in his abysmal Urdu-accented Arabic, which sounded, in Shabbir's grating voice, like a new language, a language created for the edification of apes or some intermediary human-animal species. So far, Shabbir was praying only once or twice a day. She wondered if five times a day was in the offing, but her parents—both of whom lived in the house in Jackson Heights they all shared, claiming they were so invisible in their "little corner" that Mehreen and Shabbir could pretend they lived by themselves—assured her that devoutness wasn't in Shabbir's genes. Well, pregnancy wasn't in hers.

"I wish you'd turn on your stomach," she said, appearing at the door of the bathroom. Turning on his belly meant Shabbir would get a patented Mehreen massage, especially of his beloved butt. She would squeeze clumps of flesh in her small fingers, pinching ruthlessly, until he was a quivering mass of nerves under her ministrations, ready to do her bidding, which was to go back into the box.

"Is that a new gown?" he inquired, as he often did about her clothes, retaining his posture. Next to the gigantic bed, a green night light—a remnant of Shabbir's life in Pakistan, where his parents had inflicted the light on Shabbir and his twin sister as a permanent nighttime presence, to ensure no hanky-panky went on between the siblings—illuminated Shabbir's erect penis, curving to the right. It was the only penis Mehreen was deeply acquainted with; the others had been fleeting, but this one was for keeps. The thought was too depressing to let it penetrate her conscious mind.

"I've had it for a while," she said about the gown.

Shabbir never wanted her to go fully naked. If they were alone in the house on weekends when Mehreen's parents went to New Jersey or Pennsylvania, Shabbir insisted she wear something silky, nylony, not quite see-through. She'd figured it was a way to keep him turned on; he liked to "imagine" the dénouement, even if it was the most familiar story in the world, instead of seeing the whole show at once. At night, she was supposed to wear one of the various ill-fitting "nighties" Shabbir bought from Alexander's on his way back from work. It was his idea of romance.

Shabbir looked skeptical, as though Mehreen would have a reason to hide the provenance of the nightgown, a white lacy thing with a bra too high, and panties designed for a hipless teenager.

"Turn around," Mehreen said.

"Not tonight. We need to talk about what I just said. Did you hear what I said?"

"I heard, but not tonight please."

"When?"

"Soon. Soon, I promise."

Not even the extra-attentive butt massage she gave him—rubbing his sensitive prostate, manipulating his erogenous zones for an early climax—quieted his disturbance.

She put a finger to his lips when, instead of falling asleep right away, he wanted to bring up the subject of Mehreen's unsullied belly yet again. Usually, he made a big fuss about Mehreen washing herself off after intercourse, and although he was supposed to wash his genitals too in the aftermath, according to the Islamic instruction he was acquiring on his own, he started snoring before the purifying trip to the bathroom.

In the morning, she was up before the proverbial rooster's crow, which in the case of their Queens neighborhood meant the garbage trucks and grocery delivery vans and other heavy automotive machinery making screeching, wailing, jangling sounds soon after dawn. She put down her cup of Lipton tea—Shabbir had managed to convince her, with extensive internet research, to switch from coffee, because tea wasn't as bad for teeth and gastric functions—at the kitchen sink, and stood staring outside.

It was her favorite moment of the day, and she tried to make it last as long as possible. From her angle, she could see clear through to the main street, where traffic buzzed along like a mound of disturbed ants racing for life. There was just enough space between the cumbersome trees on the boulevard for her to make out one of the melancholy brown high-rises that served as reminders to Pakistani and Greek and Bosnian families why they were so lucky to own their houses, even if their property wasn't in the nicer, distant parts of Long Island.

"It's time to take an objective look at the situation," she spoke aloud, as she was apt to in the fullness of her beautiful moment.

She was twenty-seven, according to all scientific calculations at the peak of her procreative capability. Each additional year of waiting increased the risk. The magazines were full of this information; it was inescapable. In school—she was in the fourth year of her Art History Ph.D. at Columbia—most of her friends, male and female, were married. Many had children. More than even the ethnics, it was whites these days who seemed to value having and raising children as the most heroic gestures imaginable. It was how you signified rebellion in the twenty-first century. There was an exception: Peter Hua, whom she'd known and adored from the first day she'd met him, at the incoming students orientation that beautiful September morning, when she'd found herself falling into weeping bouts for no apparent reason, escaping to the bathroom to do so, despite her newly minted status as a "wife," having spent the summer in Lahore to expropriate Shabbir from his devoted parents and sister for her exclusive use. Unlike her white friends, Peter—the sole Asian in the program other than herself—hadn't wanted to talk about Mehreen's married existence; over glasses of sherry, they chatted about the luminous quality of Jan Steen's paintings, both of them agreeing that the contributions of the Dutch to the enlightenment were vastly underappreciated. "Humor without disparagement, that's a quality that seems to have eluded the French," Peter said about the Dutch Old Masters. "Voltaire should have studied Vermeer more." Except, of course, Vermeer wasn't Vermeer in Voltaire's time, but the point stood.

She was distracted from meditating on her objective situation. That was how it was when one tried to focus on a single thing. She washed the mug, and sat at the dining table. She'd brought in the *Times* from the porch. It had the inevitable splotch of mud on the front page. Her father—also an engineer, like his son-in-law, although he'd chosen to work in the more secure realm of the state, endowing the Metropolitan Transportation Authority with the best years of his life—would take a sheet of Bounty, wet it, and wipe off the *Times* before hitting the op-ed page, at precisely seven-thirty, his routine for all of Mehreen's life. Her mother—a retired librarian—would get up at the more leisurely hour of nine, by which time Mehreen hoped to be gone from the house. She had no reason to leave so early, but if she didn't, her mother would be on her case for "inviting depression and constipation" because of laziness.

Why had she not rebelled against being married so young, before she'd had more experience with men? Her parents had looked the other way when she'd dated a few guys, none of them exciting, when she was at Barnard. She suspected one had to wait until one's thirties to taste the benefits of freedom. She'd missed out on that. Was it a forced marriage? She hadn't wanted to waste precious energy fighting off the inevitable, for it hadn't been Shabbir, it would have been some other "eligible" man of her parents' choice; if it wasn't in Pakistan, it would have been in Queens; and if it wasn't at twenty-three, it would have been at thirty-one, but the result would have been the same.

Further invitation to depression was stalled when her father clattered his way down the stairs, coughing and wheezing, his way of disapproving the cooler temperature, which she happened to love. Shabbir was long gone: he liked to wake up at six and leave soon after, taking the train to midtown before the garbage trucks started their din.

🌙

It was the first time she'd seen him at Butler Library this early in the day, and she took it as a sign. She put aside her notebook—for the last year she'd been whittling down her thesis on late French Baroque painters, but still had a great many unnecessary curlicues and flourishes to chop away—and headed over to where Peter was sunning his face in one of the windows of the reading room.

"Hey!" he said, stretching his legs and wiggling his shoulders. He needed a good massage; too bad Mehreen couldn't do it for him.

"Hey there yourself."

"Sit down, you."

There was a standing invitation from Peter for them to get drunk together at his Morningside Drive digs; Mehreen had never been drunk, and was curious to know what it felt like. At the peak of the experience, would she yell obscenities toward Allah and Muhammad, those faithless, changeable figures that tried to dominate every act in her life from two or three removes? Would she strip naked in public? Would she start doing imitations of her professors, how they turned the simplest question into a barrage of abstract answers, making her so bored she wondered in the middle of it if her Mom had had her afternoon tea back in Jackson Heights?

Peter had copies of *Architectural Digest* spread out in front of him, his usual reading at the library: anything to do with houses, solid structures, the more grandiose the better—not the flimsy fabrications of artists' puffed-up minds. She kidded him that he was in the wrong profession; it was the one subject that would get his goat, not family or personal life. And his personal life was a mess.

His father, mentally damaged in his sixties after an eighteen-wheeler crawled over his Toyota on the George Washington Bridge, had run off with a totally pierced—clit included—blue-haired angel in her twenties who called him "grandpaw" in public. Both his sisters had once been Cambodian gangbangers, although they were Chinese. And his mother had been attempting to translate the works of Gao Xingjian, without a contract, without so much as a whiff of commitment from a publisher, until the author won the Nobel Prize, on which day she gave up the labor of her life. Peter's education and lifestyle were being financed by a rich gay uncle in San Francisco, who wanted no more than to be invited to some of the flashier Columbia parties in return. Rather than the flamboyant, drag-wearing, anti-angel Mehreen expected, he turned out to be the most invisible person she'd ever met.

Peter was smart, but she wondered if he owed his success to chutzpah, his energetic flailing of himself at every opportunity, his ability to pin down people in a moment's glance yet let them know he wouldn't reveal their Achilles' heel. Being as handsome as he was, carrying that hypnotic dread in his brown eyes, made him a wonder in the groves of academe.

"What's new in the world of architecture?" she kidded him.

"Nothing I didn't already anticipate." The cynical, know-it-all, faux ironic mode was their default posture at school. It was only when they were away from Columbia that they became serious. "Wanna go over to my place and make out?"

He'd been saying that for years. She knew he was joking, and yet whenever he said it, there was a boyish glint in his eyes, like a teenager giving in to his spinster aunt's advances.

"Finish my sandwich," he said. Peter often offered his half-eaten food, and she usually took him up on it. Looking around to make sure no one was observing this breach of library etiquette—there was a limit to her levity within school confines—she started nibbling on the exquisite avocado sandwich. Culinary school was another thing Peter would have excelled at.

"Peter, do you wonder what it would have been like if you'd married Sonia?" She'd asked him before, but Peter was a generous soul who didn't mind repetition: there were, after all, only a handful of important questions and answers, so why should one scrape the bottom of the barrel?

Across from them was a tweedy, gray-toned, Edward Said copycat—perhaps an Arab, more likely a swarthy Nordic with identity confusion. He'd been sneaking glances at them, while trying to read the foreign newspaper sprawled in his hands. At last he looked straight ahead and shushed them with an erect finger before his lips.

"I think he's a fake," she whispered to Peter. "Plus, he's fifteen feet across. He has to make an effort to listen to us."

"Ignore him."

Peter, with his lean, limber body already stretched to the maximum, as though he were a heat-seeking plant drawn to the window, leaned closer to Mehreen, almost resting his head on her shoulder. He smelled good, like warm spring rain, his natural aroma.

"Sonia?" Peter picked up the earlier thread of conversation. "She should be editor-in-chief of *Architectural Digest.*"

"Be serious, Peter."

Sonia had been the great love of Peter's life. A child prodigy—math genius, nonpareil manipulator of violin strings, and star soccer player—she'd remained a phenomenon as an adult, graduating from Princeton at nineteen. Her drive for success didn't prevent her from being the most magnanimous, outward-directed person you'd ever meet. She was distantly related to Peter, through a cross-country relay of aunts and uncles who claimed to have lived through the Cultural Revolution and to be none the worse for it. Sonia had had a crush on Peter, if perfection incarnate like Sonia could be said to have a crush. She had added a dash of invention to Peter's standard repertoire of sex games. Peter's explanation for Sonia's abandonment—her by him, or him by her?—was that they'd drifted apart, but this never satisfied Mehreen. There must be something more. Peter must have some evil habit, some dark side to his character.

"She didn't tie me up hard enough when we played donkey-on-the-Rhine," he said, prompting a loud shush from the Edward Said clone again.

Mehreen returned a sullen stare, taking Peter by the arm. "Let's get out of here, to some place quiet, where we can *talk*."

She was surprised as always by how light Peter felt. How airy and frictionless, as if coated by some weight-reducing element!

Having become gloomy at the thought of Sonia, Peter said, "I'm so at odds with my adviser. Did I tell you?"

"Me too. He's an asshole." She was talking about the great Professor Bartlett, who talked to Mehreen as though she were his little daughter, all but pulling her on his lap to spank her behind. He only did it verbally, in the mildest of WASP manners, so it was excusable.

They welcomed the sunshine in the quad facing Butler Library. If she slipped her arm into Peter's, someone from the department was bound to see them—some married woman, setting the rumor mills buzzing the next day.

It was early fall and the tourist contingents of the summer, Spaniards and Swedes, had been replaced by Indians and Chinese who seemed to be dating races as different from their own as possible. Shabbir had never

111

been to the Columbia campus in the daytime, although it was possible for him to do so on weekends and holidays. There had been a couple of uncomfortable school parties, where he insinuated that there were worthy, practical professions, and then there were the rest. She hadn't yet met anyone truly brilliant in the department, someone whose piercing insight would make her see things differently. They repeated what had been said before; they were the window cleaners and pipe fitters of the Gothic cathedral already constructed, eternally dominant, their job but to admire from street level.

"The Hungarian Café?" Peter said.

"The Hungarian Café," she agreed.

They'd have a serious discussion about art. She'd wasted another morning when she was supposed to read at the library, and narrow down her thesis just a bit more. Perhaps Shabbir was right. Perhaps she was in one of the less worthy professions.

On an evening promising to be like most others since her so-called married life began—that is, either her parents were busily making themselves invisible, or her cooking was being praised or dismissed in the momentous tones suited for imperial wars, or she was figuring out what she could say about herself that would be new to someone she'd been eating with for fourteen hundred days—Shabbir managed to change the equation.

Her parents were gone, for one thing. Without so much as a ragged note on her bedroom door asking her not to wait for them, they'd vanished into the seductive ether, the part of Queens that resembled real suburbia. Her father's only friend with whom he was intimate enough to have a weeknight dinner was a permanently unemployed Pakistani engineer named Rocco—to strangers, he claimed to be Italian—and her mother hated to go to anyone's home because of the guilt induced by more beautifully kept properties.

The lights in the house were lowered, a history of Turkish art fresh off the Barnes & Noble shelves stood like a cultural reproach on the table next to the flat screen television, and a wreath of flowers graced the front door, making her think of Christmas. None of this did anything to keep out the smell of rotting curry leftovers in the garbage bin that had eluded Shabbir's makeover plan.

"Oh Shabbir." She struggled to feel the right emotions. "I'll go upstairs and change."

"Put on something nice." He gripped her hand tightly, like he had on their wedding night, when he'd held hands much too long for comfort.

He was trying, he was trying, she ought not to be so cruel. In the bedroom, she was confronted by a spray of roses, laid on the bed like a sacrifice. Shabbir hadn't given her flowers on their four anniversaries.

He shouted from downstairs, "I would have had them delivered during the day, if you had a fixed work address."

Nervous about what was coming next—tales of Shabbir's own secret Sonia, revelation that he had prostate cancer, simultaneous orgasm matching the descriptions in romance novels?—she changed into her short pink dress, which Shabbir liked, despite his reluctance for her to wear it outside.

The lights downstairs were dimmed. Bats would feel at home. So would Dracula. She needed a drink. That was *Peter's* mantra, not hers. Shabbir had cooked broasted chicken, Lahori-style—a first, the other occasion being when he barbequed ribs for his first Super Bowl, for Pakistani coworkers who looked like they'd never attempted badminton or ping-pong, and nearly set the house on fire. It was free of spices, a concession to her tastes. Seated across from him at the dining table, yearning for the forbidden wine, she noticed that the stack of theological books constituting Shabbir's auto-induced curriculum was missing from the armchair in the corner. No one ever occupied the armchair; the books did, as a strategically placed beacon of guilt.

"What happened to the books, Shabbir?"

"First tell me, do you like the food?"

"Um, yes, very good, I love it. Your own formulation?"

"My own," he said with a broad grin. Good, the evening was already a success for him, no matter what happened next.

"So the books?"

"Ah yes." He bent forward, shifting his hands behind his head, which according to the body language experts reflected great confidence, but to her suggested a man cradling his most precious instrument in a last loving gesture before the guillotine fell. "Mehreen, I think I've been going too far with my religious studies. A reasonable amount of devotion is fine, especially when a man is in his thirties, trying to find his identity in an unfamiliar country." He shifted his hands to cradle his chin. A beard would look monstrous on him. He had asked her, loathing the time it took to shave, if it would look good on him. It would scare the bejeesus out of his coworkers. "Mehreen, I apologize if I haven't been paying attention to your needs. The work, you see, it gets to me. And then the politics."

Until dinner got cold, Shabbir brought her up-to-date on the machinations of various factions seeking to disenfranchise him of legitimate authority in his division of the firm: the dastardly Singhs and Kumars, infinitely more hostile to Shabbir's advancement as fellow South Asians than regular white folks could ever be, figured prominently in the tale. At the last moment, however, Shabbir realized his long-windedness, and rescued himself by pulling up next to her and feeding her a few bites. The candles, still flickering, were in league with him.

She'd never once mentioned Peter to him, even in the most casual of references. She fulfilled her wifely role by chattering about the hapless women in her department, so gullible, so uninformed about world events, so American in their lust for popular culture and material objects, without hinting about the resentment boiling inside her toward the stupidities of the profession of art historian.

"Shall we have a drink?" She was pushing it. It was against the religion. Shabbir never drank. They kept some bottles for guests, but when did their guests ever have any?

"You may," Shabbir said. "I can't, you know that." He had to answer to his God.

"I don't feel like it," she corrected herself, feeling drowsy. She was ready to be seduced by her husband of four years.

"Mehreen, this could be the night," he said to her when she was undressed and for once not going out of her way to make Shabbir's dick responsive to the occasion. "You didn't take protection, did you?" When she looked at him as if he'd lost his mind, he said, "I hope you're following through.." The politeness of his request only infuriated her. She wanted to tell him she'd failed to follow through, to put a damper on his physical exertions, but chose silence.

Not that silence offended Shabbir. When she'd been vocal in bed at the beginning of their marital odyssey, he showed fear. Tonight, he was making an all-out effort to please her different body parts—feet, calves, knees, thighs, stomach, shoulders, chin, nothing escaped him. Yet Mehreen had never felt so distanced from the very idea of sex. Why did people do it? It was the most ridiculous activity imaginable. For this, the world went around? For this? Art history came off better in comparison.

She forced herself to think of Peter on top of her, but didn't succeed. Shabbir's visage drowned her mind in a pool of self-pity. Objectively speaking, he was quite handsome. Fat hadn't invaded his flesh, and didn't seem likely to. He could be charming to "aunties" and "uncles," especially those whose children had driven them crazy with marital misalliances. Tonight, he felt like an alien— in every sense of the word. He'd be a citizen in another year. A United States citizen. Then he'd be free to marry anyone. He'd be equal to the Singh and Kumar factions in that respect. He'd be his own man.

Sex could be so disgusting. Imagine the consequences if it led to a naturally produced clone—a child, hungering for your nipple and oozing anger and desire from every pore, monopolizing your every waking and sleeping moment, binding you forever to your sex partner, the one who'd gifted you the perpetual shadow. Ugh!

She'd never let Shabbir have the satisfaction. She started feigning orgasm, catching at that precise moment the way to whittle down her thesis to manageable levels.

It began as a wicked glimmer in her eye when Shabbir said at dinner, with more bravado than Arthur Danto might have mustered on Native American tapestries, "The Chinese will take over the world."

Mehreen's father looked up from *Pakistan Link*, the community newspaper published in America and available alongside DVDs of Shahrukh and Madhuri movies at South Asian groceries everywhere. There were those who read *Pakistan Link* and those who read *India Abroad*, and never would the twain meet.

"The population growth works in their favor," her father agreed. "The development community was trying to pull a fast one when they said the third world would go hungry. It never happened."

"At work, Chang and Tang are like monkeys," Shabbir said. "They show off. They want everything instantly. They have no shame."

"Chang and Tang?" Mehreen's mother wondered.

"If they could, they'd plot to be my direct bosses."

"What does this have to do with China's population?" Mehreen's father asked.

"The Chinese immigrant. He used to be lost, wherever he went, even when he made it big. He could never call a place home. He was always an alien. Now he's getting a nerve. He's not afraid of being persecuted for his yellow skin. That's when his race gets dangerous."

"So Chang and Tang have taken over from Singh and Kumar?" Mehreen asked.

She was trying to be civil, to compensate for the opposite tendency in Shabbir lately. Since the night of the attempted impregnation, she'd been quieter at home than ever before. She derived guilty pleasure from her silence, acting like the Tibetan monk Milarepa, whom she used to fantasize about deflowering before she got married, or like a female basketball coach gone quiet on her felonious protégées. Talking made her feel like an anorexic experiencing sinful gastronomic pleasure.

"I try not to split the world into factions," declared Shabbir.

He was beginning to sound like one of those dime a dozen aging Pakistani uncles, with tufts of hair growing out of their ears and shapeless beige safari suits from the seventies adorning their flabby bodies, but with iron wills and know-it-all personas when it came to "world affairs." Shabbir was emitting the first signs of turning into one of these anti-womanizers.

"It's better not to divide the world," Mehreen's mother agreed.

"I think I'll go outside for a walk," said Mehreen.

Shabbir didn't ask if he could accompany her. The walks were a new phenomenon, unique to their current cold spell—so Shabbir hadn't been able to integrate it yet within his response mechanisms.

"Be careful," Mehreen's father warned. "The crime rate is going up, now that the economy is in the dumpster."

"Put on your beige sweater," Mehreen's mother advised. "It can get chilly all of a sudden."

The religious books were still missing from the armchair, although no one used it, as though it were sacred space reserved for the books, which might demand reseating at any moment.

In the bedroom, she mechanically put on her sweater, before realizing she didn't need to follow every word of her mother's, and taking it off. She put it back on again, because to rebel like a robot seemed even more obtuse.

"May I come with you?" Shabbir had snuck up behind her, placing his palm on her buttock, not yet caressing it.

"No. I'm going to see a colleague. A fellow student. Peter. Peter Hua. He's Chinese."

"Oh."

"I don't socialize enough. But this is more than socializing. I have to refine my thesis."

"You're always refining your thesis."

"But not enough."

"What time will you be home?" Shabbir was holding up well. "Is there a number we can reach you in case…in case there's a problem?"

"What kind of a problem would there be?"

He didn't answer that directly. "Go ahead then. You can go."

He was acting proprietarily. This was the effect she'd wanted to elicit from him—if she'd wanted any response at all—but it felt disconcerting.

"Peter's a nice guy. He's suffered a lot. Family problems. That's why I think he'll be a great art historian. You need to have suffered a great deal to understand art."

"So this Peter, is he married?"

"No, but he could have been."

This conversation went on at length, Mehreen being mendacious by building up a portrait of Peter as a haunted, melancholy, unpredictable fellow with designs on all the married women in the department, blondes and brunettes. Her voice became squeaky and high-pitched as she uttered her false spiel.

"You can't meet with him at school tomorrow? At the library?"

"I could. But I want to go now."

"No one's stopping you."

Sex between them since the climactic night had been labored, also far less frequent. She hadn't initiated it once, a departure from their equal sharing of the motivational burden.

There had been no more grand romantic gestures. She wasn't sure if Shabbir understood that she felt differently toward him now. How could she ever talk to him about it? It would be like going to the Russians at the height of the cold war and asking them if your own missile silos were in the best strategic location.

Instead, she started talking to Peter, that night, and many nights after that, about the degeneration of her *objective situation*. Peter reciprocated by letting on that his narrative about his wacky family was a tad exaggerated. He was never more adorable than when he tried to be ordinary, a Joe Average accepting that heroism was out of reach.

When she taunted Shabbir with the rope-for-a-sinking-woman attraction Peter held for her, it felt so good she made a habit of it. Day after day, she would erupt into enthusiasm about how great it was to share her innermost feelings—not only about art—with Peter, how much insight he had into the arc of her professional career, how thoroughly trained he was in the classical ethos, so that to talk to him was to talk to a Leonardo or Goethe.

She felt her strategy was working. The more she talked with Shabbir about Peter, the less time she needed to spend with Peter, or indeed any other friends and acquaintances, and the less important the travails of her married life seemed to become.

At some point, however, she became obsessed by what Shabbir might be thinking about her. Was he wracked by jealousy? If so, why was he so calm? Why did he still bring up Chang and Tang at the dinner table, as though ignorant of the allusion to Peter? Why was he always polite to her? Why had he started asking again for butt massages? Was he on to her game? Did he know it was only platonic?

She'd prove him wrong. The two men in her life would have to meet. She was at a loss as to how to orchestrate this. The direct approach was bound to fail. It was a good thing Peter was handsome enough to make other men suspect he was gay, but turned them green with envy when they realized he was as heterosexual as they came.

Shabbir had given her a cell phone, which she kept turned off. "You can keep it in vibrating mode, if you're afraid it'll go off at the library," he'd instructed. To her protest that cell phones were carried by teenagers with nothing to talk about and businesspeople having affairs, he'd responded, "Just for emergencies, please."

Sitting with her feet on one of Peter's desks, looking out the window at the tops of the trees in Central Park, she wondered if the switched-off cell phone in her brown jacket hanging on the door was attempting to vibrate. Was Shabbir calling her, instead of putting the pieces into place for his final assault against both factions, Singh and Kumar, and Chang and Tang? Had he refused dinner last night with her parents, sulking in the bedroom with microwaved halal hot dogs—his latest pique—to prove he could eat on his own?

"Does he even give a fuck?" she yelled at Peter, even though he was at the desk next to her. Having two desks side by side was Peter's way of suggesting to the world, should he ever have a decent party or invite an eligible girl for a drink, that he was ready for a relationship. Peter's narration of wild parties at his apartment had turned out to be a bit on the purple side.

"Does who give a fuck?" Peter was absorbed in the new Eco book, which to Mehreen's mind was like the old Eco books. Writers these days came in brands: the Rushdie brand, the DeLillo brand, the Foster Wallace brand. To be associated with a certain brand said something about you as a human being.

"My dear husband, is who."

"Why, because you're here?"

"Peter, how come we've never gotten drunk?"

"Because it's bad for your liver."

"You're a health freak all of a sudden?" She glared at him, and he lost himself in the fat hardback again. He had a girlish habit of licking his fingers when turning the page, something she'd never have guessed had she not gotten to know him so intimately—she wasn't *living* with him, but she'd come as close to cohabitation with another man as she could while staying married.

She wondered if she'd turned Peter's apartment, after weeks of regular visits, into something that looked more lived-in, rather than the Gobi desert of transparent solitude it had been when she first saw it. He'd filled it with contemporary streamlined European pseudo-furniture. It lacked solidity.

"Peter, would you like a massage?"

"I want to say yes, and I really appreciate your offer, but I think I'll take a rain check this time. I'm really into this book, and I want to finish it today."

"Whatever you say."

So now Peter didn't want her massages? Had she become so unattractive after regular daily visits? When he did agree to a massage, he kept his tight briefs on—she would have guessed he wore boxers—and when she spent too much time squeezing his ass, he would become eager to wrap it up. It was true his skin was soft and babyish, but there too she missed solidity. Her conclusion after knowing Peter in the flesh was that she preferred big men.

"You can finish the strawberry shake," he offered.

"I think I'll go out for a walk."

Peter didn't respond.

Who wanted to get serious with a married woman? But you could get unserious with her, couldn't you? She put on her brown jacket, patting the cell phone as practical people did all day long, to feel connected.

She slammed the door on her way out. Peter had given her the key to his apartment within a week, but kept asking her all the time if she'd lost it. If she returned it to him, or even suggested it, it would signify the closure of something for which she wasn't ready.

She walked around Morningside Heights in a rising fury, not deigning to acknowledge the nods of the plump Mediterranean-type joggers who invariably had a thing for her. Lingering outside the Hungarian Café, she wondered if she dared go in by herself, as her professors did, not giving a damn whether the world thought them old and lonely. She waited outside for so long that a waitress treated her like a homeless bum.

These occasions of frenzied self-disgust used to produce worthwhile insights. The thought was occurring to her now that her thesis was becoming an endless nightmare—the last narrowing of the path having turned into yet another divergence to an open road—because doctoral candidates didn't want to finish and get out of school into the real world of jobs and savings. This didn't mean it was a valid perception. It was only the thought of the moment, no more valuable than the fleeting enlightenment from a Woody Allen movie or a Philip Glass score.

"Fuck all that," she said when she arrived at the Amsterdam Avenue entrance to Columbia University. Why didn't her parents get involved in her deteriorating marital situation? The first part of their job was done when she got the acceptance letter from Columbia, and the rest when they nodded solemnly at the mullah's nikah recitation in Lahore. She'd been her parents' Sonia, a convenient crutch, and Shabbir their Peter, the man who came to the rescue. So there was redundancy in the story? She turned on her cell phone, expecting it to vibrate right away.

Still peeved, she entered Lerner Hall to buy some ice cream. It was much too cold, but she found a spot in Low Plaza where she could exercise her ossifying licking skills on the hapless cone. A pair of toddlers, paradisiacally blond as in some patriotic artist's rendition, came up to her and matched her lick for lick, their ice-cream cones dribbling and making a mess. Their lithe and ethereal mother—a fully-realized exercise in blonde ecstasy herself—watched from across the pathway, oozing pride of possession. *See, I'm a mother,* she seemed to say, *I didn't refuse my husband when he wanted to make me pregnant. Fact is, I initiated the pregnancy. I'm hard-wired the right way.*

It was definitely a good idea to prolong schooling; she sure didn't want to deal with what her father and Shabbir and Peter's uncle confronted on a day-to-day basis. Come to think of it, she'd never not been in school.

"Oh God, I'm so glad I found you."

It was Shabbir, dressed in a dark suit and red tie, his work uniform.

"You?" Mehreen stuttered. "What're you doing here?"

"Looking for my dear wife, on a beautiful Thursday afternoon, to see what she's up to."

He settled unselfconsciously on the stone bench, putting an arm around her with the ease of the practiced husband. She panicked, afraid that Myrna the Vanderbilt girl, Professor Bartlett's daughter, Jolene the department secretary, anyone she knew might see her.

"Don't," she said, pushing his hand away, and quickly finishing the ice cream.

As if on cue, the blonde mother signaled her kids, and they marched off into the world beyond Columbia's gates.

"I just thought, you know, since I never visit you here," said Shabbir. "I left work early today. The library is beautiful. If I were a student here, wow, what wouldn't I do."

"You get used to it."

They sat quietly on the bench, the afternoon fading into gloom. Another blinding flash: Sonia was a figment of Peter's imagination. He'd never shown Mehreen any pictures of her, despite his tendency to accumulate everyone else's pictures.

"Shabbir, I'm having an affair."

The words came out of her mouth before she'd planned it. It was a patent lie, and the most beautiful and correct one she'd ever told. It felt good, it felt exhilarating, and she constructed, for Shabbir's benefit, a full-fledged fantasy of hot, steamy afternoons with Peter, whom she said Shabbir should meet—he lived close by—so they could talk about it like adults, work it out "amicably," leaving no hard feelings, though of course she would understand if he did feel mad at her, if he wanted to hit her.

Shabbir listened to the tale without interrupting. He'd want a divorce now, of course. She'd move into a cheap Bronx apartment, take the train every morning to Columbia, finish her dissertation in one year, and get a job teaching on the West Coast. Eventually, her parents would move close to her, though not in the same house. Shabbir would be fine on his own, he would take care of himself. Would he be fine? Would he manage? He didn't know how to cook. Would he become a religious fanatic, memorizing what he could of the books still missing from the armchair?

"Come, we should go home." He took off his coat and put it around her. "It's getting late."

"That's it?" she said. "That's all you're going to say?"

He reflected, playing with his wedding ring. "For now," he sighed. He sounded adult and mature, like the man she thought she'd married, trusting despite herself in her parents' superior judgment. Perhaps she'd found that man after all. But was it too late?

If she said, let's not tell my parents, he'd be on to her lie right away. She was choking. Trying to get an edge on another human being was futile. The best thing was to let other people be, to just let go.

GROWING UP BLIND IN A HOTLY CONTESTED STATE

I never know how to deflect one of those hijab-wearing, round-faced, thick-nosed, Near Eastern women who come on to me in class. They think a teacher in his prime, if he doesn't declare his attachment, must be ready for the plucking. Mind you, none of them—virgins all—would have the guts to follow through with it, were I to show the least sign of interest.

This one girl in my Middle Eastern History class, a nineteen-year-old of Lebanese extraction named Huda, says to me after class, when the seven others have left—we have a wonderful faculty-student ratio—if I wouldn't mind giving her private instruction in some of the intricacies of the Great Game, since she finds the constant barrage of questions from her classmates distracting. I'm too stunned to reply, and tell her I'll get back to her, at which she flutters her eyelids the way I thought women stopped doing sometime in 1979. If I have any extra time, I'd rather write for the *Boston Review*, thank you very much;

or be on more panels in Washington, D.C., hopefully televised by C-Span, now that my specialty has suddenly become the hottest thing in town. I'm what they used to call in less politically correct times an Arabist.

Of course, I can't tell my wife about these come-ons; she'd take it the wrong way. When I married Shifa at Yale's Battell chapel in a multireligious ceremony—to satisfy my parents, we performed a private nikah, with our closest relatives in attendance, in my hometown of Marietta, Georgia, some months later—the understanding, which had ripened over four years while she finished her undergraduate degree and I watched her from my teaching fellow's perch, was that we would leave each other alone in our professional lives as much as possible. For although we'd started off spending hours every night talking in my Grove Street office at Yale about all sorts of esoteric subjects—whether Hassan Al-Banna was of a terrorist mold, how many decades before India would become a superpower, and what would be the best ways to address stereotypes among Yale's students toward Muslims—we'd soon figured out that Shifa had a more scientific bent of mind that didn't always sympathize with my impressionistic methods.

I teach at Mount Holyoke College, which would have caused titters among my Yale classmates even in the tightest days of the job market. Real men teach at Georgetown. Shifa is now in the last year of her M.D. at Harvard Medical School. For her to avoid a commute, we have rented a small studio in Boston, which I hardly ever visit. I don't mind paying for it out of my salary; we can easily afford it. Depending on how busy she is, she stays there several nights a week. I have no reason to suspect any kind of hanky-panky—there, I'll say it straight out; on my part, the slate is clean.

A colleague's wife, Guftar, an Iranian with a headful of quaint notions about freedom and democracy, stops by my Skinner Hall office after class—the same girls who desire private tutoring or ask nettlesome questions in class rarely take advantage of office hours—to give me a reproduction of a nineteenth-century Persian painting. I'm proud of my growing Near Eastern art collection, which now covers a room in our house.

"Safdar," she says, "I hope I won't be diminishing the art collection in the Prophet's home."

It must be a tongue-in-cheek comment; she's secular down to her painted toenails. She uses the appellation "Prophet" because both Shifa and I are direct descendants of Muhammad—herself a Hashmi, myself a Jaffrey, with roots in the Quraysh tribe to which the Prophet belonged. The ancestry is easily traceable over fourteen centuries. We're also both unusually tall—well over six feet, both of us—so we stand out in a crowd, and attract many moths to our flame, like Guftar.

"This is beautiful, thank you." I caress the reproduction on delicate linen canvas, while envying and pitying Guftar's husband, an idiotic little Malaysian who teaches linguistics to the Mount Holyoke virgins, and misses all our parties when Shifa is around and we have time to host, with excuses that he's preparing for one conference or another.

"Safdar, if I didn't know any better, I'd say you were ogling me." Guftar takes me aback, until she suddenly pulls back and bursts into laughter.

"Oh, you're just kidding."

A woman like Guftar can never be the full-fledged partner and bearer of burdens Shifa has been for me. Early on, we decided we wouldn't let our religious commitment get in the way of professional advancement. Too many of our fellow Muslims burn out, defending lost causes like Palestine, and interjecting religion in secular matters, where it doesn't belong. True, I've written about what a caliphate might look like in the twenty-first century, but I've done it to explore the contradictions between religious and secular law, often irreconcilable, not because I'm some starry-eyed dreamer.

"Pick up some curios for me next time you're in the Holy Land," says Guftar.

I'm the only Muslim in these parts who's actually visited Israel and Palestine, so I know what I'm talking about when I write about the conflict. I'm fond of traveling all over the Muslim world, from Indonesia to Morocco—only Nigeria is missing from my list of major countries in the Islamic zone. It tickles me to think I bought one of my precious golden urns from a dealer mere blocks from where Shifa grew up in Amman, before I ever knew her.

Guftar's visit has made me desire Shifa all the more. I call her at work, where they get a hold of her after much paging, but she says this week is not a good time to visit her at her Boston studio. I agree.

In those days, we used to live in an ordinary ranch house next to another with a shell on top, like a concert hall's, the quirky expression of an art dealer and his submissive wife. My mother used to call the dealer a fake, the wife a moron, and their house a vulgarity. When I was much younger, my father, a reserved and ghostly man not inclined to being contemptuous, clutched my hand tight when we were walking home from the A&P, as if to protect me from their evil spell. The other couples on our street had children I'd grown up playing with, so I knew the parents from their regimes of strictness or permissiveness, except for this couple.

I used to want to spurn my scholarly side, doing only enough in high school to assure me a spot in a good university. My father, a disciplined professor of economics who'd emigrated from Delhi in 1965, the first year Lyndon Johnson threw open the floodgates of immigration, and was now chairman of his department and an expert on foreign aid dilemmas, assumed I would take more responsibility for my future once I crossed a certain age threshold.

I had plenty of spare time on my hand, not engaged in relationships like most of my teenaged friends, with only a couple of fumbling experiences with girls that left me wondering what all the hoopla was about. Naturally I turned my curiosity to what went on next door.

There was much to investigate. Often, big trucks parked in their driveway, unloading loud men and women who were dressed in bright Kmart polyester suits although they could obviously afford better, and who spoke fast and laughed hard as I imagined people in the Northeast did. Over Thanksgiving, Christmas, and other holidays, Mr. and Mrs. Robarts disappeared, and always returned utterly exhausted: you could see it in the way they stooped when they watered the crumbling plants in their yard. The mayor was impressed with them, mentioning them as a valuable presence in the community, with "hearts of gold" and "wisdom acquired from tough experience," adding that he respected their privacy. He made them sound as though they were sociable survivors of the Nazi camps.

The lights there would go out at eight in the evening on the dot. Why so early? One night, as my parents and sister watched a PBS documentary on the Khmer Rouge, I slipped out the door, and jumped over the hedge to land in the neighbors' backyard. The flower beds were freshly dug up. I thought this was an activity for spring; here, it was fall already, and it was nippy. I tiptoed over to what looked like the kitchen window and peeked in. Nothing there, but I could make out the sounds of music playing upstairs—it sounded like Haydn. A ladder was conveniently in place, and I climbed on it, the absurdity of the shell, in imitation of music halls I'd seen pictures of, hitting me like a bawdy joke.

On the top rung of the ladder, if I strained to my left, I could see inside the bedroom window. It was dark, but I sensed movement. Perhaps the old couple were making love. I thought the idea disgusting and was about to climb down, when Mrs. Robarts started speaking loudly to bursts of approval from Mr. Robarts. I began to suspect she was reading aloud from some French absurdist play, Giraudoux or Anouilh, but if she was, how could she do it in the dark? Had she got the whole thing memorized? There were three different parts, and she was assuming different voices for each. At the end, Mr. Robarts yelled "Bravo, bravo!" and then there was silence.

I lost hold of my footing and fell off the ladder, luckily on my back in one of the soft, freshly dug flower beds. Picking myself up, I resolved to get to the root of the mystery of our neighbors.

My sister, Irum, was waiting on my bed, victory in her eyes. "I saw you spying on the neighbors. I'll tell Dad unless you tell me what you saw."

"Get away from me! You can't make me do stuff I don't want to do. Go tell Dad, I'm not scared." But I was. My sister left, vowing to revisit the matter. I wished she'd leave me alone. She was rumored to be an "item" with Abel Goldstein, the only Jew in the school; if my parents knew, they'd lose their minds. Not because the guy was Jewish, but because they truly believed Irum would be a model Muslim girl despite their own earlier shenanigans—as a graduate student, my mother had aggressively courted my father, when he was a graduate student in Michigan already betrothed to a girl in Delhi, compelling him to break off his engagement.

I'm a little peeved to have to introduce the panel on "Democracy in the Middle East." In my opinion, there's only one democracy in that part of the world, and the only one in the foreseeable future: Israel. The rest can only be shams. It's a matter of habit, custom, ingrained until it becomes second nature. It takes centuries. But I hold my tongue and introduce the Tunisian and Algerian professors of democracy, not to mention the Jordanians and Syrians—the Syrians, my God, the Syrians!—all of them with French accents and European-cut suits, although their base of operations is the U.S.

Shifa couldn't come, although she knows the Jordanian professor's family; or rather, her father does. But my student Huda is in the audience at Hooker Auditorium, making up for my wife's absence by sprawling in the front row and staring at me all through the presentation.

"Professor, it's imperative I talk to you afterward," Huda says, as the panel breaks up to wild applause. The consensus tonight has been that the Middle East is more than ready for democracy, and that the disgruntled Arab street is in no way immune to its charms. Just to get rid of Huda's cloying nearness, I say, "Yes, of course, in my office please, meet me there."

Guftar, whose breasts look heavier than usual as does her belly—is she pregnant? Why is she wearing a see-through gray silk top?—accuses me of carrying on affairs with innocent students, while my poor, unsuspecting, loving wife slaves away in the grimy hospitals of Boston. At least she only makes these jokes in Persian, which I happen to speak fluently. Her husband may be the linguist, but he doesn't speak any of the Oriental languages. "This isn't the time or place," I tell Guftar, leaving her annoyed, since her little Malaysian husband walks up just then, in an unusual appearance at a campus event.

"Two hundred people came," I tell him. "Not a bad showing."

"Not bad at all," he leers at me, his tiny ugly teeth showing. "Come Guftar, let's meet the panelists."

I leave early to prevent Huda from barging in again; besides, the North Africans bore me with their assurances that once they come to power democratically, they won't cancel future elections and permanently install their own faction.

In my office, after much tears and histrionics, Huda declares her undying love for me, love that I'm led to believe occurred at first glance and continues unabated eight weeks into the semester. While she's performing from her script, I sneak a glance at the computer records; it's as I suspect: Huda has a C minus average, which seems unforgivable, given that she speaks Arabic, and should have a ready stock of knowledge not available to her non-Muslim classmates. She can't be an affirmative action kid; Muslims aren't. They'd be there, along with the Jews, if all affirmative action were ended.

When it looks like she's done—wiping away illusory tears—I tell her, "I'm sorry to disappoint you, but I'm married. Besides, it would be against college rules. I could get in serious trouble. We both could." She stops crying. I pull out my wallet and show her a picture of Shifa; she's dressed in an Indian getup, with red sari, a tikka on her forehead, and tons of jewelry. Why don't I keep pictures of her in my office? A lot of my married colleagues display pictures of their spouses. "We can talk about your grades, your class performance," I console her.

"Can we please?" She looks up expectantly, drying her false tears with the tissue I've offered her. "I'll do anything, Professor, *anything* at all, to help with my grades. My father would be very upset if I ended up with a C. He'd kill me."

"He wouldn't kill you—this isn't the Middle East, my dear—but I agree, he might get mad. Let's talk about extra credit, makeup work, although strictly speaking I should be granting you no special favors. But I see you're sincere about improving."

I do my best imitation of a neutered imminently middle-aged professor of Middle Eastern Studies, unexpectedly beginning to enjoy Huda's company, as she sidles up close to listen intently, her perfume causing my head to buzz. I can't help sneaking glances at her heavy thighs, her full bottom shifting on the hard chair, and her thick breasts shaking with every tremor of the body. Oh the breasts, the full breasts, which Middle Eastern women seem to possess in such abundance, like fields of fruit going to waste—except my own Shifa, thin as a reed, with a boyish figure ill-designed to produce children or comfort a man in the slough of his misery.

Job well done, Professor, I congratulate myself when she's gone without further incident. I open a tin of English digestives to nibble through, as I pen a tepid introduction to a non-Muslim Yale colleague's hypothesization of a universal Islamic constitution.

"Dear, if you must spy on us, do so in the light of day, when you can see things." Mrs. Robarts had walked right up to me as I was hunched over my broken bicycle, trying to fix it.

I turned red all over. "What?" I wondered if I should deny everything.

"It's all right. We don't mind. My husband and I—we came of age during a world war and a holocaust, you know. We've seen it all. I just came over to invite you to a party we're having Saturday night. Some special friends from Boston. I think you'd like them. A low-key affair."

She took my stunned silence for acceptance, and floated back into her house. So she knew! And she didn't care. At such close quarters, despite her clothing for the aged, she showed definite signs of youth. Her eyes were mischievous. Perhaps she and her husband did get randy after all. Perhaps the reading and appreciation of plays was their postcoital expression of bliss.

I didn't yet realize this was to be the beginning of my real education.

It took all the courage I possessed to go over to the Robartses' that Saturday night. I made an excuse to my parents that I was going into town to watch a movie with friends from school. I wasn't much of a moviegoer. My sister was suspicious.

I got on my bike and started heading into town, before making a circle and arriving at the Robartses' from the other direction.

That night I met the most interesting people in my life. The house was alive, throbbing, buzzing with European and Eastern languages, music of heterogeneous, hodgepodge, hybrid varieties, and attitudes and customs that seamlessly blended the Southern cavalier tone with Yankee bohemianism. I met jazz and blues musicians who performed all over Georgia and the Southeast, a Guggenheim-winning poet who told me about his summer of residency at some place called Yaddo, a haunted mansion in the resort town of Saratoga Springs, New York, and a Cuban artist from Miami who explained why she couldn't help being an abstract expressionist even though the "field was crowded like refugees in a boat off Key West."

A blonde named Jeanine—more graceful than any Southern woman I'd met, making the beauties in my high school look like tramps—took to me as if I was her charge, asking me to be sure to apply to Harvard or Yale, but not Princeton, because Princeton had stuffy eating clubs and because Princetonians didn't have the global consciousness of Harvardians and Yalies. When she offered me a drink, I couldn't refuse, breaking the last injunction of my parents. I was afraid of becoming tipsy, falling over, but after a couple of drinks I felt little effects, except finding it easier to talk to people, a welcome consequence.

The Robartses had easily welcomed me, as if it had only been a matter of time before I would join their fold. Mrs. Robarts played Chopin études on their Steinway grand piano. When she performed, years fell off her appearance. In a sweet voice, she started singing French songs of the interwar years, shot through with yearning. I looked at Jeanine across the crowded room, and she nodded back at me, as if saying, *It's a privilege to be alive, treasure these moments*, and I did, I really did that night, and all the other nights I spent in their company.

The insight occurred to me: creativity kept people young. No one made an issue of why I—an Indian, albeit with very light coloring—was present among meticulously pedigreed people, who'd rubbed shoulders with movers and shakers, who'd known cabinet secretaries and visited the secluded corners of the White House and spoke about *Brown v. Board* or the Cuban Missile Crisis with the authority of insiders.

Where did these people come from? The word that passed their lips most often in describing themselves was "exile," even if they were born and bred Southerners. They spoke of living in the South as if it were a temporary phenomenon without quite knowing how they got there, a state of being that had to be tolerated with good humor but not fully embraced. They were from Alabama and Mississippi and Florida and the Carolinas and Tennessee; they shared the trait of wide travel at the least instigation.

I met the Greek architect who'd designed the shell. The Robartses' house was already showing wear when my parents bought ours eighteen years ago, once my father got his tenure track position at the university, shortly before I was born. I learned from the architect that the

Robartses had been famous patrons of the arts in what he called "the lower depths of Connecticut." I'd read one John Cheever story in my high-school anthology, and the architect's description of that lost, more innocent time— "the nonconformist conformist fifties"—reminded me of that fairy tale WASP world of drinking and flirting, risk-taking and abandonment, loyalty and betrayal. Mr. Robarts had received a huge legacy from his investment banker father and had decided to spend it all for the benefit of assorted artists needing help, instead of indulging in personal luxury. "Now we have the damn Ford Foundation and NEA setting rules for what you can and can't do, killing the spirit in young people, awarding millions right and left to nobodies. Damn foundations," the architect declaimed, and I had to agree.

By the end of the evening, I felt like an honored guest free to come and go. When I went back home, the desolation of my parents' world, the views they'd boxed themselves in, the dos and don'ts to maintain their sense of religious and cultural identification, seemed so overwhelming I couldn't even cry. I was speechless for days afterward at the dining table, hearing my family go on being themselves. At school, I found new confidence, both boys and girls gravitating toward me as though wanting to benefit from the fountain of youth I'd discovered. Mrs. Robarts's parting words kept coming back to me: "Dear, spying can be a rewarding business, don't you think?"

I'm surprised when Guftar knocks on my door at home. Shifa is too tired to have parties on weekends. When she's home, she likes to relax in front of the video, watching intolerably melancholic Egyptian movies from the fifties. So Guftar has only been to our house on the rare occasion.

"Come Guftar, come." I'm acting calmly. She's wearing one of her tight, see-through silk outfits. Her black hair is done up in a fetching way, and I ache to run a finger over her painted lips. For once, all my efforts at suppressing lust are failing me.

When confronted by an unexpected encounter like this, I try to set the right tone early, moving the exchange in safe directions and closing off the risky ones. But tonight I make no such effort. I let Guftar take the lead, wait passively for whatever will happen.

She fixes herself a drink, and I have one too. We sit on the patio chairs, appreciating the cool evening. It's chilly enough for her nipples to get hard; I notice through her thin top. I cross my legs in the slack chair, covering my hard-on. I try to think of the last time I had sex with Shifa, and can't remember.

Guftar talks about her marriage—it's in a shambles, what else?—but this doesn't interest me. My father admonished me, when I reached puberty, not to read too many novels, for they would make me unable to recognize real love. What he meant was that I would become jaded. He was right, and I know from experience, because I violated his injunction. Guftar's tale is familiar, as predictable as the locusts descending on Marietta every summer.

We drink some more. I'm fading out, convinced of the futility of all conversation, which amounts to nothing more than solipsists missing their own demons by a wide mark each time.

Suddenly Guftar makes me alert. "My husband and I have been thinking of a ménage à trois. He's agreeable to watching me. Safdar, you're a married man, mature about these things, and I never see you flirt with anyone. You have your marbles all in place. Would you be interested?"

"What did you say? Me interested in what?"

Guftar keeps a straight face, looking at me with yearning.

I see myself from a distance, as I must appear to women in general—handsome, tall, in good shape, with a full head of hair and ready wit. I'm susceptible to the charge of being supercilious, but there's so much stupidity in the world. I'm convinced neither of my parents ever felt the temptation to cheat; as for my sister, she went on to have an ideal marriage at twenty-one, finished her doctorate at twenty-five, became an award-winning teacher, and raised two healthy sons with no developmental problems. We still congregate at our house in Marietta; my father grows old, in his tenured tracks, my mother remains curious and perky, and I see them every year at Christmas, when I'm not traveling in the Middle East. It's all as it should be.

Guftar is waiting for an answer. The very thought of the Malaysian watching me perform is repelling. Would he have to be in the room? Could the act be videotaped for him? I would be making love to the physical parts of Guftar the Malaysian claimed as familiar territory.

"Guftar, I love you"—I don't know where the word "love" comes from—"but I don't like your husband."

I'm hoping she'll offer to make love then and there, out of sight of her husband. Reading my mind, she says, "I can't be disloyal to my husband. I'm sorry, Safdar."

More than my other colleagues, I'm on track to become what they call a "public intellectual." I've been on C-Span's *Washington Journal* a few times. Is that part of what draws women to me? They're not interested in who I am, but what I do? Oh, how silly, what a women's magazine formulation!

I spend the evening moping, after Guftar is gone. I frantically try to reach Shifa—it's a Thursday, and she's supposed to be back in western Massachusetts tonight—but no one at the hospital knows where she is. The phone at her studio rings and rings.

I start pulling together the things I'll need to spend the night at the studio in Boston—primarily the class preparation for tomorrow. I wanted a Friday afternoon class, unlike most of my colleagues. Perhaps the desire to stay busy on Fridays is to compensate for the old legacy of Friday prayers, which was the one religious obligation my father unfailingly performed, as we went to the main mosque in Atlanta in the middle of my school day. Shifa and I have agreed I'll never interrupt her at the studio; we need to keep our professional lives separate. But today I feel like breaking all the rules.

The phone rings; it must be her. Before I can say anything, a distraught male voice says, "Shifa?" He sobs. "Who is this?" I utter sternly. "Hullo, hullo?" the voice trails off into incoherence, then hangs up. The empty dial tone accuses me of ignorance.

I try to convince myself that the voice on the phone didn't say the name Shifa. It would have been impossible. No one calls for her during the day. It couldn't be her father in Jordan, because he's had a stroke recently and prefers not to speak.

It's been disturbing anyway, and I wait around, fully dressed, the upturned collar of my old raincoat tickling my earlobes. What do manly men do in these circumstances? What would Hemingway do?

When I call Shifa one last time at the studio—more than an hour later—the same man who'd called mistakenly at my home, sobbing the name Shifa, picks up. Unmistakably, it's him. "Hullo, hullo?" he says. I ask in my befuddled voice, "Who's this?" He hangs up.

Suddenly, the nature of the matter is clear to me. I'm the last one to know, as is usual with these things. Does everyone know? Do my colleagues and students know? Is that why Guftar and Huda come on to me? Does the Malaysian know?

My life as I know it is over. I try to feel within me waves of anger and hurt, but it doesn't happen. I pick up the phone, dialing my father's number. I won't tell him what's happened. I hope he won't be able to tell from my voice. I won't be a sobbing, wailing, heartbroken man, I promise myself. I won't be angry at her. I won't be angry at the world.

I got my real education during the last two years of high school in Marietta, at the Robartses' home, week after week. My parents and sister joked I was turning into a regular movie buff—was I secretly writing a column for the local newspaper?—but eventually left me alone. There was an unspoken agreement between the Robartses and me for them not to acknowledge me in front of my parents—should we ever collide in the street or the grocery store—and instead maintain respectful distance.

After my sister got into my parents' bad graces—for getting pregnant by Abel, and enlisting their help in getting an abortion—I had nothing to fear from her. Having met girls like Jeanine, who acted as if equality with men wasn't a legislative dictum but came gracefully, I saw my sister as irredeemably provincial. She would always remain that way, even if she ended up getting a doctorate in literature from Emory, which is what she wanted to do.

After the abortion incident, my parents softened toward me, allowing me greater latitude in personal and academic life. Had my sister not committed her unforgivable sin, I might have rebelled more than I did, and reacted against the pressure to enter academics by becoming a bum instead. My parents actively started encouraging me to date—there were Muslim girls in my high school—to keep me out of trouble.

I got to know the characters in the Robartses' pantheon of heroes all too well: the minimalist poets and abstract expressionists, and their hangers-on, no longer surprised me with a well-chosen word or quotation from obscure European intellectual texts. Rather, I'd come to understand how much more I knew than I'd realized. Mrs. Robarts seemed to be the only one who grasped the balance between delicacy and firmness with which I had to be handled.

Eddie the New Orleans jazz trumpeter once treated us to an exposé of the protocols of homosexual hookups in the seedy bars and gay clubs of that frightening city that left me aghast. I asked him, "Eddie, don't you think you were too explicit?"

Eddie looked at me pityingly. "The last thing this fuckin' country needs is censorship. Get out of my sight, pretty boy."

Luckily, no one heard this exchange. But the perfect mood in the Robartses' universe changed from that night. I started wondering if I'd neglected my formal studies by attending the Robartses' soirées so diligently. If Mr. Robarts had so much money to give away, how come I hadn't met anyone who'd been the personal beneficiary of the largesse? How come it was all rumor and innuendo, word of mouth and urban legend, from so long ago? Were the Robartses really contemporary?

There was still a semester to go in my Marietta incarnation—I was waiting to hear from the Ivy League colleges to which I'd applied—when Jeanine invited me to visit her "other" home in Princeton, New Jersey, for spring break. Her parents were away in Europe; her brother wasn't going to return from his investment banking gig in London anytime soon.

"What do you say, Safdar? You and I, you know, we could have a good time together. I could teach you horseback riding and tennis and swimming. I always thought you'd be a great swimmer. I'm surprised you're not taking better advantage of your body. We could go to museums in New York, and we could hang out with my cousin at Yale. She has to finish her senior thesis by the end of April, so she's staying on campus."

"That's a lot to do in a week." I was acting cool, although my heart was churning at the possibilities and dangers of such an adventure. "I've never been to that part of the country. I've only heard. I don't know." My parents would never agree.

"Come on, don't hesitate. Seize the day, man. I won't bite you—except, as they say, where it pleases." She batted her eyes in the best Marietta tradition.

"Are you harassing my boy?" Mrs. Robarts joined us. "Are you trying to kidnap him?"

I was eternally grateful to Mrs. Robarts; she'd punctured the unbearable tension that had built up. I felt like I no longer needed to respond right away, that an ambiguous answer would suffice.

"I'll sleep on it," I said.

"Safdar, Safdar!" Jeanine seemed to be suggesting that a couple of years of hobnobbing with the Southeastern artistic elite had taught me nothing about human affairs. "You sleep on it well, you do that now." She sounded as if she'd already given up on me, and knew my answer.

The rest of the evening she flirted with people I'd seen her avoid in the past—Eddie the trumpeter, and Mulroney the antiques collector without a shop.

My father broke the unspoken rule in our family never to discuss embarrassing acts already committed. On Sunday morning, the neighbors were dressed up and marching off to church, looking like the Pied Piper's followers, their movements synchronized and their minds emptied of thought for a few hours. My father talked about the duty of every human being to take curiosity where it would go—up to a limit. He talked about the belief of the great enlightenment philosophes—Franklin and Voltaire, Jefferson and Diderot—that happiness was bound to necessary constraints. Only then was freedom meaningful. "You need to figure out for yourself, what are your bounds." I felt sure he was talking about the experience with the Robartses.

I resolved never to go there again. I was my own man, and I could find all the truths I needed in my beloved books, which only addressed me at the level I was ready to bear.

THE HOUSE ON
BAHADUR
SHAH
ZAFAR ROAD

The stuffed parrot from Alexandria. Any moment I expect it to erupt into song, or ecstasy, or whatever parrots do. The Tibetan mandala, woven on a red rug. It hangs from the back of the door. The brick that is supposed to be from the wall of China. I think of China as a place one goes to without being able to fully return. The spittoon Hitler used in prison. He was there for a brief time. The broken set of antlers used by a Chippewa tribe as talisman. It didn't save them from genocide.

It's an alternative education, once you get grandfather talking about the context in which he acquired each of the objects. More often though, he'll forget the history lessons and let me feel the texture of the piece in question, as if I can tune into the spiritual vibes of a certain era by holding on to things.

His study is usually dark, even at noon. I used to like to sit in his lap, even after I was too old. He asks me how my A-level preparations are going, and I complain about how difficult I find math. "Don't worry, Abid," he'll say, "not having an aptitude for math didn't hold anyone back." He's right. He also attempts from time to time to offer impromptu (but they're really deliberate) lectures on Kinsey, Ellis, Freud, Reich, Jung, and Mead—that is to say, sex—but I change the subject to the mating habits of turtles or gorillas, the kind of thing he can be passionate about.

I already know all about sex. I don't need instruction in that department. Besides, in less than a year, I'll be in England. I hear they're pretty cold-blooded there.

One of the servant girls is pregnant, that's why we have to let her go.

That's how my mother introduces the subject at breakfast on Friday. My father looks up from the newspaper and, without comment, goes back to it. My grandfather never joins us for meals. He always eats in his study, sometimes as early as six in the morning. A servant girl is what I called her now, but my mother refers to her by her first name, Zainab. She's been with us since my mother was pregnant with me, Zainab herself not much more than a child then. "She has good manners," my mother often says about Zainab. Seventeen years of employment, and she looks none the worse for wear since she came from upcountry, with a strong recommendation from her aunt, who used to be in my mother's family's service.

"Everyone gets corrupted in the big city," my mother addresses me.

"Hunh. Look at grandfather. He's uncorrupted."

"He's also inexperienced," my mother says. "If you're not really engaged with the world, there are no temptations."

"How was Zainab engaged with the world?"

"She was...she was..." my mother sputters, not knowing where to take this question.

She's aware that I despise the idea of rich people employing servants, especially females, exploiting the best years of their lives, and doing it as if it were the most natural thing in the world.

"The price of sugar is going up again," my father mutters. The price of sugar is supposed to affect the well-being of servants. As is that of atta and ghee and chawal, though none of our servants have to buy their own provisions. But this is how my father expresses his compassion.

☾

Grandfather is agitated when I return from school today. He's wearing his favorite red pajamas, nineteen-thirties vintage. The hem for the drawstring is unraveling, but he refuses to have it sewn. His beige slippers come from a vintage shoemaker in Delhi, who recently passed away.

I like to eat watermelon on the patio, as I think the plantation owners of the American South used to do in the nineteenth century, before the civil war put an end to their lassitude.

There seems to be a gathering storm. Time for a proper monsoon bath, which would be the first this June. In the garden, Meimoona, the fifteen-year-old who's set to take Zainab's place—Zainab's understudy, you might call her—talks to some of the older servants' grandchildren. She's telling them how Moses flung down his stick, turning it into the largest of the serpents, scaring off the competing magicians in the Pharaoh's employ. The children sit in front of a basket of jamuns, the purple juice of the fruit dripping down their chins and necks.

Grandfather walks up to me in short, shuffling steps. "You heard the news?"

I assume he's talking about Zainab's impending departure. He has a soft spot for her. I know because whenever she doesn't bring him breakfast to his study, he spends the whole day being cross. And I've had occasion to pick up other, more obvious signals.

"The news these days is all predictable, unexciting," I say with a worldly air. It's the kind of attitude that drives my friends and family nuts, except for grandfather, who accepts it on level terms.

"She must take care of it, of course. We must help her take care of it."

What he's saying sinks in. "You mean, an…an abortion? Is that what you mean?"

Frail and blue-veined, the sparse frizzy hair on his head standing up, his bifocals hanging on a string reaching his midsection, outside the sacred precincts of his study grandfather is just another old man, waiting for death. The aura is missing. But his words still have the power to stun.

"We also have to find the bastard who did it. And put him out of business."

"The bastard who did it is probably one of the servants next door," I reply. "Some stud who can't keep it under control."

"What are these children doing here?" grandfather says, noticing the kids congregated around the jamun basket. "And who's this girl?" He stares at Meimoona.

"Because I could not stop for Death, He kindly stopped for me." Mishal rests her head on my shoulder. "Oh, Abid, doesn't she have a way with words? I wish I could write poetry like that."

I put away the bottle of domestic beer that tastes like stale piss. "But you *do* write poetry."

"I don't know how to write poetry," says Mishal.

I'm beginning to feel drowsy. The news from England isn't good. My aunt Riffat—a spinster of forty-five, rumored to have a bevy of admirers—has written from Oxford, where she is a lecturer in sociology, that admissions are tougher than ever. I can't understand her demeaning attitude. I resent anyone who implies anything is too difficult for me.

"To write great poetry, you need great material," Mishal continues. "Like Wordsworth in the woods, Byron at war, Hardy with his country girls."

I try to placate her. "Being in love is usually enough."

She talks about the aforementioned three poets, giving far too much credibility to their idiosyncratic perceptions. But I remain quiet.

At the end of the harangue, she starts saying, "Before you go to England—"

I know what's coming next. "I can't, I really can't. It wouldn't be fair to you."

I'm being a cold-hearted monster, but I think it's best for her. She's been carrying around a secret engagement ring from me. Until now, she's wanted no one else to know.

"I knew you'd say that." She moves her head from my shoulder, then turns her face away. I know she's crying, but I can't bring myself to put a comforting hand on her back.

"I think you should go now," I say wearily.

Tomorrow evening, she'll be back, and we'll perform the same routine. We'll start off by talking about something intellectual, the way we began two years ago, then it'll turn into reproach and weeping. I hate this melodrama.

I'm surprised when she doesn't depart in a huff, leaving no trace of her behind, as she normally does at the end of one of our disputes. Today, she breaks into a weird laugh. Then she talks about how she'd like to travel the world and become a peacemaker, directly contradicting her usual conviction that she'd like nothing better than to stay at home and read novels and poetry until she loses eyesight, like Milton and Joyce.

"You must get engaged before you leave," my mother announces at breakfast one morning in July. I've decided to skip school today, but haven't told my parents.

My father nods in agreement. "Plenty of good girls, where your mother came from."

"Daanish!" my mother silences him.

A new feeling of dejection has come over me. Zainab's departure is only a few weeks away. She's been collecting her things from her quarters and assembling them outside her door, as though putting together the remains of a deceased relative she barely knew. But she doesn't complain. Her condition is now more obvious for everyone to note.

"I'm not just talking about anyone, Abid," my mother goes on. "Mishal is a good girl. You seem to like her. I think she has a promising future. Her mother has dropped hints the family might be interested. After all, we have a reputation too. What is it we can't offer?"

I switch strategies. Until now, I've always resisted. "Okay, go ahead then. I like her too."

My mother is shocked. She never expected me to bend so easily. "But...but...what will I say your long-term plans are? What will I say—"

I smile triumphantly. "You wanted a match, you got it." I leave my toast unfinished. When I look back from the dining room door, her face has turned blue. It's all bravado and bluff. They never expect sons to be easy.

Several times this summer—it's August now—the monsoons have threatened but not yet come. There have been years in the past when there has been no rain. I've spent summers in London with cousins, and when it rains there, it doesn't mean so much. Life goes on. I can't imagine how Arthur Conan Doyle conveyed such menace with description of fog. Londoners have internalized the deepest, brownest, sickliest fog in their psyches. But when it rains here, the skies splatter open, as if Mr. Hyde had taken a knife to a beautiful woman, ripping her apart, smiling thunderously over her remains. It's a brutal rain here, like everything else. Still, it's nice to go to the roof, and lie naked in the stream of water, afloat in the roaring flood that makes it look as if the roof will go under, the house will crumble. The rain here is destructive.

I hope this doesn't sound like my father trying to be poetic. I resent his being an engineer only a little less than my being an only child.

I venture into one of the rooms meant to be off-limits. My great-grandmother is supposed to have died there. She was one hundred and six, and remembered the Indian Mutiny well. The War of Independence, as they call it in the local Urdu-medium schools. She's said to have rebuffed the approaches of prominent U.P. landowners, preferring to marry a sad, dislocated writer from Agra, whose family had fallen on hard times. Competent charcoal portraits of him adorn this room, evoking a sense of futility in the face of great historical change that I find hypnotizing. He looks like a young T. S. Eliot, without the missionary zeal. He's invariably dressed in black sherwani. I had Zainab steal a key of this room for me, from my mother's treasure trove.

I fall asleep on the velvet bedspread covering the grand four-poster bed that must have needed a miracle to be carried inside. The teak doors in the house spread wide, to try to accommodate just such furniture. Once it's there, it's never meant to be moved. Not even Zainab is delegated the job of cleaning this room. It's the job of an older male servant, who never had any family.

Grandfather has a stroke. The rains never come. I connect the two facts in my mind, over and over.

Mishal reassures me, as we sit watching over him, late one afternoon. "It's a mild stroke. He'll be good as new in a few months."

"A stroke is a stroke is a stroke," I protest.

Grandfather returns home quicker than we expect. Indeed, since he's been out of the hospital, his recovery seems to be proceeding faster. I haven't visited his study while he's on his back. From time to time, he opens his eyes and asks for old friends of his, friends who died years, even decades ago. "Where's Sikander?" he says. "Tell him not to marry that woman. She'll drain his energy." Sikander had ended up playing for the Indian national cricket team in the years after partition, scoring a double-century at Edgbaston one gray, foggy week. The match ended in a draw.

"You shouldn't think the Brits have the monopoly on truth," he says in one of his lucid moments during the convalescence. "They lie, as often as we do. Their lies are just sugarcoated."

"But they're such great poets," says Mishal.

"Precisely my point," grandfather says. "Poetry is lying."

My father hasn't shown much emotion at grandfather's decline. My mother has acted acceptingly, as if nothing else could be expected at his age.

One afternoon he tells us it's not true that he ever visited Burma. It was his best friend in high school who did, and who bargained for some of the treasures that now adorn grandfather's study. Grandfather was flirting with a second cousin of his that summer. "So don't take everything I say seriously," he admonishes.

The last evening of summer, not only my mother and father, but aunts and uncles we're on speaking terms with, are gathered around his bed because he's been in a particularly ebullient mood.

Grandfather says, "You must take special care of Zainab. She is—part of the family—if you know what I mean."

The insinuation hangs in the air. But no one dares come close to it.

My mother adopts a tone of blasé indifference. "Of course, we treat our servants as family. We always have. She's only going away for a few months. Then she'll be back, no question she'll be back. The country air will do her good. She might come back married, who knows, with one of her cousins."

"Be quiet!" grandfather roars. Mishal acts afraid, squeezing my arm. "She'll do no such thing. Zainab will stay here and have the child. The child will be named Jauhar." Jauhar is my grandfather's name.

My mother gasps in disbelief.

"I think we'll leave now," one of my aunts says, and the other aunts and uncles also rise soon and follow her out.

"What's the meaning of this?" my mother challenges. I've never seen her talk so confrontationally with grandfather.

"The meaning of all things is clear." Grandfather falls asleep, or pretends to. He snores.

Long after my mother and father and Mishal have left, I sit by the bed, pondering the implications of what he's been saying. A great burden has been lifted off my shoulders. He didn't have to do this. It's the noble, self-sacrificing part of his character again. Perhaps illness has prompted him to assume the role of fall guy. Still, it's praiseworthy.

"Abid." He opens his eyes, scaring me, and putting his gnarly hand on mine. "I really mean it. She's to be treated as family. She *is* family."

For an awful moment, the strength of his grip makes me think he's sincere. Then I put aside the unimaginable thought.

ALIENATION, JIHAD, BURQA, APOSTASY

The dictator Zia ul-Haq had just been blown up in the skies. A C-130 plane, full of his lieutenants and American officials, right after takeoff from the dusty, forsaken city of Bahawalpur, had taken Zia to his fiery grave in the heavens after eleven years of martial law.

I was with Mark Moneymaker and Deepak Chawla, both of whom had always been eager to be my friends, in the Japanese gardens at UCLA, having our daily lunch of turkey sandwiches and fresh orange juice.

Mark read aloud the story of the dictator's grisly death in the *Los Angeles Times* and the *Daily Bruin*.

Deepak, with his bloodshot eyes and fakir's long, unruly hair, devoured the headlines, exclaiming, "Far out, man! The CIA, of course, is who did it. Damn CIA."

"This woman Benazir is attractive, Salman!" Mark said. "You've gotta write her. Tell her you're a highly-educated

Pakistani, willing to give back to the country some of what you got. Heck, the way you are with words, you could be her speechwriter or something. Adviser on relations with the U.S., I don't know."

"What?" I said uncomprehendingly. I felt no connection to Pakistan after spending the eighties in Southern California. Anyone who met me for the first time assumed I was born here. I used to lie about it too—I was born in Anaheim, or Fresno, I used to say—without going into details. I had not a trace of accent left. I didn't know the first thing about Pakistani politics. The only thing I cared about was to bring out the college vote for Michael Dukakis that fall.

"You've gotta go back," Mark insisted. "What are you gonna do here? All the big questions have been settled. Go back to Pakistan, and make a difference. Oh man, this Benazir is hot!"

"He'd have to finish up at UCLA first," Deepak objected.

"Yeah, I guess." Matt paused. "We've gotta decide what courses you'll take the next couple of years. More politics and economics. But write to Benazir *now*. Tell her you're on your way."

I let the two carry on, as I sneaked glances at the passing Asian girls in tight white shorts, carrying miniscule amounts of food on their trays. I hadn't made it with an Asian girl yet. For that matter, I hadn't made it with any girl yet. If Mark and Deepak knew that, they'd laugh until all of the memorized Shakespeare drained out of their heads.

I'd been only fifteen when Zia took over, eventually hanging Bhutto on the unprovable charge of ordering the assassination of a political opponent. But I'd been old enough to feel the impact of the repression. Overnight, Pakistan—including cosmopolitan Karachi—went from having a lively culture harboring eccentrics and goofballs, to a night of gloom descending over it, everyone trying to outdo others in piety and devotion.

The first years of puberty tend to be the most difficult, and it was no different for me. I was from a middle-class family that had come into wealth, but middle-class habits die hard. My family lacked the ability to talk easily about intimate matters. Sex was a dark mystery haunting every moment of my days and nights, leaving me an exhausted wastrel in the wake of its metaphysical impossibilities. The first time I had a wet dream, the thick semen congealed on my pajama front like frozen egg white, I panicked into insensibility. I didn't know whom to ask about my constantly hard penis, stuck in attack mode.

My father, who'd immigrated from Porbander, India—Gandhi's birthplace—soon after partition, and had been a low-paid school teacher, and then a clerk at a travel agency on McLeod Road, eventually made it big in the seventies, when he signed up with my maternal uncle in Japan, acting as his import agent in Pakistan for synthetic yarns. Toyobo was the brand name. It was the biggest thing around. Pakistani men didn't mind wearing polyester shalwar kameez in the boiling heat, nor did Pakistani women during long wedding celebrations.

We moved from a rundown two-room fourth-floor apartment facing Nishtar Park—we had front row seats, from our balcony, to the procession of mourners flagellating themselves with spiked chains during Muharram, and to Bhutto promising roti, kapra, aur makan to more than a hundred thousand people at a time—to a newer apartment at Muhammad Ali Mansion, a bright pink triangular building, and finally to a decent sized bungalow in P.E.C.H.S., a middle-class housing colony settled mostly by retired civil servants living off overseas remittances.

On the ground level of the bungalow, my frustrated father made moves on my teenage sister, while my mother chose to ignore this activity; meanwhile, I preferred to escape to the ramshackle room on the roof, next to the water tank. The room offered little protection from the blistering summer heat, but I was content to get by with a fan, as long as I could be out of reach of the quarreling family downstairs, catch BBC's *Top of the Pops* on shortwave radio, and spy on the neighbor Mr. Haq's oldest daughter, whom I presumed to be a frustrated virgin in her twenties. I listened to Abba and Queen, and watched Mr. Haq's daughter prance around in skimpy white kurta, her short hair and sophisticated makeup convincing me that she must have been a habitué of the discos before Zulfiqar Ali Bhutto banned them.

I was a top student, although standing first in the class month after month was weakened by the reality that I wasn't at Karachi Grammar School, the breeding ground for the elite. I went to lowly Mehre-Neem-Roz school in Soldier Bazar—the name translates from the Persian as "blinding sun of the midday afternoon." The legend was that my father had taken me to Grammar School and the equally elite St. Patrick's school as well as Mehre-Neem-Roz when I was five and ready to make my choice, and I picked the latter. The truth, I suspect, had to do with the higher fees at Grammar School, as well as proximity, which was always a big point with my father.

The teachers, mostly from the minority Ismaili sect, tolerated my antics, and frequently awarded me prizes, which I nervously acknowledged in front of the morning assembly of a thousand students. When I "topped"—stood first—in the citywide Matriculation examinations, it got a lot of attention. I told the *Dawn* reporter that the Beatles were my idols, although he changed that in the published interview to "the Prophet Muhammad is his idol." I repeated the feat in the Intermediate examinations, as a student at National College. Again, I wasn't enrolled at the prestigious Commerce College favored by the scions of the business establishment, but the lesser National College, close to home, boasting professors who often didn't show up, or if they did, lectured in ridiculous English accents. I repeated the feat citywide in the B. Com. examinations, confounding my Commerce College competitors.

In my teens, I liked to imagine I'd become a famous research scientist. My dream was to make some breakthrough in physics or chemistry that would earn me immortality. But my father's obsession was to recruit me for his business. In Pakistan, businesses expanded in proportion to the size of the immediate family. As early as age seven or eight, I would type letters for my father on the ancient red Olivetti at the office. In my teens, every day after school, some factotum from the office would come and pick me up, and I would stay until eight or nine in the evening, listening in on my father's dealmaking.

In 1978, a year after Zia took over, when I was only sixteen, my father got religion in a big way, and wanted to perform the hajj. Before that, he'd had a falling-out with my uncle in Japan, who'd gotten rich because of my father's efforts. One day, my father discovered that my uncle's loyalists had taken over the godowns full of bales of yarn, worth many lacs of rupees, and locked my father out of the office. There was nothing my father could do. Going to the police or approaching the courts would have meant inviting both his and my uncle's downfall, since most transactions, even in legitimate businesses, were "number two," or off-the-books. My father started his own, scaled-down, yarn import business. During the month my father was performing the hajj, I held the fort, playing cards in the afternoons with the office staff, chatting about American politics with the dallals, or brokers, who wanted me to seize the day and commit to one or the other deal, which I shunned in favor of a wait-and-see attitude.

The eighties began. Another uncle, this one my mother's older brother in Singapore, invited me to live with him. This uncle had had businesses expropriated in Aden, Burma, and other places when the communists took over, but always got back on his feet as though nothing had happened. I was never clear as to why this uncle asked me to come to Singapore. The unspoken expectation was that he would teach me the business—he was running a money-losing garment factory—but in truth he probably only used me as a competitive threat to whip his rebellious son into obedience. This was the youngest of his eight sons, who was more interested in Abba than abatements.

I shopped till I dropped at the malls on Orchard Road, and when I returned to Pakistan I realized I couldn't stay there a day longer. Then began a frantic rush to get an I-20 to an American college—some college, any college, it didn't matter. It was the safest way to get a visa. The consular official in Karachi was surprised that a student of my caliber would want to go to Fort Lauderdale Junior College, instead of, say, Columbia or Stanford University. At the consulate, I seethed with anger at Pakistanis who retained their pathetic accents after living for decades in the land of the free, acting obsequiously toward consular officials. I made up my mind never to be like them.

I never showed up at the Florida college. I went to New York, looked for a job—something, anything, because I'd arrived with only five hundred dollars in my pocket—and soon moved to Southern California, where I had better luck. My father and I hadn't parted on the best of terms, because he was disappointed that his grooming of me to take over the business hadn't worked out. When I merrily signed away stacks of blank powers of attorney for our old family lawyer, Suleman Gandhi, the guy had the nerve to say, "Why are you going to America? If you want to let off steam, you can always go to Bangkok." Bangkok was the place for the choicest Asian prostitutes. I glared in anger.

My father was mad at me also because I had openly rebelled against religion. When I was twelve, a schoolteacher uncle—my father's older, less ambitious brother—planted Bertrand Russell's *Why I am Not a Christian* at our home. From then on, I snickered with contempt whenever my father and sister asked, "If there's no God, then who created all the wonderful things in nature?" Matters weren't helped by my father beating me up—stuffing red chili powder in my mouth was part of the treatment—and locking me in the bathroom when I refused to accompany him for the obligatory Friday prayers.

Soon after arriving in Southern California, I ran out of money. My father instructed my rich uncles in Japan and Singapore, and everyone else associated with the family, not to help. He figured I'd come back to Pakistan, begging on my knees. I remember meeting my cousin Haseeb, a successful military defense contractor, at a mithai and paan shop on Pioneer Boulevard in Artesia. He drove a shiny black BMW. I asked him for five hundred bucks. He refused it, saying I had to make it on my own if I wanted to survive in America. It was for my own good, he said.

I'd had no contacts with Pakistanis or Muslims in the years since then. I believe I underwent a literal transformation in appearance and demeanor so no one could tell where I was from.

For four years, when I should have been in college, I worked for management consulting firms, although I did tend to exaggerate the importance of my duties. If I assisted on a project for Dan Farrell at McKinsey & Company, getting paid eight bucks an hour, on my résumé it became, "Consultant for McKinsey." With my uncertain immigration status, my boss for much of this time, a thirtyish blonde devoted to a Kundalini yoga cult, took advantage of me, promising all the time she'd look into ways of getting me enrolled at a community college. In the mid-eighties, having gotten a boost of confidence after successfully passing an extension course at UCLA, I quit my job and lived off unemployment until finding myself in UCLA's regular undergraduate program. I loved college, figuring I'd discovered my destiny as an academic, after all the distractions.

Mark and Deepak were waiting for me to respond to their suggestions.

"Pakistan? I don't know shit about Pakistan."

But the seeds of self-doubt had been sown.

That chilly October afternoon in 1989, I found myself standing in front of the Friday namazis in the basement of Harvard's ancient Mem Hall, imitating as best as I could the mellifluous Arabic recitation of the Qur'an by the grand imam of the Ka'aba, before launching into the khutba in English. I wore a perfectly ironed white kurta pajama, reading from a twenty-page dot matrix printout, complete with quotations from authentic hadith and Qur'anic verses. I also tore out pages from Abdullah Yusuf's venerable English translation of the Qur'an, fumbling through them during the khutba.

My delivery was convincing. Years later, when I was in such demand at Boston area university mosques that I began rotating on Fridays at Northeastern, BU, MIT, and other venues, a man once passed out during my khutba at Tufts. I was talking that afternoon on the subject of death, the gory details of what happens when farishtas and shaitan visit the dead person in the grave, all of it taken from the literalist eleventh-century reformer Imam Ghazali's treatises. The man in the audience at Tufts probably lost consciousness due to heat exhaustion or something, but I entertained the possibility that it was because of my terrifying rhetoric. I didn't even pause during the khutba to inquire if he was all right.

The two rooms in the basement of Mem Hall had come our way through serendipity. Soon after I arrived on campus, Harvard's United Ministry asked Safdar Jaffrey— longtime graduate adviser and mild-mannered shepherd of the Islamic flock, officially the United Ministry chaplain—him if the Harvard Islamic Society (HIS) would like to take over two precious rooms in Mem Hall, vacant because the organization previously holding them, the Appleton Fellowship, was defunct. Would we ever like those rooms! HIS members painted and refurbished the dilapidated basement rooms with the undiluted glee of tribal villagers after a conquest. Over time the legend grew among freshmen that when I arrived HIS was in the doldrums and I had single-handedly revived it, beginning with acquiring permanent space for the five daily prayers. I didn't discount the speculation.

We became obsessed with head counts, proudly noting the uptick in the number of people attending Friday prayers, from ten to twenty to fifty. Among them were secretive members of the community—doctors, lawyers, and engineers who lived with their families in the Boston suburbs, worked downtown or in Cambridge, and chose to come to Harvard rather than the established mosques.

After I'd delivered the khutba that Friday and led the namazis in a long recitation during the two mandatory raka'ahs, Mr. Qureishi, an engineer with the Massachusetts Bay Transportation Authority, admonished me, "You shouldn't be tearing pages out of the Qur'an, Salman. It shows disrespect." Muslims from the subcontinent like to store the Qur'an at the highest possible elevation, on top of a cupboard if possible. Tearing pages is sacrilege.

Another stalwart, Mr. Waheed, a man in his sixties with the habit of ending every sentence with the tag, "Question of," and about whom I'd wondered if he worked for the CIA or the Pakistan Atomic Energy Commission or some similar dark enterprise, came to my defense. "Leave Salman alone. At least he has the enthusiasm, the motivation, *question of.* Do any of us have a fraction of his passion, *question of?* Carry on, young man, *question of.*"

I wanted to be president of HIS before I ever set foot on campus. The idea had come to me when I pored over *The Unofficial Guide to Life at Harvard*, which listed hundreds of student organizations. Everyone was president of something.

The day after I arrived at Harvard, I called Mujeeb Beg, president of HIS. "Do you need any help?" He asked me to come right over to his room in Quincy House.

I licked stamps for mass mailings to anyone at Harvard with a remotely Muslim-sounding name, all of them pulled out at random from the crimson phone book. Many turned out to be Indian Hindus, Christian Egyptians, or secular Turks, although some came anyway to our events, lectures on sufism by Annemarie Schimmel or by black female converts who'd become experts in fiqh at American universities. Free samosas and mithai recruited audiences.

My UCLA professors had castigated the American way of life as genocidal. I hoped my new path was a better alternative. Before I'd left Southern California for Harvard, I visited my cousin Haseeb, the one who'd refused me five hundred dollars years ago. Haseeb mocked my new status as "Harvard man" and showed me *Crescent International*, a newsletter published by a British scholar named Kalim Siddiqui, an acolyte of Ayatollah Khomeini. Activism, patchwork solutions, wouldn't reform American society; only radical surgery would do the job.

There was also the path not taken. My first day at Harvard, I met someone who developed a huge crush on me. Cassandra was a lovely, intelligent blonde from St. Paul, Minnesota, with a taste for Gucci bags and Phil Glass. She was a transfer student from Dartmouth, and had a history of crushes on South Asian men. Her last flame, Krishna Kumar, a cold aristocratic Brahmin from North India, had also transferred to Harvard at the same time. I was a virgin still; I believe she was too.

In those first weeks of rapid-fire introduction to the Harvard system, as Cassandra and I attended endless parties and meetings all designed to make us think we were indispensable to the world, we drew close even as the rift started showing.

I wouldn't say that my alternative life was secret from Cassandra: my involvement with HIS; my enrollment in Professor Schlegel's introductory Arabic class (in which I struggled desperately, my Indo-European patterns of thought unable to keep up with Semitic logic, while a brilliant young Jew, the future architect of the Iraqi constitution, left me and the other South Asians in the dust); my impassioned conversations with Middle Eastern exiles like the Iranian physics postdoctoral fellow Suroosh Montazeri (I tried to find something positive about Khomeini's reign, while he was more critical); and my obsession with the BP call letters in the Widener Library stacks, where obscure tomes on the Islamic polity and economy drew me like a bee to honey (the difference between me and other members of HIS was that I pursued Islamic scholarship to the hilt, while they were content to show up once a week in the basement of Mem Hall, being able to compartmentalize their drinking and clubbing). True, I chose to share the depth of my passion with Muslims alone. But at some level, Cassandra knew.

Cassandra had been in therapy all her life. Although she came from a middle-class family, her ideas of transcendence were more suited to old-money offspring. One Friday night, in the middle of the fall semester, after we watched a video of my sister's traditional wedding—back in Pakistan, she'd chosen to escape my father's attentions, if they were still continuing, by marrying an illiterate man, older but very rich, with whom she went on to have six children—Cassandra and I found ourselves making out at her apartment in Botanic Gardens, while her roommate Shoshanna was at the Yale campus consummating her passion for her boyfriend Eli.

It was an odd, fumbling night of endless tantalization. Often we came close to consummation, but one of us would always draw back. As I licked her, I marveled at Cassandra's dark pubic hair, when she was otherwise so blonde. At the end of the sleepless night, when the cold sun came up, she sucked me, although I wouldn't let her make me come; I did that with my own hand, coming on her chest.

When we emerged Saturday morning for brunch at one of the Quad houses, Cassandra wanted to hold my hand. I was afraid someone from HIS might witness the Friday khateeb indulging in hypocrisy, so I said no. Cassandra wanted me to return to her Botanic Gardens apartment for the rest of the weekend, but I said I couldn't because I needed to write a paper on the Iranian Revolution for Professor Hormuz's class. I wanted to blow away the students in section with my understanding of Khomeini's concept of the velayat-e-faqih, the rule of the jurisconsult.

All semester long, Cassandra and I remained on the threshold of consummation. The more she drew toward me, the more I pushed her away. I didn't lack for girls' attention; my chiseled looks took care of that. I started turning away everyone's least affections. When I ignored her phone calls, Cassandra had no recourse but to leave gifts and cards for me in the lobby of my Banks Street apartment.

In early January, during reading period, she called me and begged me to come over because she was experiencing heart palpitations. I told her I was busy studying and couldn't. I added for good measure that I was engaged to be married to a Pakistani girl, which was a complete lie.

That night she tried to kill herself with an overdose of sleeping pills. I didn't find out until later. I never went to see her at Stillman Infirmary. She was asked to take a semester's leave of absence—Harvard's standard protocol in such cases—by the feared Ad Board. Others in the transfer student group treated me like a murderer. I pretended I'd done nothing wrong; weren't Cassandra's overwrought nerves to blame?

Soon afterward, I was elected president of HIS, after giving a visionary speech outlining my agenda. The same day I got food poisoned at a Korean restaurant in Harvard Square, where Safdar Jaffrey and the rest of the HIS board had taken me to celebrate. I found myself in Stillman Infirmary, where Shifa Hashmi, the six-foot-tall Jordanian girl who'd been my only real competition for president, and was elected vice president in the end, brought me my favorite British chocolates.

"Tijana, an observant Muslim girl hardly nineteen, gang-raped by brutal Serbian soldiers, killed one hundred enemy soldiers all by herself, with her bare hands, with nothing more than her dead brother's old army gun."

At an MIT auditorium in 1993, the Bosnian mujahid Saleem Hadjic, dressed in army fatigues and bandying a Kalashnikov, held the attention of hundreds of Boston area Muslim students and professionals at his latest fundraiser. Saleem's story about Tijana was evolving by the day. In his first speech, Tijana had been a married woman of forty-nine, raped by her landlord, and killer of two soldiers.

Also, the rewards of martyrdom in the otherworldly realm were steadily escalating. Saleem's stories about the corpses of mujahids that smelled like gardens of roses days after death were becoming his most elaborate set pieces, and extended now to description of the corpses of women, in loving detail. This part always brought tears to the audience's eyes.

I said to Zameer, a Tufts ophthalmology student from Delaware who'd done time with the American military in Korea but was secretive about it, "What a load of bull! The bastard's lying!"

Zameer agreed. "Yeah, he is. But he rakes in the money."

Indeed, Saleem was a phenomenal fundraiser. Zameer and I put aside our suspicions of the globe-trotting mujahid—had he ever been a soldier? What organization did he front for?—and focused on the hundred thousand dollars he brought in from computer scientists at DEC and biochemists at MIT that night.

How much better off I was with this activist group of Muslims than with the apolitical tablighi jama'at! My flirtation with the tablighis hadn't lasted long. I was visiting the MIT mosque one night when I noticed a circle of worshipers sharing food from a bronze thali, drawing around their leader, Taha, an intimidating African American convert, and listening attentively as he read hadith and gave a short lecture. At the end of the talk, each of the brothers affirmed their intention to spend a weekend or ten days or forty days for the purpose of da'wah, inviting wayward Muslims back to the straight path.

It was easy to fall in with them, even if I didn't like their embarrassing talk, such as the Prophet's approved way of purifying oneself after a wet dream. Did grown men have wet dreams? I had no such problem, being a compulsive masturbator.

That summer, my Harvard housing arrangement having fallen through, I was allowed to stay at the Botanic Gardens apartment of a young Indian economics professor and his liberal activist wife, by my friend Dilruba, daughter of a famous Nepali banker, who was house-sitting for the couple. While she and her Asian girlfriends cooked for hours and watched movies like *Heathers*, I masturbated to the Indian economist's *Penthouses* and *Playboys* in the bathroom. When the tablighis, with whom I was intrigued enough to regularly attend their sessions at local mosques, insisted I take a trip to an annual tablighi convention in Oneida, in upstate New York, Dilruba encouraged me to go so she could be relieved of my brooding presence.

My questions to the tablighi elders were tough—why restrict the mission to inviting only Muslims? Why didn't the tablighi movement take any political stands? Why should all the emphasis be on small deeds in literal imitation of the Prophet?—but they were willing to entertain my skepticism because of my high value as a Harvard-trained asset.

After Oneida, I became accustomed to the tablighis' itinerant lifestyle, sleeping in dingy mosque basements, satisfying the pangs of hunger with meat curry diluted by water, and perfecting my own short speech from the tablighis' Bible, the *Fadail-e-Aa'mal*, or virtues of acts, a compilation of mostly inauthentic hadith recounting the quantitative blessings of each act imitating the Prophet Muhammad, including sleeping, defecating, and fornicating.

Back at Harvard, I started visiting Muslim acquaintances—sometimes only those with Muslim-sounding names—accompanied by more experienced tablighis, inviting the misguided Harvard brother to come along with us to the prayer rooms at Mem Hall. The idea was to tempt him to the mosque, then pitch for the new recruit to join the tablighis for a weekend or ten or forty days on a da'wah mission.

I'm not sure about the precipitating event for my falling out, but it was bound to happen. Lack of excitement was part of it. I hated endless meetings to discuss which breakfast or lunch menu would most please the Prophet. With tablighis, results didn't matter, only intentions. How could tabligh compete against jihad? One day, I broke Taha's frightening walking stick—which he used only to imitate the Prophet—on the balustrade of the stairs to the Mem Hall basement, threatening that I would call the Harvard police if he or other tablighis not affiliated with Harvard ever stepped foot on campus.

After the disappointing tablighi experience, I was thrilled to be in the company of men and women who understood the politics of worldwide Muslim oppression. The evening of the fundraiser at the MIT auditorium, I fell in love with the sound of my own voice as I pranced on stage and recited the impressive amounts of pledges. A lovely girl who worked at DEC, Salma Bayabani, wanted to get my attention for other reasons, inviting me to her home in the suburbs to "have an intellectual discussion about world politics," but I ignored her.

Zameer came to the stage to rebuke me about my repetitive announcements.

"Where's the jihad sister?" I asked him.

"She's in conference with the Afghan Arabs. In the back

room." He was referring to the Egyptians and Syrians who claimed to have fought in the Afghan crusade of the eighties, but were now Ph.D. students at MIT and other area schools in high-value disciplines like nuclear physics.

"You're right, I don't see any of them in the auditorium," I said.

"They don't believe in naked public relations," said Zameer. "Even if it's for jihad."

The *jihad sister*, the instigator of that night's event—indeed, the person who'd shifted the attention of the loosely associated group of Boston area Muslim Student Associations, to which I'd brought reluctant HIS members–was Ayesha Rehmani, a girl on whom I had an unrequited crush.

Ayesha, a wisp of a girl who liked to wear pink hijab over pink shalwar kameez, was the beneficiary of an MIT policy aggressively recruiting female undergraduates, particularly minorities, to correct the school's skewed male-female ratio, even if the female student in question underperformed compared to males. Ayesha's mother had been in a long-running legal battle with Zia ul-Haq and his successors, to fulfill Zia's promise to her foundation of a large piece of land in Karachi for a madrassa to train mujahids from an early age. Even the sciences at this madrassa were envisioned as part of jihad as a way of life.

The only thing Ayesha ever talked about was jihad. In the early nineties, we were a bunch of soft college students, who'd never imagined jihad as a viable option. A year later, we were going to target shooting practice, which consisted mostly of gun safety instruction, with guys like Fayyaz Kashmiri of BU and Arsalan Ayoob of Tufts, guys who came from suburban Ohio and Illinois and found it difficult to deflect the jihad sister's admonitions to the Muslim brothers.

The gun training was supposed to be part of a strict regimen of physical strengthening. Some took it more seriously than others, making the brothers punch them in the stomach to show off their iron abs. Zameer, the ophthalmologist, was mad when I kept turning the unloaded gun to my head. That was a safety no-no: never point a gun at oneself or others, even if it wasn't loaded. For fifty bucks, we got certificates authorizing us to own and use guns.

The jihad sister wasn't optimistic that the U.S. government would intervene in the Bosnian slaughter, since no U.S. self-interest was involved in saving the Muslim innocents, but she accompanied us to the protest marches in Washington anyway. When Bill Clinton visited Boston's Copley Square, we organized quickly, showing up with placards that read "Arm the Bosnians." We performed the same routine outside the Massachusetts State House. Brother Saleem Hadjic had asked for nothing else. The Bosnian Muslims didn't need the help of Western soldiers, but they did need the West to lift its arms embargo so they could defend themselves against the Serbs.

This made sense to us. Instead of supporting Western charities that channeled money to shelter refugees or other recourses after the fact, Saleem Hadjic and Ayesha Rehmani wanted the money to go to Midwestern "charities," about whom everyone knew that they would get arms to the Bosnians, smuggled in from willing countries like Pakistan and Iran. We weren't comfortable with the jihad sister's enthusiasms, but went along anyway.

When I headed down to Washington marches with carloads of Muslim students, whose parents were some of the most prosperous doctors and engineers in New England, I harangued them that we were ignoring jihad, sounding like Ayesha. I drove one poor sister who was infatuated with me—a Catholic girl from Smith College, Sophia, who had converted to Islam without her mother's knowledge and secretly prayed in the basement of their Brooklyn home—almost to tears as I resorted to my rhetorical fireworks to demolish her "soft" interpretation of the Qur'an. The sister who drove the car, Tarannum Khan, a Mount Holyoke graduate eager to get into Professor David Miller's Harvard Islamic Legal Studies program, generously funded by Saudis and Gulf Arabs, also had a crush on me. Since the day I launched my tirade against Sophia, however, Tarannum became wary of me.

When we showed up at conferences designed to encourage Muslim involvement in American politics—numerous organizations were sprouting up then, educating Muslims about the benefits of running for office—some bored student in the audience would prompt me at the end of the lecture to "throw him off" by asking the speaker some devastating question. I obliged by pointing out logical contradictions within the speaker's presentation, tying him up in knots as I spoke of the Qur'an's skepticism toward taking help from nonbelievers.

We went to summer camps in the forests of Virginia to help high-school brothers and sisters learn the essentials of the faith. We lusted after the nubile Egyptian and Lebanese sisters, who showed not a single hair through their tight hijabs.

At the Worcester and Wayland mosques, young Turks like me tried to coax the elderly board members, physicians and engineers from Pakistan and Egypt, into explicitly supporting jihad, taking a harsher line on religious law.

My connection with Harvard was becoming tenuous. I felt like an unwanted guest, using and abusing its hospitality, while I carried on another agenda far removed from Harvard's aims. I desultorily read through books on the Austrian economist Bohm-Bawerk's theory of interest and capital, in preparation for writing my senior thesis, but this was only a roundabout way of confirming Islam's prohibition of interest on capital.

Once at a restaurant near MIT, where I was with Fayyaz Kashmiri's hijab-wearing sisters and cousins—all of them from rich Midwestern families, but willing to listen to radical philosophies—I was embarrassed when Laura Braden, a buxom blonde Southerner who was part of our original transfer group to Harvard and knew Cassandra well, showed up as our waitress. She'd always flirted with me and continued to do so in front of the sober Muslims. "I'll take you to the Astrodome, if you ever come and visit me in Texas," she said. She'd transferred back to MIT from Harvard.

Cassandra called to tell me she was joining the Peace Corps in Nigeria. I barely paid attention. She said my accent sounded different, more Muslim, more Pakistani.

Zameer and Fayyaz and I helped the jihad sister cook meals for a hundred Muslims at a time at one of MIT's all-female dorms. Ayesha's friends in the dorm, Asian and white girls, pitched in for the jihad cause, knowing what it stood for. "We're for arming defenseless people," they said. "The holocaust must never happen again."

I didn't lust for Ayesha; she wasn't that kind of girl. But I felt an obligation to fall in love with her, marry her. I told my senior tutor at Dunster House that I was engaged to a Pakistani girl, and that I would be getting married right after graduation. My senior tutor was stunned. It began as an excuse to explain why I was behind in one of my courses, but the myth became self-perpetuating.

I bought an engagement ring and carried it on me at all times, expecting to present it to Ayesha on the right occasion. Instead, I ended up giving a gold necklace to her visiting mother.

"Qabool haiy." I accept. I said these words to the turbaned mullah in the heat and dust of the huge maidan at Sohrab Goth on the outskirts of Karachi, confirming my marriage to Nasreen. I was one among scores of couples collectively wedded that afternoon. It was one of those mass weddings that tablighis like Nasreen were devoted to, because of the simplicity. No pictures of the ceremony, or indeed of Nasreen and me, were ever taken, since she and her family believed that photography was haram—forbidden as was all image-making.

My uncle from Japan, whose sons had all married daughters of tycoons in grand ceremonies replicated in Osaka and Bombay and New York, was baffled. Why would I, a Harvard man, go through with this?

"Is she attractive?" my uncle wanted to know. Everyone assumed that if I was going for a lower-middle-class girl— she lived in a poorer section of Dhoraji Colony, with her three married tablighi brothers, whom she revealed to me one by one—she must be unbelievably beautiful. In truth, she wasn't even presentable.

"I haven't seen much of her," I confessed to my uncle.

Most would have considered her unattractive. She was mannish, with a manual worker's build and weight. My mother mocked Nasreen's big behind when she plunked down on the floor to shell shrimp or separate the chaff from wheat.

It was 1994, the year of O.J. and the Contract with America. It wasn't my first trip back. I'd returned to Pakistan for the first time in 1991, right after the Gulf War. On the Gulf Air flight, I helped fill out immigration and customs declaration forms for illiterate Pathan and Baluch workers returning home from jobs in the Emirates. My younger brother—who'd started showing the first signs of paranoid schizophrenia as he came into adulthood—warned me at Karachi airport about my innocence: I shouldn't get too friendly with worker types. The laborers I'd helped had thanked me and shook my hands on their way out of the airport.

It felt funny to hug my father after a decade. I arrived in the middle of Ramadan. My family had moved from the bungalow in P.E.C.H.S. to a fourth-floor apartment nearby, because of the frequent kidnappings and burglaries that occurred in houses. They were safer in the apartment. In the building's parking lot, after my brother drove me home from the airport, my father spent only a few moments with me before heading over to the neighborhood mosque for maghrib prayers.

I fasted a few times that year and on my future trips to Pakistan, but it was more to please my mother than anything. My family had heard a lot about my activities as HIS president. Rumor had it that I'd converted a number of white Americans to Islam.

My father was running one of the liveliest businesses in all of Pakistan, Elite Computers, an operation on Tariq Road, a major commercial thoroughfare only a short walk from our home. He sold software. Pirated software, actually, to businesses and individuals from one end of Pakistan to another, indeed from one end of the globe to another. There isn't a diplomat or multinational player stationed in that region of the world who wouldn't remember my father. Even today, at any airport in the world, my father is likely to be accosted by clients from the past. "Elite Computers?" they exclaim in gratitude. Customers would always be packed in the store to get their copies of the latest Microsoft and Apple software for five or ten rupees. Twenty young employees manned the computers all day long, copying disks as fast as humanly possible.

My father took great delight in counting money. Sometimes, when he was sick, he would leave the fort to me, but I was too lax with the employees, so he would quickly return to take command.

Mostly I liked to sit next to his desk, a huge fan blowing into my face, dressed in a Brooks Brothers suit and perspiring profusely. Sitting next to me, my mother called one acquaintance after another to find a suitable girl for her Harvard-educated son.

At first my father took interest in the search. He liked a girl in the apartment right above Elite Computers. Khadija was a strong, chubby girl, about whom my sister said she could drop five babies without breaking a sweat. "She'll cook and clean for you, and never get tired," my father confirmed. He believed one didn't need to talk to one's wife about intellectual stuff. That's what male friends were for.

When we went to "see" Khadija, her father, a bank manager, asked about my plans for the future.

My father stepped in. "He's going to expand the business. There's much we haven't pursued yet. Like ribbons."

"Ribbons?" said Khadija's father.

"Ribbons. And printing paper. All sorts of supplies and peripherals."

"I hardly think your son would want to sell such stuff, after being educated at Harvard," Khadija's father protested.

The tightly knit business community I came from was skeptical of the new entity who'd shown up out of the blue from America. Such men got married but left their wives in Pakistan because American residency was hard to get. I visited girl after girl in stately mansions, methodically pursuing the hunt through interested aunties and matchmakers, rather than being restricted to my parents' narrow range of acquaintances. I established credibility, became a catch of sorts. The Bawanis, the Adamjees, the Tabanis, the leading families in my successful ethnic community duly handed over their jewels for inspection. The choice was endless. The girls were attractive as in an exotic dream, their parents soliciting me like a prince.

At the end of that first summer in Pakistan, I found myself fêted by the parents of one of the most attractive girls I'd ever seen. The father was rich, though a bit of a shady character. Their dark-skinned daughter had supermodel looks, and her zest for life was barely restrainable. The elaborate hosting meant that the family was prepared to give her hand to me on the spot. But I had to leave for Boston soon. My American travel document was about to expire and I couldn't risk overstaying. My father advised me that such an outgoing girl would be difficult to control. "She'll be talking to all the men on the plane when you go back to America. Is that what you want?"

During my visits to Pakistan, I ended up buying more than a hundred thousand rupees' worth of books on Islam from bookstores on Burns Road and Jamshed Road. These included esoteric tafseers and commentaries, books that were part of the centuries-old South Asian religious curriculum, the Dars-e-Nizami. My father didn't mind. Whenever I made an appearance in the steaming heat of Elite Computers, he'd open the cash drawer and push five or ten thousand rupees toward me.

Karachi was in the grip of anarchy and civil war. There were frequent strikes, during which my father kept working, as he did on Friday too, despite the danger of hooligans smashing the store if they found business going on behind the shutters. Every day a few bystanders got randomly killed. It could happen to anyone.

I drove around in our 1975 Toyota Corolla—a car so decrepit that bus conductors in the old city jeered at it. Keeping this car was another of my parents' ploys to protect themselves from kidnappers and extortionists. I spoiled the effect, however, by wearing incongruous suits, despite the car lacking an air conditioner, in the hundred degree heat. In this car I took my mother to "see" girl after girl, taking part in the unchanging ritual of the girl coming out to the living room with tea and cake as the prospect shot quick glances to gauge her curves or lack thereof underneath the formless shalwar kameez, and the prospective mother-in-law grilled her about her "hobbies."

By 1994, the well was running dry. In my three earlier trips, I'd pursued girls from reputable families but left the country just as the family was getting ready to hand her over, when my travel document was up. This time, on a yearlong trip, I began to get involved in the country's politics. I started writing for *Dawn*, Pakistan's newspaper of record. The publisher was one of my father's clients, and instructed the editors at the paper to publish whatever I wrote. My first article, an exploration of the reforms Islam needed, from the perspective of a former HIS president, caused a sensation. I had carte blanche to pursue any subject.

If only my family had owned satellite TV, exposing titillating Indian flesh round the clock—a frenzied freedom I'd lost touch with during my sedate years in America—I might never have married Nasreen. At Harvard, it was all hijabs and lowered gazes, brother this and sister that, and elaborate prayer and iftar rituals, where no one violated male-female etiquette. Pakistan was feverish, experimenting with democracy for the first time since Zia's dictatorship. Freedom of expression was rampant, anarchic, inviolable.

I started getting to know the leading intellectuals and politicians of the country. I went to conferences and workshops at Pearl Continental and Taj Mahal and other five-star hotels, dragging my poor mother along. One of them was a "jihad" conference at the Sheraton, organized by none other than Ayesha Rehmani's mother. When my mother tried to talk to Ayesha's mother, Ayesha, who was visiting Pakistan, pulled away her mother, saying, "Don't have anything to do with these people." I'd become a skeptic about jihad, so Ayesha and I had been at loggerheads in Boston.

At the same conference, Nasreen spotted me for the first time. She was dressed from head to toe in black burqa, never revealing her face to my mother as Nasreen engaged her in conversation. Later, in the middle of the incipient civil war, and my frantic writings for *Dawn*, as I recovered my original liberalism from Locke and Mill and other humanist giants desperately relevant to Pakistan, Nasreen started calling me at Elite Computers.

At first she didn't give her name. I was desperate to get married by that time. Someone, anyone. I was thirty-one, and still a virgin. I hadn't seen her face, but she sounded interested in my ideas about reforming Pakistan. She was a tablighi, but tablighis could be reformed. At least they were better than the jihadis.

The day of the mass wedding at Sohrab Goth, I got cold feet. I told my father I couldn't go through with it. At that crucial moment, Maulana Qadri, another of Elite Computer's loyal customers—the madrassas were rapidly computerizing—showed up. The maulana told me it was normal to feel anxious at such a time. He also talked about the importance of not letting the condom interfere with the pleasure of penetrating a virgin.

After the nikah at Sohrab Goth, I found myself left alone that evening with Nasreen at her apartment, allowed to do as we wished behind the curtains in the living room, while her family members excused themselves. The rukhsati—the official departure of the bride from her home—wasn't scheduled for a few more days. What was I supposed to do with Nasreen in my hour with her? Kiss her? Talk to her? I don't believe we so much as held hands.

Then came the wedding night. My female cousins, whom I'd lost all touch with since childhood, helped

Nasreen into the decorated bedroom of my apartment at Sumayya Complex, a sixth-floor residence that got a strong breeze from the Arabian Sea. When my bride and I were left alone, we prayed a lot. It seemed to take hours to get the ornaments and clothes off Nasreen. Her body was more mannish than I'd realized, her breasts small, her hips wide. Part of me was repulsed. I don't think we were able to consummate the marriage that night. We paused often for prayers—the tablighi curriculum was strong on warding off the devil at every stage of sexual communion. At the moment of climax, the male was supposed to grab the woman's forelock and yell a prayer to forestall shaitan from entering the spirit of the child at conception. I may have obliged Nasreen by doing just that.

Next morning, my mother came to my apartment and said, "You're not happy, are you?" Unlike my father, she'd wanted me to break off the engagement, word of honor be damned.

There was desultory sex a few times. I could go on for hours and hours, but Nasreen wasn't keen. She had no appreciation for closeness.

Conflicts arose quickly over religion. I used to keep the Qur'an under the bed. She claimed that I wanted to pee on her, or have her pee on me, but I can't recall if this was true. She wanted me to go on a tablighi trip for a year. To oblige her, I went to Raiwind, near Lahore, the main center of tablighi activity in the world. I spent a few days there, and got terribly sick. It was the most depressing event of my life. I returned to Karachi eager to fix whatever had gone wrong in my life. But Nasreen wasn't around anymore. She'd returned to her parents' home. I would never see her again.

My faithful cousin Imran, who'd been my best man at the wedding and was trusted by both parties, handled the negotiations with her family. They claimed I was an apostate who deserved being stoned to death. They said medical reports would verify I'd had brutal sex with Nasreen. Brutal? Okay, so I had to expend Herculean efforts for hours to ejaculate, and I was very vigorous, but brutality?

One night, Imran came over and said they wanted a divorce. The word shattered me. I smashed my hand through a thick glass coffee table, opening a wide gash on my wrist. I bled profusely at Agha Khan hospital, Karachi's best. The sympathetic young doctor, when he found out I'd been to Harvard, admonished me: "We need people like you to build the country. Don't harm yourself."

I heard Nasreen went ahead with an abortion, at Agha Khan hospital. I hadn't known she was pregnant. It had been a few weeks since she'd disappeared. I'd gone around to her friends to beg an audience with her, so I could know what was going on. When I heard about the abortion, I wept in my father's lap. "She killed my child," I cried, although I didn't know that the baby was mine, or if there was a baby.

My father took me to our longtime pir, originally from Kabul and exiled in Pakistan since the Soviet invasion. I recited my tale as truthfully as I could. The roly-poly pir wanted to know how I'd treated her. Perhaps I'd been "insensitive?"

A few days later, my father had his face covered in his hands, embarrassed to death, as I recounted the story of Nasreen's disinterest in sex to our family lawyer, Suleman Gandhi, the one who'd advised me to get my rocks off in Bangkok years ago. I spared the lawyer no graphic detail of the marital bedroom, also telling him about taking Nasreen to a gynecologist, to find out why she was uninterested in sex. It had been a busy week-long marriage.

I disengaged from the whole mess. I left it to Imran and my father and the lawyer to sort out the divorce. Nasreen soon married an older tablighi, who'd been married before. One theory proposed by the sophisticated among my acquaintances was that Nasreen only married me, a foreign patsy, to overcome an Islamic legal technicality. They assumed she must have been married to the older tablighi in the past but couldn't get back with him unless she consummated another marriage and was divorced.

I threw myself into writing, enjoying the luxury of not having to work, or the stress of Harvard, and appreciating the ocean wind blowing into the Sumayya Complex apartment. My articles for *Dawn*—attacking hijab, mullahs' fixation on obscenity in the media, and Pakistan's obsession with Kashmir—earned great accolades. For Women's Day, I penned a classic defense of women's rights, which earned me an invitation to speak at a prestigious conference at Karachi University—although I couldn't go because my travel document, even with a year to go this time, was soon expiring.

My mother regularly brought me food at my apartment, and the beautiful young Bengali servant who came every day to clean the place praised me to my mother as "the most decent human being" she'd ever seen.

"Why are you crying again?" I cradled Tarannum Khan's head in my lap.

We were sitting on the steps to her condominium complex on Massachusetts Avenue, across from Harvard Law School, that summer morning in 1995, soon after my return from Pakistan. I wondered how she could afford to live here with her younger sister, an intern at an advertising firm, but her father was a successful Northampton neurosurgeon after all.

"I don't know why I'm crying. I never know."

"Let me read you my new poem, it'll make you feel better." I read her a poem about Italy involving bike riding on narrow cobbled streets, flirting in the kitchen while making pasta, and the lovers' mothers in supportive roles.

"Pretty good, for someone who's never been to Italy."

"You think?"

"None of our Muslim friends would understand this poem. You're a pretty literary type. You have to have read Eliot and Pound to come up with stuff like that. So tell me again, what did you write for *Dawn*?" Word at HIS was that I was a popular "syndicated columnist" for South Asian newspapers.

Tarannum wasn't the only one getting my attention. I'd met Sabrina Haq, a Pakistani from Oxford, as well as some freshmen girls new to activism and awed by my recent direct involvement in the affairs of the nation.

With Sabrina, a molecular biologist, I found myself at the Office of Career Services one afternoon, both of us flipping through folders of job descriptions. I was looking into investment banking jobs in New York (I've often wondered what would have happened had I treated more seriously my all-expenses-paid trip to interview at

D.E. Shaw & Co., Jeff Bezos's early stomping grounds). We ended up confirming that doggie-style intercourse offered the deepest penetration for the woman. Both of us had thought it would have been with the woman on top.

I gave a talk to the South Asian Association, in the Adams House small dining room, about how Harvard undergraduates could make a difference on the Indian subcontinent. Those already thinking about going there were pursuing offers through formal channels—NGOs, fellowships, Harvard grants. I told them my experience— showing up and counting on serendipity—had worked out fine.

"Let's go upstairs to your room," I said to Tarannum on the evening she was crying in my lap on the steps. I was conscious of passersby staring at us.

Tarannum had worked as a model in high school (she had the Pathan's exotic high cheekbones), recovered from ovarian cancer at nineteen, and experienced a borderline gangbang. I suspected she offered sexual favors to rich Saudi students in return for support of her lavish lifestyle. She was still trying to get into Professor Miller's Harvard Islamic Legal Studies program. Mainly, she was a full-time Bosnia activist, appearing on local television shows like *The Thursday Group* and making tenured academics weep during panels at the Kennedy School.

She'd broken up with Zafrul, a Bengali graduate student in economics. I had the habit of giving away from time to time my wardrobe, including expensive suits, as well as books and other possessions. Zafrul did the same. Tarannum couldn't get over the similarity of our saintly "housecleaning." When Tarannum first invited me to her apartment, Zafrul was there to welcome me, offering his imprimatur to his replacement. Although I wrote passionate love poetry for Tarannum, inspired by Neruda and Paz, I'd only gone so far as kissing her and seeing glimpses of her white panties. Perhaps her Islamic strictures prevented her from letting go. Perhaps mine still did.

That summer, I was back on Harvard's periphery, no longer a student, but working for the National Bureau of Economic Research. I hated the stuffiness at the think tank, but I didn't know what else to do with my economics degree. The big-name Harvard and MIT economists at the NBER were into hard-core mathematical and statistical analysis. I preferred words. I was asked to write spur-of-the-moment advisories for Mexican and other Latin American governments to attract foreign direct investment, or speculate on the European Union's currency dilemmas, for professors unwilling to do the grunt work themselves.

I lived a couple of blocks away on Prescott Street in the basement apartment of Professor Richard Silverstein, who claimed to be affiliated with Harvard's psychology department. He leased the subsidized apartment from Harvard Real Estate, while teaching in San Francisco. Once a month he showed up to collect rent from me and five other Harvard students, and to put on his leather bondage outfit, jump on his pristine Harley-Davidson, and troll Boston's gay clubs.

Professor Silverstein was freshly divorced, and I discovered volumes of his diaries about that event in his tiny windowless room, the one I stayed in during his absence. I shared the find with the other tenants. One of them was a sad Japanese girl named Izumi. She was proud of holding her liquor, and I always had to resist her attempts to get me drunk. One night we came close to kissing, as Izumi showed me pictures of her at Andover, carelessly exposing her panties. I let the moment pass. Izumi was thrilled to get any dirt on Professor Silverstein. He'd admonished her she didn't act like a properly "submissive" Japanese girl.

No one was supposed to know I'd been married. My sister made the mistake of telling the current president of HIS what had happened with Nasreen, but I hoped he would be discreet. I was wrong.

When I met Fauzia Minto, a Harvard graduate from the late eighties and the daughter of a World Bank economist, at a bake sale organized to help Bosnian victims—the crisis was at its peak after the Srebrenica massacre—she said, "I hear you got married in Pakistan? What happened?" In my early days at Harvard, Fauzia used to blatantly come on to me, hugging and kissing me in front of HIS members.

"I never got married. That's a lie. Where did you hear that?"

Fauzia avoided me like the plague after that. I called her a few times, leaving messages, but she never returned my calls. I faced the same question from other girls who used to be smitten with me before the events in Pakistan. I refused to acknowledge what had happened in Pakistan, making them all react the same way. The Mount Holyoke, Smith, and Wellesley graduates, who had seemed so idealistic and verbally accomplished, baffled me with their hard-nosed practicality, an obsession with the nitty-gritty, particularly money matters.

Cassandra called me at the NBER. She'd finished her stint with the Peace Corps in Nigeria. She'd learned a lot about Islam as it was practiced in daily life. Because of her involvement with me, she'd taken introductory courses in Islam at Harvard. But dealing with the real thing—the violence fostered by the religion in West Africa—was a different matter. It left her repelled, as did Islam's treatment of women. I didn't tell her anything about Nasreen. She said I sounded depressed and recommended therapy (she'd given me the same advice all the years I'd known her). She gave me names of psychiatrists in Boston she liked, and I pretended to take notes.

At Eid prayers in the Quincy mosque outside Boston, I exchanged thoughts with Professor Gertrude Sackberg— one of Islam's biggest boosters at Harvard—on the booming militia movement in the American heartland. I'd happened to fly back from Pakistan the day after the Oklahoma City bombing. The violence in Pakistan already seemed faraway. The streets of Boston were too quiet.

Tarannum took me condo-hunting one day, while I was being derelict with my research at the NBER and in danger of being fired. We went to real estate offices along Massachusetts Avenue.

"What price range is good for you?" Tarannum asked.

I shrugged.

We looked at condos in the quarter million dollar range. I had less than five hundred dollars in my bank account.

"Can you really afford it?" Tarannum probed.

I wished I was anywhere else but one of those real estate offices. Even the dreaded hundred dollar Harvard Square manicures and pedicures and two hundred dollar facials Tarannum made me have to look good for her paled in comparison.

"I don't see why not," I said.

She took me to Bally to enroll in their fitness classes. I suspect it was to see if I passed their credit check. The girls I knew from before had noted that I'd gained a few pounds since going to Pakistan. It was odd for them to reconcile the heavier person with the still vibrant rhetoric. They all had tips for me to fix the problem.

Later in the summer, Tarannum called while I was in Professor Silverstein's tiny basement bedroom. "You liar, Salman!" You never told me you got married in Pakistan. Did you think you were going to keep it a secret from me? Were you ever going to tell me?"

"Who told you?" I whined.

"It doesn't matter. My sister. Zafrul. The Saudi contingent at Harvard Law School. The HIS people. For God's sake, *everybody* knows."

I started crying—for the first and last time in my adult life, not counting the occasion I wept in my father's lap when I found out about Nasreen's abortion.

"Stop crying! I hate men who cry."

She made me feel so small.

I wish she'd gone easier on me in our next confrontation. I'd been fired from the NBER, as expected, and couldn't afford Dr. Silverstein's rent. Having no choice, I moved in with a bunch of Muslims in a cheap Somerville apartment. One of the guys was a pucca tablighi, Osman Abdullah, HIS treasurer. There were three other South Asian Muslims in that apartment who went along with Islamic rituals, but weren't as devout as students born and raised in America. I had phone sex with new girls in San Antonio and Portland who'd heard of me as an HIS biggie on the internet, while Osman and the others conducted "shuras"—consultations, following Islamic practice—to deliberate on how much daal should go in the cooking pot, or whether ice hockey was Islamic.

Osman irked me. He would borrow my comb for his greasy hair and beard. He complained about how his uncle had got his physician father in trouble with Medicare authorities on allegations of fraud, but good Muslims that they were, Osman's family had swallowed the bitter pill and shunned revenge.

I'd written an essay, "Coming Up For Air" (Tarannum would have appreciated the literary allusion, though I wasn't sure about other readers), for the HIS newsletter while I was in Pakistan. It described my awakening as I confronted the reality of poverty. Where was the clerical elite naïve Muslims in America idolized for having the answers, when it came to dealing with the real world? I'd written about how the privileged in Pakistan normally kept a veil over their eyes, a defensive barrier against visible signs of brutal poverty, without which they wouldn't be able to justify their privilege. I wrote that I'd made the fatal choice of letting down my own defenses, allowing the full force of the brutality to penetrate my soul. I claimed to be a changed man. Osman had objected to the publication of this essay, arguing it was too close to apostasy.

In my writings for *Dawn*, and in my talks with HIS members and South Asians in general, I talked about the need for Muslims to be intentionally "naïve liberals." Classical liberalism, under the onslaught of postmodernism, stood discredited with Western academics. But it was precisely what Muslim countries needed. The weight of history would have to be set aside, as Muslims first learned the basics of liberalism.

Carried away by this injunction, I started getting into fights with Osman and the others, when I asserted there was "no such thing as the CIA." The HIS people would look at me as if I was a madman. "What do you mean there's no such thing as the CIA? Of course there is. They're behind every dirty deed in the Muslim world."

I gave my last khutba at HIS. It was Ramadan. I started talking about poverty in Pakistan, bringing up Mahbubul Haq and other U.N. and World Bank experts who looked at it hardheadedly. There was barely a link with Islamic ideology in my last sermon. The crowd was stunned and restless, though some who hadn't grown up in America seemed appreciative. I chose not to lead the prayer after the sermon, pulling an elderly sheikh from Al-Azhar, a visiting scholar at Harvard, for the duty.

When the fights with Osman and other roommates became too frequent, I decided to pack up and leave while they were out. I owed some rent, but they'd broken my computer, so I figured we were even. I took refuge at the Roxbury home of one Dr. Nizami, a talkative BU and Harvard-affiliated public health specialist.

Tarannum called me. "How dare you leave those people without paying rent, Salman? I order you to pay the four hundred bucks you owe them right now. Go there, now!"

I lamely complied.

Tarannum drove over with a friend to Dr. Nizami's apartment, wanting her framed high-school picture back. I used to keep it on my desk at the NBER during my tenure there.

I started reading Ibn Warraq's *Why I am Not a Muslim Anymore*. All my suspicions about Islam—the Prophet's brutality and misogyny, the unbroken history of hypocrisy and violence—were confirmed by this apostate Muslim.

I began to lament my lost years at Harvard. I could have made so much of myself had I not fallen into the religious trap. Just as the experience with Nasreen had begun to seem surreal soon after its conclusion, the last several years, while I'd been in the grip of religious fever, seemed to do so too. I wished I wouldn't abuse Dr. Nizami's hospitality by running up thousands of dollars in phone bills to Pakistan, money I couldn't possibly pay.

When Tarannum came to retrieve her picture, I handed it to her in the snowy parking lot of Dr. Nizami's building. I could honestly say I felt no emotion toward her.

THE RUG SELLER'S DAUGHTER

"Baba, how many people do you want me to fix dinner for?"

It was the daughter he hadn't seen before, the lone inheritor of the business and the legacy, popping the question from the back door of the shop which led into what Pathans called "the zenana," the part of their property inhabited by women. Strict segregation had been the order of the day for as long as Jim Saltzman had been acquainted with Pathans, so he was surprised by the brash intervention from the voluptuous daughter. Despite the blue and white chadar covering some of her hair and face, he glimpsed her ruddy complexion, large green eyes beholding multitudes of questions, and the fetching beauty mark beside her nose.

The father, Jamal Khan, signaled with his fingers, three. Jim wondered about the identity of the third person, because Jamal Khan had only this child, who was divorced, and no other family. Jamal Khan's wife had died twenty years ago in a typhoid epidemic. Jim noticed the surprise on the faces of the young men who worked for Jamal Khan—they hadn't taken the benevolent apparition in stride either. The daughter—with a look that lingered on Jim—disappeared with a twirl of her chadar inside the zenana.

On that hot, steamy afternoon in Peshawar—surely the last blast of summer—Jim was well-pleased with his cache, which he would send on to Intercontinental Hotel in Islamabad, preceding his own arrival. He had found the most understated, elegantly woven Bukharas, Isfahans, and Kashans in the universe of Oriental rugs, and he started composing a letter in his head to his estranged second wife, Patty, who'd shown, during the years of their marriage, appreciation for Jim's skill in picking out the best rugs. "Dear Patty: I'm sitting on top of a treasure trove. If I had the means and the money, I'd want to ship all of Jamal Khan's store, in toto, to the warehouse in San Diego, where I'd sit on the collection, and never sell a single piece. Call me an addict, but it's a good addiction."

For thirty-five years—since Ayub Khan was president of undivided Pakistan, and the tragedy that resulted in Bangladesh hadn't happened—Jim had been coming at the end of every summer to this land that hadn't learned how to dream big enough despite its wide frontiers. Each year Jamal Khan saved the best of the year's crop, acquired during trips to remote parts of Uzbekistan and northern Iran, in honor of Jim's respect for true art. Jim bargained over prices, of course—not to do so would invite disdain from Jamal Khan's associates, if not from Jamal Khan himself—but it was a pro forma activity, and he didn't derive pleasure from cutting the price by a few per cent, unlike his fellow rug dealers in America.

"You will be closing the shop?" Jamal Khan, sitting cross-legged on the floor, was asking about Jim's plan to go into semi-retirement. His English was hesitant, although they could easily have conversed in Pashto, Jim having picked up enough of the vernacular over the years. "What will you do? You are still a strong man. Retirement can be the end of ambition." Jamal Khan, with his leathery, pinched face—the antique French pince-nez he'd acquired through his former son-in-law lent him dignity—put aside the burbling hookah, to attend to what Jim would say.

"I won't let that happen to myself." Jim was plunked on a mound of carpets, enjoying the feeling of lushness. Truth be told, he didn't need the new lot of rugs. His retirement was assured through wise investing—thanks to Patty, who'd been sent to deliver him from trouble in middle-age, only to gracefully retreat from the scene herself—and buying rugs at this juncture was an indulgence. Jim knew this truth, but if he let Jamal Khan know, the thrill of the chase, the mutual excitement of a sharp-eyed seller spotting a fellow aficionado, would be gone.

"What will you do?" Jamal Khan persisted.

"I live near Escondido. Beautiful beaches. Surfing. Sailing. I have my boat. And am I too old to chase girls?"

"Girls? Well, I just said you were young and strong, so I cannot take back my own statement, can I?" He laughed self-consciously, like a young girl, like someone who'd forgotten how to laugh because of family tragedy, an early divorce maybe, and was again getting used to the sound of laughter.

Jim wanted to change the subject. "I still can't believe you're using computers for everything."

A young man stood near the entrance, entering the transactions of the day into the spanking new PC. He was one of Jamal Khan's new hires, and showed a touch of insolence, although that was perhaps only a passing phase, as the man learned to deal with the angrez, or English, the blanket Pakistani designation for white people.

"It is a necessity," Jamal Khan said. "I have to do it. Everyone is using them. If I do not use a computer, my customers think I am not up-to-date, my shop does not have the best rugs, I am missing something. Go around Peshawar, and shoe sellers, furniture makers, they are all using computers."

That was one thing—moving around Peshawar—Jim had stopped doing. The place was changing too fast. His told himself his lungs could no longer handle the pollution, but another part of his anatomy was the problem: his old heart couldn't get used to the new aggression, the passing of politeness and delicacy, the new rat race infecting the Pathans in what used to be Shangri-la but now looked like any third world sprawl with no purpose.

"I'm sorry I don't get around Peshawar."

"No worry, there is enough time." Enough time? The old rug seller knew Jim needed to catch a cab to Islamabad before sunset. "Tonight, you are eating with me. I hope you had no other plans?" Jamal Khan raised his eyebrows, daring Jim to contest him; and when he looked around the store with the same elevated eyebrows, the gesture dismissed his helpers. The two old men were soon alone in the shop.

Jamal Khan rose and put a hand on Jim's shoulder. "I did not want to discuss this in front of my shop assistants, but I am thinking of shutting down this place."

"You can't do that." Jim was shocked. "You're irreplaceable."

"No man is infallible—not even the prophets. It is inevitable. There is a season for everything. I am much older than I look. Unlike you."

Jamal Khan was being kind. Perhaps Jim's love of rugs, which had outlived economic utility, had something to do with preserving him. He looked at his bales of rugs, bound by sharp metal strips, with pure love.

A little later, Jim had become more mellow. He was sitting on the floor of the nearly bare living room—one of the largest Kirman antiques he'd ever seen occupied the center of the room—his head propped against thick, velvety, mirrored Kabuli cushions. He passed on the bowl of pistachios, cashews, and almonds—the best nuts in the world came from this region—in preference for smoking. The cigarettes Jamal Khan gave him had relaxed him. Did they only contain tobacco? They were probably smuggled from across the border. On the other side of the Hindu Kush, the magic quotient was higher.

The room was full of smoke, there was a twinge of irrevocable sadness, and only D. W. Griffith's belly dancers were needed to enter in pairs and complete the picture.

Patty's fantasy had been for them to retire while they could still enjoy themselves, and escape to some remote part of the world where the cost of living was cheaper, where there was no smog and freeway congestion, where they would have time to do things that made life worth living—reading and talking and making love. Patty understood Jim well enough to leave him alone on his rug purchasing trips; she knew it was his time for solitude, and she interfered with it at her own risk.

"We will have dinner now." Jamal Khan entered the living room, dressed in fresh white shalwar kameez, bathed in feminine perfume. The sweaty masculine aura of the shop was gone. "You must be hungry."

"I'm starved."

"We do not mean to starve you. They say, as poor as Pakistan is, nobody ever starves in this country." The sly comparison was with India. "Come, my friend." Jamal Khan lent him his arm, and Jim rose unsteadily.

"Those cigarettes were wonderful."

"Hashish." When Jim looked baffled, Jamal Khan said, "I am only joking with you."

"It'll be difficult to take the cab at night. I don't even like riding cabs in the daytime, when I fear death at every turn."

"You will not be taking the cab. You will stay here."

"Here?" But Jim had known all along this was coming. "I didn't bring any change of clothes. And the rugs. Will the rugs be okay?" Before the shop closed, a Suzuki pickup had taken them.

"The rugs will be fine. And you can wear my clothes."

The rest of the evening was an enchanting dream. At first Zahra served them lamb curry and cashew chicken from a respectful distance, her chadar sometimes slipping off her hair and face. Jim understood the privilege of being included in the family enclave. Pathans were famous for keeping their women secluded. Jamal Khan had never asked Jim to accompany him to his wife's grave; even after death, she was sacrosanct. No young Pathan male uttered the name of his mother or sister in public. Yet here was Zahra, moving around as in a hallucinatory vision, locking eyes, while Jamal Khan complimented the food.

"Sit with us," Jamal Khan invited Zahra.

Bashful, turning her face sideways, Zahra joined them, sitting next to her father.

"My daughter speaks good English—also some French. I sent her to a private school in Murree. The mullahs are shutting it down. They want only madrassas in that part of the country."

"You speak French?" Jim asked. "I had a few semesters. Very rusty, but I can manage."

Zahra answered him in French, and they stumbled along the crumbling roads and bridges of Jim's youth, education, and career. They did not speak of rugs.

"And your wife, does she not join you in your travels?" Zahra asked in English.

"My wife and I are estranged. What I'm trying to say is, while we're not officially divorced—tax reasons and whatnot—for all intents and purposes we're no longer husband and wife."

"Why not get divorced and be free?" Jamal Khan interrupted.

"I could if I wanted to. If there were compelling reasons."

Jamal Khan excused himself. Jim didn't ask where he was going. Hours seemed to pass while Jim talked to Zahra about everything under the sun—except for the love of his life, rugs—and was impressed by her knowledge. When Zahra interrogated him, she did so not with cynicism or irony, but in the spirit of getting information, like Dick Cavett or some other earnest talk show host. American women in the forties and fifties must have been like that—intelligent but sincere.

"What about your ex-husband?" Jim said. "I mean, what happened?"

"Can we not talk about it?" Zahra looked sad. "Let's just say he was a bad man. He betrayed me."

Jim guessed she meant adultery, but there had to be more. Most Pathan men had mistresses—indeed, if you were rich and didn't have any, you'd be considered worthless.

"Have you served qahwa?" Jamal Khan inquired upon his next entrance. "How about some dessert? Zahra makes excellent halwa."

"No thank you, no sweets or coffee. Unless *you* want some," Jim pointed to Zahra.

Later, when Jim was on the floor with Jamal Khan again, without Zahra present, Jamal Khan said, "Many Afghans, Pathans, have gone to America. They love that land. It is like a second home. Real initiative, and for women respect—respect all around. Pathans have great respect for America."

"We have some things going for us."

"Your land is built on family and faith—like ours." Jamal Khan spoke about numerous relations who'd gone over to America, and were now prospering. "My daughter would like very much to go to America."

Jim was about to blurt out that emigration to America was difficult these days, when at last he caught on to the meaning of the evening.

The night was as baleful as the evening had been magical. The qahwa—to which he'd relented, when Zahra made her final appearance of the night—was keeping him up. The spare room in Jamal Khan's house had large empty closets. An irritating buzz, like that of a generator, came from the next-door house—or maybe it was a factory.

The taut charpoy was hard, the thin mattress not enough to soften the roughness. Pathans considered it a matter of honor to continue to sleep on the rugged charpoys, even after they were rich enough to afford proper beds.

He wondered about Zahra's bed. Did she toss and turn? Did she suffer from insomnia? Did she need to hear stories to go to sleep? His fate had been to meet shrewd, practical women who were beyond childish needs. Not that Zahra didn't seem practical—with one marriage behind her. What *was* that dastardly husband's crime? Pathans, for all their virility on the battlefield and in the marketplace, were not known for beating up their women.

The buzz next door got louder, and he thought of getting up and investigating. At least when humans worked with hands, such white noise wasn't generated. People in the West talked about shutting down the rug industry in this part of the world. Then what would keep the young men from getting into trouble? It was a priceless apprenticeship for those lucky enough to get it.

Would he want his own son to work at a rug loom at ten or twelve years of age? His material circumstances were different, and he couldn't disown his background. Anyway, a child had never been on the cards. Patty looked at children as cute objects, related to the Toys "R" Us apparatus, not quite human. In that respect, Patty had been like his first wife. Trust Jim to find the only two women without maternal feelings in the Western hemisphere.

Zahra had been married for five years, from eighteen to twenty-three. Why wasn't there a child? Pathan wives usually got pregnant within the first year.

Had he not known better, he would have sworn that Jamal Khan was drunk by the close of the evening. He'd started bragging to Jim about the price his old house could fetch. He foresaw the neighborhood being gentrified in a few years. Already, the old Kabul elite was reorganized in the host country, replicating its segregated patterns. The creepy bastards, in love with royalty and its disreputable ways—ordinary Pathans were democratic, if they had any political creed—gave a bad name to wealth, but in one's old age, how could a property windfall be refused? He bragged about selling rugs at astonishing prices—well beyond anything Jim imagined for the most precious antiques—to European aristocrats who were worse than Americans, because they didn't admit the level of their ignorance, whereas Americans did.

Zahra was uncomfortable at Jamal Khan's volubility, putting her soft hand on his shoulder to quieten him. The old man went to bed without saying good night.

Jim was beginning to sweat, though the night outside was cool, and the fan was rotating fast enough. There was that familiar ache in the pit of his stomach, which appeared whenever he was called upon to make a decision. But was that how it was? Did he have to decide, or were decisions made for him? What was the decision he needed to make now?

Was he supposed to be the aging knight in shining armor, coming to Zahra Khan's emotional rescue? Ha, he thought, he was old enough to have grown up with the precursors to rock and roll, the ones even before Chuck Berry and Little Richard. He saw Zahra lying on his lap, in the fading light of a warm summer evening on their porch in Escondido, her soft buttocks spread out for him to slap.

He got up excitedly. The blood was rushing through his veins. He was more keyed up than he could remember being in years. He felt like a young man. Sure, he was young enough still, in all the ways that counted, to take care of the needs of a woman at her peak. Women at their peak. What an absurd popular formulation! As if women were never at their peak. It was the poor men who always fell behind in the race, at some point slowing to a crawl.

He calmed himself so he wouldn't have to masturbate. To do so in old Jamal Khan's home—despite his host's drunken performance earlier—would leave a bad memory.

He only had to wait until the morning, and then he'd be on his way, putting the incongruous situation behind him. Good, he could finally sleep now—the buzz next-door was gone, the fan was circulating hard enough to make him feel like he was floating. He would be gone at the crack of dawn, back to his gorgeous rugs in Islamabad, and then out of this weird country, with its unpredictable customs and expectations, and on the plane to sunny California, where there were never any surprises.

Zahra did the unexpected and took away his will. When the door cracked open, he thought it might be burglars—knowing that a Westerner was staying at Jamal Khan's house, some local gang must have moved into action.

"Don't be afraid, it's only me," Zahra whispered from the door.

Jim wasn't sure if he was dreaming. Zahra's hand on his arm removed any doubt. She slid under the covers with him. "If my father knew, he'd have me killed," she said. Jim realized the magnitude of what was happening. Should Jamal Khan decide to, he could kill Jim, and no court in the land would rule against him, understanding the violation of hospitality that had taken place.

"You shouldn't be here," Jim said.

Zahra started caressing his temples, his eyes. "You should not be angry at me. It's the last night of my life I can expect to have any pleasure. My father is packing up, leaving, for God knows where. What will happen to me? My father wants to become a vagabond, a homeless man, at his age. How can I be with an old man who has lost his marbles? Don't be upset with me." She sobbed, while Jim didn't know how to make her feel better.

"I'm an old man, Zahra, like your father. I have the same faults." That was how Patty felt.

"You must do whatever feels good to you, whatever feels right. The heart always knows."

Jim felt a wave of disgust toward Patty for having always underestimated him. This situation, happening now—could she ever imagine Jim being desirable from so many points of view, and ending up with this dilemma?

Zahra was eager to move on to more physical things. Her hand was fumbling over his throat, his shoulders, as though desperately searching for something.

"Go to sleep now," he said. "I'll take care of everything." He didn't feel such manly assurance, he'd never been comfortable with taking charge, but it felt like the right thing to say. "In the morning, everything will be okay."

Did he mean that in the morning, the challenge to his self-worth would be gone, that he would again be a normal rug buyer dealing with a normal rug seller? Did he mean to disappear without saying good-bye?

"Don't feel bad toward me for what I've done," Zahra said.

"How could I?" Jim choked back emotion. This was a beautiful girl. A lucky man could yet have her.

Sleep didn't come until dawn. A clamor in the street

woke him. The sun was high in the heavens. Children were shouting, vegetable and fruit vendors were shouting louder, and housewives were shouting the loudest from their windows, ordering carrots and parsley and potatoes. Jim's night of surprises was over.

Jamal Khan was nowhere to be seen. Neither was Zahra.

The youngest of the rug shop assistants, young enough to be a domestic servant without intruding on women's privacy, came around with coffee and toast.

"The master has left," the servant said. "A cab will be here for you in an hour."

"Where is Jamal Khan? Where is Zahra?" Jim was befuddled. Was this it then? He was being given marching orders? Had he so disappointed his hosts?

"They are not here." The servant observed Jim with a mixture of pity and contempt.

Further questioning would be futile. Pathans were the most stubborn people on earth. Once their mind was made up, nothing on earth could shake it.

Was he being tested? If he stayed on, despite the servant's indifference, would that mean he was committed to Zahra, not out of mercy but because of the beginnings of love?

Wearily, he told the servant, "I'll be ready soon. I need to be in Islamabad to take delivery of the rugs."

The whole world and all that mattered in it seemed to escape him, and he could do nothing about it.

Anis Shivani

DOWRY

"Can you please send someone over to pick up the medication?" Dr. Nadia Rehman said to Rachna, the mother of the girl, Sunera, she'd come to see.

Rachna nodded. Sunera, only seventeen, lay immobile on the bed, on the side of her that hadn't been burnt to a pulp, barely able to breathe.

"I'll tell the dispensary to keep it ready under your name." Where were the girl's older brothers? Nadia thought the patient history she'd read said there were several of them.

Nadia had been so rushed—it was an unusually busy day, with the imminent deadline for the mandatory mass vaccination for the state, on top of her many administrative duties—she'd forgotten her prescription slips at the hospital. Doctors no longer routinely made house calls, but this was a courtesy service of the local government hospital, to put patients at ease with physicians—a relic of the past, but it served its purpose. She refused to call it

"PR," as some of her more cynical colleagues did. To the poorer families served by the hospital, it meant a lot.

"Can I pick it up? I don't have to go to school this week," said Sunera's little brother, all of ten. He had streaks of white in his hair, perhaps crumbling choona, the whitewash that covered both the outside and inside of houses in such neighborhoods. The houses here were flattened and crumpled together, like a field of mushrooms stepped upon by a giant.

"Don't bother the lady doctor," Rachna said to the boy, slapping him on his thin, dark wrist. If he were an animal, the boy would be a mouse. Like a mouse, he'd survive and outlive smarter, bigger sentient beings. Rachna herself was affectless as though her daughter's fate was predetermined, and all she could do was accept it in the most otherworldly manner possible.

"It's all right, he can come," said Nadia, but wondered why the boy wasn't in school. These days children went to school until three in the afternoon; in her time, it had been a shorter school day.

"As you wish," Rachna said.

The only way to survive for a mother whose pretty young daughter's face and upper body had suffered third-degree burns was to put aside her natural emotions, and be all businesslike. Otherwise, she would bring the whole house down. Rachna had the right idea. She'd kept a recital of the events leading to Sunera's near-death experience out of the discussion. This was sane, but unusual in Nadia's encounters. There had been four such incidents she'd attended to this year; the female relatives tended to alternate between being berserk and frigid. Her male colleagues acted too sensitively around her when one of these cases became front and center. She wished the doctors close to her would act more normally.

Sunera lay covered in a white bed sheet, only her hair, which had been spared, visible. Nadia wondered how the poor girl could breathe, being covered so. As soon as the sheet slid a little to expose Sunera's ravaged, bandaged body, Rachna pulled it up. It wasn't the worst case of burning she'd seen. She wanted to tell Rachna that Sunera would be fine, but the words stuck in her throat—they felt like a lie. She wondered where the older brothers slept.

Nadia coughed. "Try to clean the dust more often," she chided Rachna. "I know it's hard, but try to do it. It's better for Sunera's recovery."

"Did you hear what the lady doctor said?" Rachna turned on the boy. "Clean with the jharoo after she's gone. Did you hear it?"

The boy feigned indifference.

"Do you want me to twist your ears?" Sunera's mother didn't say this in a malign manner, but it jarred Nadia.

Nadia thought of her own ailing father, now in the late stages of dementia. In his youthful days, told of an encounter like this, he'd have simultaneously acclaimed and derided Muslim-Hindu interaction at an intimate level. Yet he'd been one of the great liberals of his age—in his own mind, at least. A smile came on, when she thought of her father's verbal pyrotechnics, combined with her mother's worshipful attitude toward the linguistic facility, whether or not she understood his babblings.

"Married? Are you married?" Rachna's mother gave Nadia a cold stare.

What must the poor woman be thinking? A young obviously unmarried Muslim physician—where was the ring on Nadia's finger? Where was the self-assurance, even arrogance, of the married woman?—and she was party to the dastardly secrets of a Hindu household. The girls who ended up being burnt were overwhelmingly from Hindu families. The government tried to suppress the statistics, but the doctors knew better.

"I'm not married." Nadia wished to say no more about the matter, so she stuffed her instruments in their case. "Don't forget to come by this afternoon for the medication," she told the boy.

She sneezed on her way out, the dust bothering her.

A few years ago, there had been a proposal. She hadn't particularly remembered the man from when they were interns together at the leading hospital in the state capital, although he claimed to know every detail about her— her likes and dislikes, her taste in clothes and people, her academic odyssey. She had gone along with the pretense that it amounted to more than the usual arranged marriage preliminaries, even though the biggest marriage broker in town was involved in the matter from step one. Her mother had been keen on the "boy," although her father was always suspicious, perhaps because he would have a potential competitor in extemporaneous speechmaking.

"It's about all we can expect," her mother concluded. "We should feel lucky."

This resigned attitude, despite the match's professional qualification, was expressed because there was a fly in the ointment: the boy was Hindu.

A generation ago, the prospect of such a match across the religious divide would have been unthinkable. But times had changed. There appeared to be a global shortage of men—not statistically, despite the slight edge women maintained in birth and long-term survival rates, but because there didn't seem to be enough responsible, sober men around. "You might ask him if he'll convert," her father kidded. "But do the job yourself. If he goes to a mullah, it's all over." The mullahs would turn the sincerest seeker against religion. But they were proud Hindus, this family, and conversion came up only for Nadia's family to feel better about themselves. In the end, her father relented: "The God we worship is the same, no matter what we call him—Allah, Ram, Jesus, it's all the same."

Sudhir was a persistent, dutiful, aggressive suitor, even after the engagement. He sent expensive presents for Nadia and for her parents, hand-delivered by his servant from twenty miles away in the next town, where he lived. He wrote out epic poems by Byron and Shelley in his distraught physician's hand, which Nadia couldn't finish reading. He was a pleasant, hopeful, uncalculating partner in assembling the dowry—rather unusual, since the dowry was meant to be a surprise to the recipient. This was true beyond the lower rungs of the middle class, where such transactions were conducted in the full light of day and a with deep cynicism on both sides. He expressed preference for one bedroom set over another—his taste ran to art deco, rather than faux Raj—without the least embarrassment. He let Nadia's father win most arguments. And the parents, devout Hindus, remained invisible.

Things began to fall apart when during the course of their yearlong engagement, Nadia started getting all the professional breaks, and Sudhir experienced the reverse. He was getting outwitted in hospital politics by everyone, right and left. This was a huge obstacle to success in state-run hospitals for those with better educations than their bosses. Meanwhile, Nadia was effortlessly accumulating awards and recognitions. If the trend continued, Nadia would soon be the head of some hospital—perhaps within five years—while Sudhir could only envision clashes with his "inferior superiors," as he called them, as far as the eye could see. He started talking about emigrating to America, to play on a level field. "Meritocracy is what it's all about," became his mantra.

His way of breaking the engagement was typical of him. He came over, had a calm dinner, and afterward took Nadia to the local park, where under the stars on a beautiful late-summer evening, he accepted complete responsibility for the "mistake." He didn't deserve her, she really should be with someone of her own caliber. He was sincere, and Nadia let it go.

She'd returned all his gifts and mementos to the servant who came soon after to pick up the things, except the handwritten epic romantic poems. If Sudhir missed those, he didn't say.

As she pulled into the hospital parking lot in her shiny black Ambassador—a perk that went with her position— the old chowkidar, Izhar Khan, gave her a heartfelt salaam.

"Baji," he said respectfully, even though he was in his seventies, "there are three more emergency cases in the burn unit."

More young women attacked for buyer's remorse, not bringing enough dowry, not doing whatever it was that the husband and his family expected of the poor girl? More such cases? When would this ever stop? What was she doing as a doctor, cleaning up the messes? Shouldn't she drop this, and become an activist, fighting the government to impose severe penalties for these crimes, rather than letting the perpetrators get away under the haze of cultural justification?

As though reading her mind, Izhar Khan said, "Baji, they're all men this time."

Good, then, Nadia thought, before realizing she'd just expressed happiness, as a doctor, at men being burnt rather than women.

"Firemen," Izhar Khan added. "Their hoses didn't work."

Despite herself, she smiled.

She'd barely stepped into the hospital's lobby—she was sore that more money had gone into the marble decorations for the hospital's façade than in importing new medical equipment, and she'd made her disappointment clear to the budgeting department—when an older colleague, Dr. Kazmi, collared her.

"You've been paying a house call to the girl, the Hindu girl, who came in last week with the burns." He pulled her aside to a corner, as if imparting a great state secret.

"Yes, what of it?"

"But you're Muslim," he began. "Look, I understand your sincerity and all, but we need a little more sensitivity. Already, resentment against Muslims is rising in the hierarchy, disproportionate to our numbers. If we become too visible, especially in poorer communities—"

"I thought that was the point of these visits, to bridge all kinds of divides."

Dr. Kazmi stepped back and looked at her patronizingly. "We'll talk about this later. You know the road to hell is paved with good intentions."

A younger colleague, Dr. Shyam, who'd first treated Sunera, approached them.

"How's my patient?" he asked.

"She'll pull through."

"I saw pictures of her before...before she was hideously disfigured. A very pretty girl. Married at sixteen. The husband got a big promotion." Dr. Shyam said this as if it explained everything. In a way, it did. A promotion meant better prospects. The male shortage again. He could probably marry up now, and expect some shrew— an unmarried aunt, a tormented mother, someone who just hated women—to take care of what remained of Sunera.

Nadia was still in a rebellious mood. "So, how will you be reporting the case? Cause of accident?"

"I can only go by the official police report." Dr. Shyam's geniality dissipated. "Accidental kitchen fire. No one at fault."

Dr. Kazmi nodded approvingly. "I'll let you two get to work. Remember, staff meeting first thing tomorrow morning."

Later in the lobby, as she left work early—it had been a while since she'd taken her father to the park—she bumped into Sunera's little brother, looking lost. At least the white dust in his hair had been washed off.

"Did you get your sister's medication?"

"Yes, doctor," he said shyly. "See?" He extended his hands, which held the tubes and bottles.

"How's my patient?"

"I haven't been sick in two months."

"I meant your sister."

"Oh." He was shy again.

She gave the boy a ride home in her car. It was his first

time in an automobile, and he showed his excitement. Nadia learned that after she'd left, Rachna cried profusely, but Sunera woke up to stop her. One of the older brothers had regained his job at the auto parts factory. She promised to look in again soon.

Her father made sense in his dementia, when he said things like, "Someone should tear down all the temples and mosques, the houses of disbelief," or "When will they stop wasting money on beautiful graves?" A stray thought came to her: Sudhir would certainly be more at home in America, and she was glad for him.

WHAT IT'S LIKE
TO BE A
STRANGER
IN YOUR OWN HOME

He saw her flicking her red woolen scarf with the elegance of an actress at her door. Her graceful fingers, nails painted pink, lingered over the exposed area between her neck and the top of her white blouse, caressing her slim necklace. He wondered about the importance of the necklace—a cherished gift from a former lover, a guilt-inducing heirloom? Certainly of totemic significance, as his interrupted studies in psychology at Rutgers taught him.

Strengthened by her rituals, she approached her sleek blue BMW, her shoes crunching the bed of new leaves that had appeared overnight under lashing winds. Still toying with scarf and necklace, she acted as though recollection of her blessings overwhelmed her. She slid inside the BMW with the practiced ease of the fortunate, and cranked the engine to roaring life. The morning stillness was shattered.

In this small-town New Jersey neighborhood, forty miles from Manhattan, she was one of the last commuters to leave for work. He wished he knew what business she was in that allowed her to leave home at ten and return at three. Something to do with fashion or art, he hoped, not real estate or finance.

She was a beautiful woman by any standards. Now she was gone—the peak moment of his day over, the rest awaiting him like a horror movie forced on him by one of those freakish girls he used to be attracted to in his twenties. Ursula was the neighbor's name—Ursula Svenson, befitting her flaxen hair and lithe body—as he had learned from a piece of stray mail last month, an overdue life insurance notice mistakenly delivered to him.

Mohammad, Mo to everyone, let go of the spyhole he'd made in the Venetian blinds, sinking on the rumpled bed. He spent an hour reading and rereading the baseball news in the *Times*. In the poor Cairo neighborhood he'd lived in for the first nineteen years of his life, his delicate body had often been battered in street soccer brawls. His older brother used to mock him for daring to plunge his puny body into the mêlée, like tiny Israel in the middle of the vast Arab lands, inviting certain destruction. Of course, Israel had thrived, while the Arabs languished, but anyone who dared to acknowledge even part of the truth, like his childhood idol Anwar Sadat, faced extinction.

His estranged wife Mona, fluent in Arabic despite having lived in New Jersey since she was five, had taught Mo not to get worked up over Arab turmoil. Theirs had been a marriage based on severe attention to process, detail, function. Mona and Mo had played out for seven years the marriage counselor's fantasy of a conjugality that laid every fracture out into the open.

There hadn't been a child to show for the daily struggle. Mo wasn't sure if this was something to regret or celebrate. Now thirty-nine, feeling sure the sudden physical decline that overcame males in his family past a certain age was around the corner, he was grateful Mona hadn't made monetary demands on him, had left the house to him, and that his software company was flexible enough to grant him a six-month leave of absence while he sorted out his personal life.

This gave him time to think, an unaccustomed luxury that his parents would have considered disguise for sloth, but that in this slacker-dominated culture made him something of a hero. His immediate supervisor Bill, a Rutgers man himself, had told him when he heard of pretty Mona decamping one fine spring morning, "You do not deserve this. Repeat, you *do not* deserve this to happen to you." Bill was too kind. Mona's major complaint was that Mo crowded her emotional space like a poisonous tarantula, that he didn't know when to leave her alone. Still, all things considered, he felt he had lived up to the ideal of the sensitive husband as far as possible.

To prove his viability without doubt, he had to know if a woman like Ursula, his elusive next-door neighbor, would find him a worthy companion. He had no idea how to initiate such a friendship, but he was determined it would be tomorrow, Saturday, when Ursula woke up late and stayed home all day. He'd never seen Ursula with a man. That was a good sign.

He took time to shower and shave. It wasn't the first time he was tempted to let the razor slip and cut his throat. If he did that, everyone at the emergency room would suspect he'd tried to kill himself. His naïveté would put the doctors and nurses on greater alert. They would treat him like a child, and he would play along. It was almost worth the pain to get that sort of attention.

In the overheated bathroom, he thought of the last time he'd made love to Mona, a Friday night when he was drunk, having been out with Bill and the others in his project group, celebrating a job well done. Mona had wanted to know why after seven years as a two-income couple they hadn't made sufficient progress toward a retirement nest egg, why Mo treated her new friend Asha, from India, as a social pariah, and why Mo didn't push hard enough at work for a promotion. Mo eagerly set down to the task of edifying Mona on all these points, precisely the attitude Mona resented, making her evoke the tarantula metaphor.

That night, he felt sure he used Mona as a plastic dummy, an inflatable doll with a serviceable vagina, evident in the way he grabbed her belly on each side and thrust into her with the manic propulsion of a machine gone haywire, bent only on expelling his semen. He was sure Mona knew it too.

Getting agitated over this memory that nonetheless made him yearn for Mona's body— or really, any woman's body without the attached interrogations and demands— made him lose his grip on the razor for real, and he acquired a long gash on his throat that really did need medical attention.

Hastily bandaging it and ignoring the leaking blood soiling the collar of his white oxford shirt, he went out to struggle with the temperamental garage door to get into his Lexus SUV and head downtown.

At noon, then, once the thick mahogany door banged shut after him, he felt like a king. He was a solid taxpaying citizen, law-abiding and responsible, and if Mona never appreciated it, too bad for her.

He was excited by the idea of walking along Main Street, peeking glances into upscale stores and businesses, wondering if Ursula worked in any of these. After all, not everyone had to work in Manhattan. Where did people who worked in nondescript places downtown live? He knew the answer: not in his tony neighborhood. But that never did stop him from wanting to pop his head into every travel agency and consulting service.

He didn't enter the hospital to have his wound examined. He circled the place a few times. Swinging around the emergency room, he waved at Dr. Hammoudi, the Algerian surgeon who used to be part of Mona's circle of friends. Hammoudi was bent over, spitting on the sidewalk. It never occurred to Mo that a doctor might ever be in need of medical attention.

In the first years of Mo's marriage, Hammoudi would call Mo the evening before Eid to remind him to be at the train station at seven in the morning. They would go to a cozy Fifth Avenue mosque for prayers at eight, and later, if it wasn't a workday, they would have falafel at Habib's Shwarma Place near the mosque. Mona approved of the twice-a-year Eid ritual. Mo went along with the hypocrisy. The last time he'd remembered God was when he thought he might be falling in love with Mona's younger sister. But he'd backtracked on his call to God, counting it as a sign of weakness.

What had made him wave to Hammoudi with affection today? Hammoudi had a shriveled wife, a near illiterate, whom he kept closeted in their untidy house in a rundown neighborhood. He became the kind of person Mo had stopped consorting with once he was immersed in undergraduate life at Rutgers; Mona was the one who compelled him not to snub his nose at "his own kind," not to look down on retrogrades like Hammoudi and his wife.

Mona's trail was everywhere. Yet he was practical enough to realize he couldn't escape Mona's scent by leaving town, changing familiar surroundings. To get rid of Mona definitively, he'd have to find a human antidote.

He went in to say hello to the barber, a Lebanese man whose parents had both been killed in the civil war in Beirut in the mid-seventies. Since the attacks brought down the twin towers, Jabbar always seemed agitated. Mo wanted to linger to find out why Jabbar was bothered today, but Jabbar signaled him with his diffident gaze to be quiet. His customer at the moment was the mayor himself. It was only after Mo had left the shop that he recognized the mayor, from the placards dotting the yards and parking lots. The mayor had been married for thirty years to a plain woman. Everyone who seemed to get anywhere was happy with one woman.

He emerged on the windless street. Why couldn't he start his own software consulting firm? Utilize his niche as an Arab-American to land juicy contracts with the Kuwaitis and Saudis? This had been another of Mona's lines of attack on him. He thought of her lame reproach as he stopped in front of Castin and Sellers, a law firm that defended doctors against malpractice lawsuits, among similar activities. Could Ursula be working here?

Had he been serious about tracking down Ursula, he would have sniffed out her blue BMW around town— unless it was in an underground garage, which seemed to be the norm these days even when there was plenty of space aboveground.

No matter how much the mayor and his cohorts prettified the town, there was no getting away from the effects of industrial pollution: the perennial stink of factories doing their dirty business in the middle of the night, expelling slimy gunk, the constituents of natural life recomposed into a chemical morass that surely would come back to haunt humanity. The inevitable was only being hastened.

Mo was on top of the hill that was the highest point in town. But even from here, no part of Manhattan was visible. To watch the collapse of the twin towers, as acquaintances of his had done from other New Jersey towns with a view of Lower Manhattan, was something he was glad to have been spared.

On that fateful Tuesday, he'd been sick and at home, having turned the phones off. Mona called frantically all day. So had his parents and sister from Egypt, wanting to know if he was all right. It was only in the early evening, shortly before Mona was due to arrive at her normal time and he had gone out to the drugstore, that he was confronted with a country visited by death.

For a long time before that, everyone had stepped outside history. Had he been a believer, he would have thought of appropriate metaphors to illustrate the fall of the towers, witnessed from safe suburban domiciles about to be transformed into hostile, militant outposts, where people kept an eye on each other for no other reason than spite. Maybe that was what made Jabbar mad. Maybe Mona would still be with Mo, had not that fiendish Tuesday made everyone turn inward, in a vain attempt to confront truths better left unexplored.

At Balabian's gourmet grocery, his final stop, he bought an expensive bottle of red wine, a habit he now indulged in every Friday. Later that night, he would again thank his lucky stars that the dot-com bust had left him untouched (he hadn't diversified his portfolio to the extent his financial resources dictated, and the few firms he was heavily invested in had emerged unharmed). He would make bets with himself over ball games pitting the powerhouses against the scandalously underfunded. He would skip up and down the stairs for no reason, valuing the empty space, lacking the voice of a child or a woman or a frail parent. Being left alone felt good.

He was so caught up in looking forward to the lonesome evening that he didn't notice Ursula ahead of him in the checkout line.

The checkout girl was a typical New Jersey eighties throwback—a gum-chewing, nose-pierced, pink-haired teenager who might as well be cursing when she said thanks. This one moved jerkily, as if her body kept getting stuck.

Ursula caught his eye first. "Aren't you..." she began, looking fresh as she had in the morning.

Mo's mind cleared up, the white noise in the universe quickly solved and forgotten. "I'm your neighbor. I'm Mo." He stretched out his hand. In the slow checkout line, if they stood and chatted, who would notice or care? "We've never been introduced. My oversight."

Ursula beamed. He noticed the wine and cheese among her purchases. And the tampons. For once, this crude sign of bodily functions didn't embarrass him. When the checkout girl twice dropped Ursula's things on the counter, Mo helped bag the things.

"Well, here we are." Ursula hesitated when they were outside. An unleashed German shepherd looked indifferently at them, then drowsily lay down.

"Right, we're here," said Mo. "Are you having a party?"

Ursula laughed. "Nothing like that. My coworkers are coming over tomorrow morning to finish up a project that has gone over deadline. It's the only way we can think of not to get fired. Bosses, bosses!"

"I see. What do you do?"

Mo hoped the universe's distracting noise was still at bay, and he sounded like a man possessing self-esteem, not someone recently dumped by a wife with a seven-year itch. A red-haired traffic cop who had let him go last year for speeding on Route 3—Mo's excuse was that his speedometer was broken, and the cop hadn't checked—waved at him. Mo waved back as though the cop were a dear old friend. The prospect of falling in love made one expansive. Dogs, cops, checkout girls with mobility issues, all seemed forgivable.

"I'm a tax accountant."

"Say that again," Mo mumbled.

"I'm a tax accountant."

"Oh." Mo couldn't hide his disappointment. Was she a local then? Indeed, Ursula confirmed it. She worked for an H&R Block imitator, with ambitions to expand into Pennsylvania.

"My wife of seven years dumped me not long ago. Can you get me some tax break for that?"

"I could, if you were my client. Do you want to be my client?"

Mo felt her checking out his body. His wiry frame was his biggest asset. It made him look ten years younger.

His gloomy brown eyes, shaded by arched brows, were his other plus point. He could be a decadent aesthete, a graduate student in philosophy.

"I might want to be your client. Would you like to discuss that over drinks?"

He couldn't believe his luck. The woman whose every move he had scrutinized during the summer and early fall was coming on to him. Up close she looked older—perhaps late forties, perhaps even older—but she was a catch by any measure. The shame and melancholy after Mona's departure would at last lift. He'd be able to show his face to Bill and his other coworkers, able to reclaim his manhood among equals.

There, right in front of Balabian's, was Ursula's blue BMW, which he hadn't noticed. His own SUV was several blocks away. Ursula offered him a ride. When he got in the car, the smell of smoke offended him, but he remained quiet. Ursula's profile exaggerated the wrinkles around her eyes. He bit his lip, dismissing Mona's nagging from his mind.

There could be only one dénouement to the way things were going between him and Ursula.

The first of the calls came two weeks later.

It was the most lighthearted he'd felt since Mona left—make that, since he *met* Mona, because she had immediately forced him to be serious. He was playing with his limp dick in the bathtub, marveling at its battered state after a week of implacable, hostile sex with Ursula, wondering if it was time now to call Bill to ask to be reinstated at his old job, when the cell phone rang, ruining his reverie.

He knew it couldn't be Ursula, since she never called him once he left her place no later than ten at night, weekday or weekend, because she had to have her eight hours of sleep. It was Mona's younger sister, the woman who preached to him about the universal Abrahamic God, when he was a young man.

"Kerem, is that you?" Mo was pleased. His dick began to get hard, as he thought of Mona's sister's pointy nipples, crowning small loping breasts he yearned to witness naked. The girl on the other end had only moaned hello, but now she admitted, as though confessing a sin, "Yes, it's me."

Mo didn't know what to say. To ask about Mona would be tasteless. To express how pleased he was to hear Kerem's voice would be equally crass. Kerem, after all, was supposed to be on the other side. Or was she?

"You're still going to NYU?" Kerem, not a bright student like Mona, had been taking extension classes for a number of years, leading to no degree, accumulating credits like her religious counterparts collected blessings.

"I stopped going."

"That's a change."

"Mo, I want you to let me know if you're in trouble."

"Why would I be in trouble?"

"I mean, if there's anything you're afraid to to talk about. I'm here to listen."

Mo suddenly became mad at Mona and all that was associated with her and her cussed family. Something in him broke. He wanted to smash the cell phone against the wall of the bathroom. Psychologists might call his reaction delayed anger. Never having been able to get back at Mona—she had, after all, committed a neat disappearance trick—he was now taking it out on the next closest thing, her tempting sister.

"Fuck you. Fuck all of you."

"Mo, I'm just saying—"

"I know what you're saying. You sound like some counselor. What do you mean, if I'm in trouble? For your information, since your sister left me, I've had the time of my life. As we speak, I'm screwing my gorgeous blonde next-door neighbor. Come and see for yourself."

"Mo, stop this. You're acting childish, hysterical. I'm not talking about your sex life. I could care less about that. What have you been doing for six months, without a job, is what I'm asking? What have you been doing with your time? Are you involved in something?"

"I'm involved in resolving the Kantian dilemma once and for all. I'm involved in figuring out if there's a direct chain of connection from Kierkegaard to Nietzsche to Hitler, or if there's a Hitler in all of us."

"These are not good times to be talking of Hitler. After the attacks—I *watched* the towers come down."

"From your home in Brooklyn. From your safe distance. Did the mushroom cloud make your head go mushy? Are you still grieving? I'm not grieving."

"Mo, you're not in control of your emotions. I'll call some other time."

Before he could apologize, she had hung up.

He threw the cell phone against the wall, breaking it into black smithereens dotting the floor like dead stars.

His anger remained diffuse. He didn't know where to aim it. As different as Kerem was from Mona, lacking Mona's method of sly repetitive insinuations, Kerem did have some of her older sister's cumulative way of building a case against you. Damn Mona! Damn Kerem! Damn the whole family!

Mo let go of the air bottled inside him like an unpaid tax assessment. How little he had to worry with Ursula. Her home was as full of objects as his was empty. Ursula was the mother of three grown daughters, either in college or graduates already. They were more aligned with their father—wouldn't you know it, another tax accountant?—than with her, but Ursula was at peace. After sex, Ursula would list the favors she had done her daughters despite their enmity, and ask Mo, "Tell me, am I in the red or the black?" Mo would say, "Black, of course." After which, Ursula would promptly fall asleep.

He understood he was being used. Ursula didn't want to date any of the men in her office, let alone her clients, for fear something serious might develop. With Mo, she was safe. After his recent estrangement, he was unlikely to take anyone seriously. Ursula had read him correctly. They still joked about Mo turning over his tax records to her, so he could become her "client."

She was the first woman he'd been with in nearly nine years, other than Mona. Each time he fucked Ursula, regret over Mona's loss seemed to fall away a bit. He was screwing himself into wholesomeness. What would his aging parents—thank heavens, they were in good health, otherwise he would have to bring them to America to ease his guilt—think of Mo's M.O.? Were they really as tolerant as Mo credited his parents' generation—those who came of age before the new fundamentalisms?

The phone rang again, this time his landline. Mo's skin was shriveled. He went to pick it up—it could be Bill or someone else from work. He'd left a message for Bill earlier in the day, and hadn't heard from him.

It was Ursula, wanting a favor of Mo. Her oldest daughter, Shirley, would be visiting for the weekend from

San Francisco. She wanted Mo to make himself scarce. It wouldn't do to have Shirley tell her father that Ursula was seeing someone. Not that Ursula's ex-husband was subsidizing her in any way, but Ursula wanted to protect her image of loyalty. At first, Mo thought Ursula was going to ask him to meet with Shirley, be the badge of normality a relationship with him would represent to an anxious, liberated daughter out West. But Ursula only wanted him to disappear from sight. He found the request insulting and told Ursula so. Ursula retorted that perhaps they should see each other less often—their schedules, different lifestyles, etc. Mo tuned out the rest of her justification.

When he hung up, he left a frantic message for Bill. He felt ready to head back to work. Maybe not this month. But soon, before he fell out of practice altogether.

The next day, he didn't wake up until two in the afternoon.

Since the attacks, he'd been afraid to wake up any later than nine, in case he missed another spectacle. His reason told him what had happened that day was unlikely ever to occur again, but his heart was attached to the idea of witnessing another debacle, this time live. Not that he wished murder and mayhem, innocent people dying, but if it was going to happen anyway, he wanted to have an unfiltered look.

The day Ursula's daughter was supposed to arrive, Mo resisted the temptation to look through his window at Ursula's home. Ursula had served her purpose. He was over the heartbreak of women, and could get back to real life.

He wasn't surprised when Ursula showed up late in the evening, explaining that Shirley had decided to cut her visit short and head over to her father's place in Connecticut. There was more going on between mother and daughter than met the eye—probably a dysfunctional relationship—but Mo restrained his curiosity.

Sunday evening, while Mo and Ursula ate chips and watched the Giants lose, Mona called. Mo was flustered. Should he take the call in front of Ursula?

After this weekend, he wasn't sure this was just a short-term fling. Ursula was giving signals she might be in for the long haul. How could he speak to Mona in front of Ursula? He took the phone to the kitchen area, plopping his elbows on the counter, so Ursula could still see him from the couch. He kept an eye on her throughout the conversation, which lasted long, keeping his voice low to suggest he was beyond surprise.

But Mona's call had surprised him; unsteadied his world, in fact. He was in love with her all over again, the minute he heard her calm, pragmatic voice, the peaks and valleys smoothed out for better effect.

Mona was with her parents in a different New Jersey town, twenty miles away. She had yet to serve him divorce papers; there was always hope. But he understood that Mona's friendship with a Moroccan pizza deliverer, struggling to get through community college while his parents sent him money they could ill afford, had moved beyond the platonic stage since Mona had moved out.

Scrawny Abdallah, with a teenager's beard struggling to cover his monkey face, was one of those pseudo-warrior types come lately to religion. This loser, Abdallah, future college dropout, infatuated with the past, present, and future glories of the Islamic world (a world he had left without a qualm, given the first chance to emigrate to the land of the infidel), was the proximate cause of Mona leaving him. How sad! How tired! How anticlimactic!

Mona spoke to Mo of Abdallah as though she were the boy's mother, detailing how she tried to sever him from his troublesome friends, how she tried to keep his emotions in check, especially in the dark days after the attacks, when the slightest public difficulty could get a boy like Abdallah—of the wrong age, race, and religion—in trouble with the authorities.

Mona wanted to speak more about the authorities— the best ways to reassure "them" of your patriotism and loyalty to the homeland—than about herself and Mo. Her outlook as college counselor—this was how she met Abdallah three years ago, fresh off the boat, paranoid about being under constant surveillance—had reduced Mo to just another troubled client.

Toward the end of the discussion, he became disgusted with Mona. His liberation had received another big spur. He raised his voice to a normal level, feeling he didn't need to hide anything.

"You're still in love with her, aren't you?" Ursula said, when he joined her on the couch.

He hated Ursula for this question. How could she be so obtuse? Wasn't it obvious that Mo was getting over Mona, with every sentence he'd uttered during the phone call? When Mona mentioned at the end that the divorce papers would be on their way by the end of the month, had he not taken it calmly, relieved that Abdallah the boy-warrior would be taking her off his hands for good?

"No, I don't still love her. How could you say that?"

"Maybe you're right. You're with me, after all."

"I *am* with you."

Mo kissed Ursula's full lips. It revived his heart, made him want to live on despite police brutality and child poverty in the richest country in the world. He was abstracting Ursula's physical presence from her intellectual self. It was reactionary, lavishing such sentiment on a woman's physicality, but he didn't care.

Ursula kidded him about his job, telling him he'd already been fired but didn't know it. This had a ring of truth, especially in the fluid high-tech job market. For every experienced programmer, there were ten new ones eager to work for half the pay and none of the benefits. Mo resisted getting even with Ursula, when she teased him about his "insecure status" in the fragile economy of the twenty-first century, by taunting her in turn about her estranged daughters. Yet he was also irritated that Ursula didn't wonder why Mo kept silent about her messy family situation.

Mo went into a funk the following week. He started sleeping until later and later in the day, when the plop of the mail would at last awaken him. The bills, which hadn't frightened him when memories of his large paycheck were still fresh, now seemed ominous. He'd bargained poorly when he leased his SUV.

One of these days, instead of the always friendly black mail lady, he would be woken by a sharp knock on the door. It would be an authority figure—what type of human being performed such duties?—serving him divorce papers. Mona moved quickly. If she said within a month, it would more likely be within a week.

She would be reveling these days in her regained position as darling of the local Egyptian community, having shed attachment to Mo's scattershot persona. She was unfailingly boisterous, capable of the withering glance that put any man in his place—especially if he happened to be an Arab in love with newfangled effeminacy. She was probably again the center of attention of males from eighteen to eighty, everyone glad that Mo the monster was gone. No one would blame her for the breakup of the marriage.

That afternoon, when he got up at four, he was surprised by Dr. Hammoudi's visit. His mind scanned the Islamic calendar in his clouded memory and couldn't recall Eid or any other religious event.

Hammoudi acted as though Mona's absence was no big deal; in fact, he was disguising his discomfort. He mentioned his wife taking a yearlong cooking course at a vocational school, and his daughter having done well on her SAT's. Hammoudi had more white hairs in his wispy beard than before.

He wanted to drop off a booklet about emergency precautions in case of a bioterror attack. It was written in the language of schoolchildren, and probably had as much value. Mo dismissed it as something meant for people scared of monsters in the dark.

Mo had no wish to partake of such phobia. "We'd be better off worrying about being struck by lightning. I don't do that either."

Hammoudi was taken aback by Mo's lightheartedness. He talked about the revolution underway at the local hospital. Everyone was on the frontlines of homeland defense now. Hospitals were being reconceptualized as first responders to large man-made catastrophes. Disease would henceforth arise from nowhere, be incalculable in damage, and require permanent war footing—necessary preparedness which might never need to be executed. As Hammoudi talked, Mo couldn't be sure if he was delirious. Was he actually anticipating a catastrophe that would wipe out the town, leaving the doctor alone as master of the decimated domain?

"Bring me some of your wife's kebabs next time," Mo said, as Hammoudi left. What a waste of time! All because Mona felt the need to be "on good terms" with anyone remotely Islamic.

Mo began to time waking up with the start of the late *Oprah* rerun, even though he didn't stay up correspondingly late at night. As early as midnight, drowsiness overcame him. He slept as much as twelve hours a day, and still felt tired.

Having failed to catch up with Bill on the phone— some major new project must be keeping everyone busy at ungodly hours!—he decided to check in at the office. He couldn't sleep a wink that night. He was a wreck, with dark circles under his eyes, and his face looking puffed up and older. Perhaps the abrupt physical decline had commenced.

In the morning, he was anxious to get out of the house. He realized he no longer watched Ursula's movements from his window. What had been the nature of that obsession? Why had he been so childish?

He drove the car along the well-traveled New Jersey highway that no longer felt as familiar to him. The polluted rivers, masquerading as freshly drained and cleaned ones, the gigantic chemical and plastics factories with castle-like visages, the landfills that could be seen from the road rather than being hidden away, all left him with revulsion for the obvious corruption. For the sake of disposable diapers and hemorrhoid treatments, humanity was leaving a wasteland for future generations.

At work his former colleagues slapped their hands on his back, squeezed him in bear hugs, as though everything had stalled without Mo. Nobody looked him straight in the eye though.

His office had been turned into a cramped conference room—"temporary, what else do you do with empty space?"—one of his coworkers explained.

Bill was overwhelmed with a project that needed to be wrapped up by the end of the day, so he regretted not being able to hang out with Mo, but instead Mo was shown straight to the "headman" himself, Joe Salvi, the boss of bosses, who'd only spent significant time with Mo his first day on the job.

Joe spoke at length about the state of the industry, the challenges ahead for the firm. Mo patiently listened, hiding his worry. To listen to Joe, the business had seen its glory days a few years ago, even if no one had realized it at the time. There would be no more "excess capacity" in the industry for the foreseeable future, not when it came to human input.

Joe had, in his shirt pocket, Mo's final check neatly printed and folded. It was a generous settlement, and Mo was allowed to have access to health insurance for six months.

He didn't make a fuss, took it like a man. His old father in Cairo would be proud of his aplomb. Twenty years in this country, and he was equal to the bosses. He could go toe-to-toe with the sharpest of them and not be embarrassed for himself.

This sentiment barely lasted the afternoon. Depressed, he left a note on Ursula's door saying he wouldn't be around that evening, and headed to the public library.

"Give me everything on bioterror," he told the silver-haired librarian, who looked astonished. Mo realized he'd committed a faux pas. You didn't talk to your grandmotherly librarian that way. You asked her gently for the call letters to a subject, the rough location on the shelves where you might find the object of your pursuit. It had been a while since he was in a library. As an undergraduate and while pursuing his master's degree in engineering, he'd been fond of spending hours on end in the library, researching subjects with little or no relevance to his field: sailboat construction before the age of plastics, Japanese armament improvements in the wake of the Western onslaught, the long-term effects of atomic explosions on the health of Pacific Islanders.

Next to him, as he fiddled with nonexistent coins in his pockets, was a divorced woman he remembered Mona pointing out as someone who had survived wife battering and formed an organization to promote victims' rights. This buxom woman with large ears and gigantic hands hardly seemed the type a man could beat up.

Mo leaned right into her and said, "Hello! I think I know you."

The woman backed off as though touched by a red-hot poker, pulling her young son close to her bosom as though Mo was about to snatch him. "I don't think so!" Rather than finishing her business at the circulation desk, she left the library.

"What the..." Mo said loudly, complaining to the librarian when she returned with a handful of books. "That woman left. She just left. Am I a pariah now? Is it my skin color? My accent?" He realized he was losing it. If he had an accent, it was barely detectable. His skin color, in these northern latitudes, was rosy white. He didn't have the thick curly hair of the typical Egyptian but rather the delicate hair of the Syrian or Lebanese.

"Sir, this is all we have," the librarian said. Mo was surprised she'd followed his bidding and got him the books. He barely glanced at the titles, not having expected there to be any books on the specialized topic.

"I'm not sure I really care for the subject. It's on the advice of a doctor friend of mine. Self-improvement. What to do in case of an emergency."

The librarian wanted him to take care of overdue fines from five years ago. The fines were for books on pregnancy Mo and Mona had checked out when there was a false alarm that Mona might be pregnant. The fines had a cap. At twenty dollars, a book was declared missing. The librarian didn't want him to return the books, just pay the fines.

The day was still young. Mo wondered if he should leave a phone message for Ursula that he couldn't see her anymore. But he lacked the courage. He needed the physical closeness. His was in the subservient position and he couldn't help it. He wondered if he should call Kerem and ask her if she wanted to meet him for coffee. Maybe she'd have tidbits about Abdallah that Mona was embarrassed to share: how Abdallah was in every way inferior to Mo, how any day the dreaded authorities would be on to his game, as they picked him and locked him away in some godforsaken detention facility. He wondered if he should hang out at Bill's favorite bar that night, to show there were no hard feelings. Or should he dump the terror preparedness books at Hammoudi's home, without an explanation, and trust him to return the books to the library?

Instead, at a gas station he cleaned out the seats and trunk of his SUV, filled up the tank, and headed for Las Vegas. He didn't care about gambling. He'd never even been to Atlantic City. But it seemed time to get away from everything.

Along the way, he stopped for a full day in Lincoln, Nebraska. He became attached to a century-old Lutheran church with a grandiose bell tower, and ambled to the top to see how the bell worked. He felt people resenting his curiosity, just as he had felt with the librarian back home. What was it, people were not allowed to pursue interests for their own sake anymore? Did there need to be a reason to ask questions of strangers, of functionaries and clerks?

In Lincoln, he stayed at a bed-and-breakfast run by a half-deaf couple—luckily, either the man or the woman seemed to catch his comment or question—and composed a lengthy letter to his parents, his first in years, describing the beauty of life in the land of opportunity where he, a poor Egyptian immigrant, could realize the American dream in all its glory. He wrote about how his boss at the software company—while reluctantly letting him go because of industry constraints—had nonetheless shown him maximum dignity under the circumstances, how he had shared confidences about the business intended for insiders only. What more could a man ask for than dignity? It made up for every other deprivation.

That night at the bed-and-breakfast as he gobbled a steak—Mona shunned meat, and since she'd left he'd tried to make up for lost time—an Arab-looking couple, with a daughter around three, showed up for dinner. The couple looked exhausted. Mo recognized their Palestinian dialect. Both were overweight, and suffered from bad skin. Mo couldn't help chatting with them. Too busy feeding their recalcitrant daughter, the couple barely had time for their own meal.

They were from Detroit and, like Mo, were out of work. The husband used to work on the assembly line in a tire factory, and the wife used to have a retail job. Their stuff packed in a Dodge van, they were headed to Alabama to stay with the wife's parents. Already, they were wondering if leaving Detroit's large Arab community had been a mistake. Mo assured them that they'd made the right decision.

The couple started treating him like a long-lost friend. Invitations to visit them in Alabama, or Detroit should the South fail to work out, were duly issued. The man and the woman had separate cell phones. That was not an area, apparently, in which to economize. With his straggly beard and slightly askew face, the man could have been an older, more decrepit Abdallah—in fact, the couple could have been Abdallah and Mona, their restless daughter the child Mona never had with Mo and might still have with Abdallah.

Later, Mo wouldn't be able to recall all he did for two weeks in Las Vegas. He gave rides to scruffy hitchhikers, shared beers and meals with strangers at disreputable joints. He sang Monkees and Animals songs he'd liked in college, but had given up at Mona's insistence—Mona was fond of Umm Kulthum and other wailing Arab singers of previous generations. He set himself a limit of losing no more than a thousand dollars a day. The fortnight finished as he exhausted his credit cards—thanks to Mona, who'd never believed in carrying too many credit cards. When he was checking out of his hotel, the clerk was looking at him with disdain. He was sobering up with the prospect of departing sin city.

"You know, I honestly couldn't tell you what I've been doing here for two damn weeks," he told the woman standing next to him. She drew back at Mo's confession. The odor from his armpits and crotch was substantial.

He made it back to New Jersey in two days, driving nonstop. If he'd hoped for clarity—should he sell the house? Should he start over in a new profession? Should he visit Egypt after twenty years?—he'd acquired none. He felt as bereft of hope as the day he'd confused the librarian.

Two weeks is a long time in the new millennium. Entire universes are replaced with new participants, new protagonists, new pogroms.

Mo found a letter from the FBI sticking on his door.

For hours, as he guzzled the brand of coffee favored by Ursula, he was afraid to open the envelope. The FBI was now leaving messages for people on their doors? For everyone to see? What could it be about?

Suddenly, it came to him. Everything he'd done in recent days could be seen as suspicious activity. The visit to the library, when he was overwhelmed by having been fired, was the worst. Asking a librarian to hand him "everything on bioterror"—in this day and age? He couldn't believe his stupidity. Was his normal life, as he had come to know and love it, finished? Was he about to enter a Kafkaesque nightmare, making the rounds of the FBI, not to mention more shadowy intelligence agencies that had sprouted in this land like the environmental and consumer protection agencies did in the despised age of Nixon?

The blunder at the library hadn't been his only sin. He fit the profile perfectly: of the lone madman, the gunman, the bomb thrower, in short the terrorist, terror having recently impinged on every aspect of his life, his severance from Mona, his lost job, his unnatural alliance with Ursula. Was he not the most fearful man in the land? Was he not afraid of his own shadow? Wasn't this what compelled people to terrorize others—the great reversal, the weapon of the weak, the only power of the impotent, having recently exploded into bright daylight and become the magnificent universal obsession?

His age, thirty-nine, on the borderline of youth and maturity, was itself suspicious. Had things gone well, he would have made a smooth transition to middle age. But with things going wrong at this critical juncture, aging was deadly. He'd been sleeping late. He'd lost his job. Wasn't it usually techies—especially out-of-work techies— that were most susceptible to being recruited by terror networks? The preponderance among terror masterminds was engineer types from middle-tier schools like Rutgers.

More details from the recent past bothered him as he ruminated in the kitchen. Observing Ursula from his bedroom window. He might well have been observed observing for months. He remembered leaving messages late at night for Bill, when he was drunk. Had he rambled about the inborn treacherousness of Arabs? If he had, he meant Mona, of course, but wasn't Mo an Arab? To take the axe to one's own side, even in the heat of misunderstanding, was to throw into doubt one's own loyalty.

What about his lack of responsiveness to Hammoudi? Had Hammoudi turned against him? In this era of Stalinist confessions and exonerating rituals, he wouldn't be surprised. Hammoudi, like anyone else, had to get ahead. Why should he prefer Mo over his own pathetic wife and daughter? What business could Hammoudi have had, as a surgeon dealing with people's cysts and tumors, with bioterror preparedness? Hadn't his spiel been fishy? Why had he come to Mo with the silly brochures? That seemed right out of FBI 101, covert agent training for the unimaginative.

And that bloody shirt of Mo's, the day he'd cut himself shaving, when he circled the hospital he didn't remember how many times. Hadn't he seen Hammoudi that day? Hammoudi had visited him soon after that. And the mayor, the very day of his Ulysses-like wanderings around town, had seen him silently leave the Lebanese barber after one meaningful glance.

By now Mo was convinced of his own guilt, ready to turn himself in to the FBI as a prime candidate for terror recruiting.

His coy, fatalistic acceptance of being fired, that was another of the X factors. Would any self-respecting programmer have taken it sitting down as he had? Why the lack of protest? How else could people read it except as the final stage of apathy?

Mona's sister Kerem—she'd called him asking if he was in trouble. Mona had called soon thereafter—at the time, he'd assumed Abdallah was the one to be watched, but was it Mo everyone was concerned about? To top it off, if the spooks had been on his trail, was his two-week disappearance, in Las Vegas of all places. Las Vegas, where the greatest terrorists in the world make their final stop before going over the brink, before executing the best-laid plans of decades, for a last moment of recognition at the altar of narcissism blown up to continental scale.

Ursula knocked on the door.

Yes, he was back, and no, he didn't need any help. He looked at her suspiciously. He wondered if she was a paid informant. What role did she have in the hot pursuit by the FBI? She was curious about his activities of the last two weeks. Did he need any money? Why hadn't he shaved? He didn't look good with his stubble. Yes, he knew that.

He opened the FBI letter in front of her, wondering if this bold action would make her give herself away.

The FBI, he found as Ursula started chopping vegetables, was interested in having him visit their local office—there was one right next to the Lebanese barber, upstairs from a bankrupt insurance office—to tell them whatever he knew about Abdallah!

It was about Abdallah, not him!

Abdallah, that asshole, fresh off the boat, able to work a magic spell on his beloved wife Mona, who before his sneakiness belonged to Mo!

Abdallah, the real deal—not Mo, with his harmless accent, bargain clothes, and moderate exercise regimen. Abdallah, who no doubt underwent marathon sessions in target shooting, who must be a martial arts expert behind his flabbiness, and who certainly frequented penniless exiled sheikhs with rabid followers on every continent. Abdallah, who doubtless made Mona stop in the middle of the New Jersey Turnpike when the sun went down, so he could figure out the direction of Mecca on a portable compass and bang his head on a dusty straw mat to beg Allah's mercy. Abdallah, who surely fed his imagination on visions of world conquest, a band of raggedy one-eyed and one-armed men taking over the world's greatest power with nothing but their chilly magnetism.

It was Abdallah, not him! Thank heavens! Mo laughed hard.

Ursula stared. "Is it really good news?"

"Oh Ursula, I'm so happy. I love you, I love you, I love the whole world. I can't tell you how lucky I am, in every way."

"What's in that letter? Did you win the lottery?"

"Ursula, I'm the happiest person in the world right now. I have nothing, but I have everything. I don't even have you. I lost you somewhere in Vegas. Maybe the day I got fired. No, the day I met you at Balabian's, already that day. But it doesn't matter. I can go on without you. I have everything I want."

"Oh Mo, you must be getting a fever or something. Let's get you to bed."

"I'm fine. Don't talk to me like that. Don't try to bring me down."

"I'm not trying to bring you down."

"You are. You're acting like all wives do. And you're not even a wife. Nor will you ever be again."

"Mo, don't be cruel."

"Ah, cruelty, you don't know the meaning of the word!"

That night, he feverishly plotted his indictment of Abdallah. The FBI was right to suspect him. He would do it in such a way that Mona was kept out of it. The FBI would know that Mona was no more than an unsuspecting pawn in the saga. She was not to be held responsible. If anyone was to be accused, it was Mo himself, who had taken Mona for granted. How could Mona be blamed if she had run into Abdallah's arms? Abdallah had the charm of the young working for him, while Mo was middle-aged before his time—not when it came to looks, but attitude. Discipline, rigid patterns and habits, reliability. Would the FBI care about Mona and Mo's love life? They would only want the facts about Abdallah. That's what he would offer them, just the facts, nothing but the facts.

Toward dawn, he dozed off. He slept dreamlessly for the first time in months. No more roulette wheels, no more blackjack tables, no more asphyxiated librarians sprawled on the spotlessly clean white circulation desk.

When he woke up, his feverish energy was gone. He pushed up the blinds. What a beautiful sun, strong for this time of year! Ursula was paused as ever before her BMW, caught in rapture.

He waved at her. When she didn't notice, he forced the window open. "Hey, I'm up early!" She seemed disturbed by his announcement. Instead of smoothly easing into the car and swooshing out of her driveway like the sleekest of animals, she awkwardly jumped in and jerked the BMW forward..

He hadn't slept much, but he knew what he had to do.

He scanned the job ads in the *Times* (he was proud not to glance at the baseball scores), marking out unusual openings he wouldn't have considered in the past. Marketing jobs with niche dot-coms lucky to have survived the bust. Government-subsidized institutions where he might be treated as an individual, and where there would at least be a pretence of doing some social good.

He called his lawyer, a stringy white guy he'd met at Rutgers, and who celebrated each of Mo's milestones with fervor. Mo instructed him to go forward with whatever had to be done to resolve the divorce to Mona's satisfaction—and to spare him the details. He told his lawyer he would hand-deliver the FBI letter, which he wanted nothing to do with. He didn't want to visit the FBI office to cooperate with them. If he took that attitude, could they force him to talk? But if he was compelled to go, could he take the line of least resistance by not telling them anything they didn't already know? Would he need to be accompanied by his lawyer at such a meeting? Mo's lawyer wasn't surprised by the questions, but promised to find the answers.

Having put that to rest, Mo decided to declare a sort of hello-goodbye to Hammoudi, and the Lebanese barber, and the owners of restaurants and boutiques, and everyone else in town he had more than a nodding acquaintance with. He hoped his dignity would be reciprocated. His mind was made up. Henceforth, he would live in Manhattan, lost in the anonymity, dissolved in the crowd, and he would value it. He'd come close to losing everything. He wanted to regain it all with the calm deliberation of a man on a mission.

He decided to go to a park near the highway—one that he and Mona used to frequent in the early days of their marriage—and write Mona a decent letter, the first since her departure. He would tell her how he was coping with the practical details she used to take care of. She would be pleased to know his progress.

He would tell Ursula he couldn't see her anymore. He had no desire to be someone's part-time toy. Her insistence that Mo not have even a fleeting encounter with her daughters still rankled.

What he couldn't anticipate was that Ursula would turn his dismissal of her into an outspoken liberal defense of cross-cultural relationships. Mo was apparently a cultural exercise for her, a reclamation project designed to ease her own guilt as well as his insecurity. What he also couldn't anticipate was that at the moment of his peak vulnerability, with the FBI trying to entangle him in a shady net of evidence and disclosure, he would once and for all reject Ursula, refuse her comforting hand on his shoulder as he faced alone the rampaging witch-hunters now roaming the land.

He was through with others trying to define him, for good or ill. His rite of citizenship would finally take place, years after the formal ceremony. His pride would henceforth be earned.

THE CENSOR

1.

The new rules on kissing are, it's allowed if it's done Indian-style—lips breathing close, behind smoke and mirrors, or more often hazy bushes. But no American kissing. Couples can approach, entangle, embrace, depending on where their hands rest during the peak moment. Hands must be off, so to speak. Definitely European shamelessness is still out. But I wonder. There are times when eroticism becomes so flat, so predictable, it becomes the kind of safe thing a capitalist might pursue in leisure-time, not a driving obsession. So shouldn't we be disallowing discreet snuggles, the sneakings and maneuverings of our own dainty heroines, as posing far the greater danger? I wonder, I wonder.

Not a word of these doubts to my superiors.

2.

Yesterday afternoon, at the awards ceremony, on Islamabad's most pristinely boring boulevard, surrounded on both sides by castles of bureaucratic rectitude, my supervisor's supervisor is bestowed a medal of honor by the Culture Minister: "In these times of global strife and misunderstanding, you perform an invaluable service by removing the distractions diluting the pure cultural artifact. Without your intervention, what we would get is enhancement of conflict, not its lessening." Everyone, politely dressed in seventies safari suits, open at the collar despite the wintry chill, claps, looking glassy-eyed. A waiter, balancing a huge tray of comestibles, trips on the microphone wires, to collective applause when he corrects himself at the last second, like an experienced ballet dancer. I suppose he is gay. Half the population in the city is gay—that is, the permanent part of it. The transients tend to be more correct in their sexual preferences. It has been a long time since the openly gay people have bothered to storm the ministers at their lavish soirées. The cheering in the auditorium suddenly escalates. A midget-sized man is raising his hands in the air, like the Shi'ites at prayer, appraising the acclaim. The holy month of Ramadan is just around the corner. It will interfere with the diet, ruin many delicate constitutions which will not be able to handle the rigors of abstention.

3.

"Khan sahib, do you remember when we were at the Sorbonne, and those long-haired students asked our delegation why the Bengalis were thriving after severing themselves from the western part of the country, and that was in the middle of one of their worst famines ever? When they were the basket case of the world? Thriving, they said, in French, I forget the phrase they used, but certainly that was the meaning. What is the purpose of such bias, do you think?" I have survived every regime, democratic, pseudo-democratic, dictatorial, fascist, virtual, and yet I can keep every ruler's face distinct from the others', as though I had gone to school with them, had helped them cheat on exams, and was obligated to protect them because we played cricket on the same field.

4.

One's colleagues, one regrets to report, are often so enamored of the dead past, venerated for the common mudslinging that came one's way, that one had rather not face mornings at all. Anyway, it is a satisfyingly cold day, and I suspect the fruit stalls will be open later than usual in the evening. The wind blows as though straight from the other side of the border, from the height of the Karakorams, bringing in its wake the smell of cashews and pistachios, and of women whose unveiled face no man has ever seen.

5.

It is an old American classic, a Jimmy Stewart movie, and I doubt there can be anything worth excising here, but I am obligated go through the motions. "Cut," I tell myself, making the snip-snip gesture honored by mimes. "Cut! This is a piece of shit, this will ruin our young minds." I read somewhere that nearly a quarter of the university-educated have access to high-speed Internet. Yet my job persists, in fact becomes more tenured than ever, more secure by the day, like the guards at the Quaid's mausoleum, protecting the honor of the founder with their waxed faces and immobile bodies, looking past the ticking hour, past paupers and princes alike. "Unity, faith, and discipline," the Quaid's motto holds, and I suspect my late bachelorhood has something to do with getting bogged down in its mechanics. Each part contradicts the other. You cannot have two of the elements at the same time, let alone three.

6.

The new rules say we can show the Taliban's faces, instead of blurring them. Individually they are no longer terrorist threats. However, talk of Russian influence in the border areas is still forbidden. The mullahs in Karachi have made a new deal, so we no longer need to pretend the urban madrassas don't exist. The price of wheat is going to skyrocket this year, so it is all right to mention travel to India (if you don't see the connection, well...). This need to hold many contradictory thoughts in my head at the same time is the price I have to pay for versatility. Colleagues who have stuck to one genre, movies, say, or television documentaries, have smaller guts, more hair, whiter teeth.

7.

There is an explosion at ten in the morning, and the lights go out. We are prevented from leaving the building by the guard, "for our own security." There is no window in my office, a "security measure" from the time the building was inaugurated. I don't know what is happening outside. Many hours go by, during which I ponder why the movie *Network* is so objectionable that despite my work on it, it is still considered an affront to the country's sensibility. It is a relic of the past, laughable in its pretensions—yet *All the President's Men* is okay, because relations with America are cooler, now that our ruler is paying the price at the polls. Also, it is time to take another look at *One Flew Over the Cuckoo's Nest*, and *The Deer Hunter*, and *Julia*. They tell me someone blew himself up in a suicide truck not far away, but what is curious is that he didn't aim for any structure in the vicinity—he meant to kill only himself. So suicide bombers are now committing only individual suicide, and leaving the public alone. This must be some new stage of the dialectic.

8.

After all my education, my foreign hopes and diversionary dreams, this! It's all because I couldn't lose my shyness around white women. Or at least not until it was too late, and I found myself back in the country, through no fault of mine, hypnotized by the train wreck, the streaking vehicle of failure on which was loaded all the artistic dreck of the century, heading for utter collapse. They say Hitler was a failed artist in prewar Vienna. I understand how small frustrations multiply into world-altering resentments. People everywhere are bitter, secret poets, mystics at the breakfast table. There is a steep ravine behind my house, ending in utter murk. Our very own Grand Canyon. Sometimes the moon tramps so slow over the horizon that we feel it pausing over

Islamabad, for a special blessing. "O ye failed romantics, exude not too much faith in the land of the pure, because the centuries are relativistic anyway." The rising price of flour and sugar, the proverbial insult against the common man, is insinuated in this independently-produced movie I have been screening now for possible lapses this last week, only to conclude that its realism is so banal, it's the most threatening thing to come across my desk in years. I make a special note of the director's name, a young man who claims to have learned his art in Canada. I can do him no favors, his fate is sealed.

9.

A woman who claims to have known me as a soldier on the Wah front in the 1965 war calls me out of the blue. She has a noticeable North Indian accent. "I'm sorry, I was never a soldier in my life," I apologize. She won't accept my version of the past, and insists on her narrative. It is too sophisticated to be a prank, and besides I no longer keep up with such frisky people. "No, this is how it happened, you can't tell me otherwise," she says, hanging up on me.

10.

The new rules about political speech have come out. It is okay to say "terrorists" now. For years we have been saying "extremists," or "fanatics," or "militants." But now the word of choice is terrorists. Only the president used to be able to say terrorists. But now all must be encouraged to say terrorists. It is the new honesty. I notice, at the proverbial water-cooler, my colleagues throwing out the word at the slightest opportunity. "The chowkidar is a bloody terrorist, he wants to open the trunk of my car to inspect it. Imagine, I have been coming to work here for ten years, he sees my bloody face every day, and he wants to know what's in the trunk of my little Daihatsu?" Another says, "My mother-in-law is a terrorist, she wants us to spend the entire holidays at her ancestral home in Abbotabad." There is a coldness in my walk back to my office that I cannot explain to myself.

11.

Imagine having a daughter. Imagine having to explain the facts of life to her. I would have lied. I would never have been able to imagine her grown up. One has children only to keep them childlike, for ever, despite the harm to them. Yes, that is the most benign parental impulse, and cultures that don't allow children to be children suffer in the long run. I speak like a retrograde fossil, but in return for my silence, I am entitled to my opinions.

12.

There is a state funeral for a former prime minister, a figurehead who had served under one of those pseudo-dictatorial presidents long ago. There is disagreement over how to present the news to the country. It evokes memories of when we were entangled in the fine print of constitution-making, to the extent that we never got a workable one. His legacy is beyond reach. It is at such moments of uncertainty, when the definition of the truth becomes a question of priorities in flux, that those much higher up than me, dealing with such subjects as Olympics preparedness and tamping down the blasphemy lawsuits, suddenly start acknowledging me in the hallways and parking lots. I too inflate to monster-like proportions during certain times of the day when my services are in such acute need. Of course, the independent satellite channels are officially beyond our reach, as is the vast expanse of the Internet, a universe unto itself (we can try blocking and jamming, as we do from time to time, even if I've never approved of this kind of underhanded tactic), but they do not speak for the government, so this is not how we judge ourselves. I would say that our minority status in a world of proliferating media is what gives us endless vigor, to fight on and on, and I would say that this is what keeps me youthful, at least in spirit.

13.

What is the fight all about? Who knows. I recall a Beckett play in which nothing happens. Every morning at seven a vegetable-wallah rolls his cart past my house. His specialty is bright green cucumbers, fresh as though washed in the sea, a thousand miles to the south. I stretch on my lawn, or sometimes on my roof, in clear sight of the Margallas, mountains for the bourgeois, unlike those other mountains for the Taliban, which rise like infallible towers for the icon-busters. I idolize my physical and spiritual remains, in the best sense of the word. One side of my body is a little shorter than the other, without having been a problem. A callus that threatened to erupt on the back of my hand has receded spontaneously. "Sahibji, shall I wash the car?" my driver interrupts me. "Of course, wash it thoroughly, leave not a scratch, not a spot of dust. If I see so much as a speck…" I have teased him like this for years, and yet he has never got the joke.

IN THE SHADE
OF
THE WAVERING

PALMS

Tawfiq's mother Salma wakes up before first light as always. Tawfiq's children—Uzma, twelve, and Asma, eight—will be up in a couple of hours for school. Salma is careful not to make noise as she washes her hands and feet during wudu in the bathroom and walks downstairs to the patio with red velvet prayer rug in hand to offer fajr prayers.

Salma's retired husband Sikander, sixty-five and a walking encyclopedia of hypochondria, neither joins Salma in her five daily prayers nor reproves her, telling the family that long ago Allah has "settled his case." Taking her cue from Sikander, Salma never pressures Tawfiq and his wife and children to pray either.

As long as Tawfiq remains an honest businessman, not cutting corners as he produces fighter jet spare parts at his Whittier factory for the Department of Defense, and as long as Uzma and Asma keep making good grades, it's all a doting mother and grandmother can ask for.

Salma is grateful for the daily miracle of the Southern California sunrise, the sky blooming with cool orange hues, a lazy painter's palette. At such moments, she doesn't want to be reminded of her thinning hair, her own aches and pains. Dawn comes leisurely in this corner of the world, unlike the abruptness with which the sky harshly changes color and the earth becomes warm in Karachi, or in Salma's native Ahmedabad.

Tawfiq's sprawling five-bedroom house in the foothills of San Dimas, where Salma and Sikander have now lived for ten years, astonishes her for its low maintenance. This is just as well because Tawfiq's wife Firdaus is a former philosophy student, an Iranian woman eight years younger than him, who likes to indulge in pie-in-the-sky plots of vast business enterprises that will make work unnecessary for future generations, but who doesn't so much as pick up after Uzma and Asma finish breakfast.

It's Firdaus who both irks and charms Salma. Firdaus doesn't keep her heavy breasts tethered firmly enough under her flimsy blouses. Her plumpness makes her look always pregnant.

Salma has read enough heart-wrenching short stories by Ismat Chughtai, Qurratulain Haider, and other feminist writers in Urdu to understand the typical resentments of the mother-in-law. Yet she can't bring herself to forgive Firdaus for her cheapness: how she drives from store to store to save pennies on groceries, even as she sends thousands of dollars to charities whenever there's an earthquake in some poor country; how she encourages Uzma and Asma to have meals and sleepovers at friends' homes rather than inviting them over, to avoid the extra strain on the household; and how she comes up with ludicrous quotations from Hafez and Rumi to refute Tawfiq's logical arguments about practical matters.

Firdaus calls Salma "Amma," conversing with her in the fluent Urdu she's picked up after fourteen years with Tawfiq, and always waits for her to start eating before she begins, but Salma suspects bitterness under the surface. She won't be surprised if any day now Firdaus complains about the amount of water Salma spills over the bathroom floor as she performs wudu.

In Salma's family, ambition comes in spurts. Sikander, after having made imitation French Baroque furniture for Karachi's elite for thirty years, now shows no interest in Tawfiq's business, although Salma encourages him to stay busy by helping out with accounting, if nothing else. She believes that the brain withers from disuse. Sikander has lost interest in politics too, just when ancient hostilities have returned to the surface, and people are at each other's throats again.

Once Sikander pronounces at dinner, one of Firdaus's luscious kebab and kufte affairs, "Nostradamus predicted the collapse of the twin towers in the world's leading city." This is a superstitious bend Salma doesn't like.

Firdaus counters, "Abba, what does Nostradamus say about bearded men ruling the world, and daughters reaching puberty at nine and ten?"

Sikander doesn't reply, having always been neutral about the rule of the ayatollahs in Iran, seeing both positive and negative sides to it, while for Firdaus it is a calumny that in liberal Iran mullahs should have put women behind the chadar and sent little boys to die in trench warfare. Sikander dare not go near the puberty question.

Salma can't disagree with Firdaus, but it's Firdaus's

manner of putting herself in the forefront, blurting out the disagreeable truth, that she can't stand.

Salma is disconcerted that after loudly having sex with Tawfiq, Firdaus goes about the house without taking a shower or washing herself, showing no embarrassment about her wet, tousled hair, and the bite marks over her arms and legs.

Out on the patio this morning, Salma raises her hands to Allah in prayer, ending with an appeal for a secure homeland for the Palestinians, a dua that comes naturally to her after witnessing a disturbing CNN video of the mistreatment of Palestinian boys at the hands of Israeli soldiers. Tawfiq's prosperity depends on war between nations remaining a fact of life, but this is a link she isn't able to pursue to its end.

Next door, she can hear Arlene—the redheaded fifty-five-year-old manic divorcée who speeds around the neighborhood in her red Porsche—getting a boisterous early start on her gardening.

Arlene had once asked Salma to teach her a few words of Urdu—"kya haal hai," "theek hai," "achha, khuda hafiz"—but then lost all interest in Salma and Sikander. That was many years ago. Firdaus says Arlene is the "neighborhood slut," with an eye for every man, including Tawfiq, while Tawfiq always defends Arlene, saying she's never gotten over the loss of her older husband, a decent man who was one of the pioneers of the personal computer. Firdaus has trained Uzma and Asma to be wary of Arlene, despite Arlene making the effort to remember both girls' birthdays and giving expensive presents. Salma is pleased that Asma and her friends don't make up derisory songs rhyming with Arlene's name, as they sometimes do with the other neighbors.

Salma wishes her concentration wouldn't wander during prayer. She hopes Allah will forgive her for this weakness. It's less excusable because her progeny seem to have their lives in order. It isn't as if she has to worry about livelihood, survival, or security. Salma and Sikander's decade of immigrant life in Southern California has been incident free, a blessing after the riots, strikes, assassinations, and turmoil in Pakistan. Tawfiq's twenty-five years here have been marked by one success after another, his first year at Cal State Fullerton the only time he needed his father's help. Arlene once commented on the ease with which Salma and Sikander had "adjusted" to life in America, like "ducks taking to water," noting that some of her Mexican friends had trouble with the basics after decades in the country.

Salma folds the prayer rug and faces the screen door, unwilling to enter the fray of the household. Firdaus swings opens the door, standing face to face.

"The sun will burn your skin. It's detrimental to older people." Firdaus is dressed in a skimpy spring dress, her broad shoulders standing out.

"The sun is gentle. Have you forgotten how harsh the sun is in our part of the world?"

"*This* is now our part of the world," says Firdaus, "or *mine* anyway. I was only in Iran until I was eight years old. One forgets. False memories are worse than no memories."

Daughter-in-law, why do you always have to be so argumentative?, Salma wants to say, but holds her tongue. She offers to help get Uzma and Asma ready for school, but Firdaus declines, because the girls have to be more "self-motivated" now.

Tawfiq joins them on the patio. He's already dressed in a crisp white button-down shirt and red paisley tie. His hair is beginning to thin, which worries Salma, although Firdaus thinks it lends him an aura of gravity.

"So this is where the women of the household plot conspiracies against me," Tawfiq teases, tying plump Firdaus in a bear hug, and pinching Firdaus's behind, trying to keep it secret.

"Tawfiq, is your father still sleeping?" Salma asks.

"Yes, let him. It's his golden age of retirement. He doesn't have to get up before the crack of dawn. Unlike some of us, who can't let go of the old dogmas."

"Tawfiq!" Firdaus silences her husband. "Have more respect for your mother."

Tawfiq is visibly upset. "I think I'll skip breakfast and go to work early today."

He claims his barbs against religion are "ironic," although Salma doesn't get the point. He has turned out like his father in taking the line of least resistance. Salma also wishes he would put up more of a fight against Firdaus.

Salma wishes Firdaus would ask Tawfiq to eat before he goes, but she doesn't. After he leaves, Salma and Firdaus don't know what to say to each other.

Salma can't make up her mind about Firdaus. She feels no such conflict toward Uzma and Asma. The girls are too direct. Americans are simple-hearted, but this can be a virtue when families have to solve their problems.

"I guess Arlene didn't get laid last night," Firdaus complains about the ruckus next door, provoking Salma, who looks ashamed. "The girls ought to get up by themselves. I shouldn't have to go through the song and dance every morning."

"Come quick!" shouts Firdaus, rousing Tawfiq from the kitchen the following Saturday afternoon. He's been nibbling at salad olovieh, and studying an intricate golf manual. "On CNN. They're showing a Pakistani businessman in handcuffs. The owner of a high-tech firm, in Orange County."

Tawfiq enters the living room reluctantly. "All this sensationalism, I tell you I don't care about it." Since the episode at fajr prayers, he's been irritable. The inability to let go of minor flare-ups is new. Tawfiq used to be like his father in quickly letting go of grudges. If Firdaus and Tawfiq don't watch out, Uzma and Asma will grow up to be sourpusses, unable to please any man.

Firdaus is undeterred by Tawfiq's disinterest. "Abba," she pins Sikander, who's watching the wide screen with glazed eyes, "don't you think Tawfiq should care? Who's next? This man on TV looks respectable enough. First they come for the Jews, then they come for the priests, then they come for the communists, and then for me. The old story." Firdaus was proud of her education at Cal State Fullerton.

Sikander stirs himself. "Tawfiq's been here for a solid quarter-century. I feel like a newcomer still. He knows what's best."

"There you go," says Tawfiq.

"Do you know the man?" Firdaus insists. "You must know him. They say he made aircraft spare parts for the DoD. Sounds suspiciously like the man of this household."

Salma wants to silence Firdaus's impetuosity. But another side of her admires her practicality. It's better to be anxious than to daydream.

Firdaus repeats, "Do you know the man?"

"Yeah, I know him. It's a small community. We all know each other."

"Daddy, did you notice his beard is white but his hair is black?" says Uzma, who with Asma has joined the adult audience of the CNN proceedings. "That makes him look odd."

"That's because he forgot to color his beard," says Asma.

"No, he didn't," says Uzma.

"Did too," says Asma.

"So is he a bad guy?" Firdaus interjects.

"Bad?" Tawfiq says. "How could he be bad? How could any of us be bad when we serve our country by making essential military parts at the cheapest cost, without having the work outsourced to desperate and untrustworthy Asian countries?"

"Must you always be sarcastic?" Firdaus wonders.

"It's better to be safe than sorry," Sikander says. "Why don't we let Tawfiq make the judgment? Is anything at stake for this family?"

"Do we even know the facts in the case?" Tawfiq says. "Why is this man being arrested? Maybe it's a mistake. They'll probably let him go by the end of the day. Hs reputation will have been ruined for good. That's too bad."

"The facts in the case," says Firdaus, "since you haven't been paying attention, are that he's being charged with assisting terrorists, of making illegal purchases and sales."

"Bah!" protests Tawfiq. "Asim! Poor Asim, obsessed with his golf handicap and impressing his new blonde wife, assisting terrorists! He'd be scared to death if he saw a terrorist in full regalia. Long beard and nasty smell and all."

"Tawfiq, your father has a beard," Salma says.

"Abba's beard is different," Tawfiq says.

"And weren't you his golf buddy?" Firdaus asks.

"Was?" says Tawfiq. "Am."

"You're choosing to be blind," says Firdaus. "Deaf and dumb, and blind." She gets up in a huff and strides to her room.

"I think I'll take the girls for a walk," Tawfiq announces, but doesn't move from his awkward perch on a stool in front of the television.

"Grandpa, I want you to be my horse," Asma says, climbing on Sikander's back. "Grandpa, ride around the house on your hands and knees, like Daddy used to do."

"You mean hooves, silly," Uzma says.

"Hands and knees," says Asma.

"Leave him alone," orders Tawfiq.

Now Tawfiq is watching television with interest. Asim's neighbors are aghast. The scared employees at his company refuse to comment. A picture of the skinny Asim when he was an engineering student at UC Irvine, with a wisp of a beard, is shown over and over.

Taking the girls out for walks is a duty Sikander likes to perform, but Tawfiq has been spending unusual amounts of time at home, especially on weekends. His calendar used to be filled with social events when he wasn't putting in twelve-hour days at the factory. Now, even though the war on terror is picking up, which should be a boon to companies like his, business hasn't kept pace with the ideal conditions.

Firdaus, changed into a miniskirt that shows off her fleshy legs and rump, comes stamping down the stairs. "Uzma, Asma, let's go."

Salma makes an effort to ignore Tawfiq's sullenness—he can't take his girls for a walk, because their mother has preempted him—and Sikander's equal apathy. "Firdaus, can I come with you? Please?"

Firdaus takes out the SUV keys from her pink purse. "Come, Amma, come. It'll be a girls' night out."

Salma doesn't bother changing out of her blue shalwar kameez and stringy dupatta for the outing. She slips into her comfortable old Bata slippers. Tawfiq looks like a lost boy as they leave the house.

"Where are we going?" Asma wants to know.

"I told you, ice cream at Bernaducci's," Firdaus says. "And we can shop on Melrose afterward."

"I want to watch *The Simpsons*," Asma whines.

"*The Simpsons* is not on tonight," Uzma says.

"Is too," says Asma.

"I hate that show," says Uzma. "Apu. Like there are any Indians who really talk like that."

"Be quiet." Firdaus is irritated. "Next you'll be watching *Buffy the Vampire Slayer*. How come you don't watch cartoons on Saturdays?"

"Mommy," Asma says, "*The Simpsons* is a cartoon show."

"It's an animated show for grown-ups," says Uzma.

"No more *Simpsons*," warns Firdaus.

A wise parent must exercise authority judiciously, Salma thinks, or else rebellion is guaranteed.

"Tawfiq wasn't always like this," laments Firdaus.

She makes good speed on the 210 and then the 10 freeway. Salma used to be afraid of Firdaus's careening turns, but now her heart doesn't flutter when Firdaus blindly barrels up a hill or misses falling into a ravine by inches.

"Tawfiq loves you," says Salma.

"Of course he does. Who else would love him like I do?"

If Salma were to say something too strong on behalf of Tawfiq, she would alienate Firdaus, so she only says, "Go easy on him."

Uzma and Asma, in the SUV's backseat, have a verbal game going on, the outcome of which will decide which of them gets to have the double fudge sundae at the ice-cream parlor in West Hollywood, whose European name Salma can never correctly pronounce.

"These Indian kids," says Firdaus, "always winning the spelling bees. Poor Americans, can't spell their own language."

"I bet no one in my class can spell Tehran," says Uzma.

"I can spell I-*ran*," says Asma. "I ran so hard I fell on Tehran," making it sound like "terrain."

"Very smart," says Firdaus, "and very unnecessary."

Both girls, especially Uzma with her light hair and fragile features, look vulnerable to Salma. They might grow up to be the type of women men take advantage of. And that swimsuit of Uzma's, which leaves nothing to the imagination, has got to go. If only she felt comfortable enough to talk to Firdaus about this. Firdaus doesn't want them to watch that harmless animated show, but lets Uzma put on makeup and take boys' calls, even if she claims it's only about homework.

More of Tawfiq's friends in the business are arrested. These events usually occur on Friday afternoons. The location is always some spotless business park in a city like Anaheim or Tustin, the name of the company never displayed on the building, the on-air reporter a breathless blonde having difficulty pronouncing the names of the principals, and the parade of stunned employees and associates colorless like Talmudic scholars, not traitors and assassins.

The family gathers more seriously around television. No one can feign disinterest any longer.

"Did you notice how they fit the same profile?" Firdaus asks.

"Profile?" Tawfiq is having trouble matching the law enforcement jargon with the banality of his profession.

"South Asian male in mid to late forties. The man has kept his Muslim name, even if it's a tongue-twister like Muzammil or Inzimam, rather than switch to Mo or Sam. He goes to Friday prayers at the Garden Grove mosque or the one downtown. He isn't known to have had zealous sympathies. His business partners are Americans so naïve and trusting they can't tell Iraq from Iran. He used to have business dealings with Kuwait or Abu Dhabi or some other Arab country back when it was okay to do so. He gave money to charities for Palestine, Afghanistan, Kashmir." Firdaus pauses for effect. "All of which reminds you of whom?"

"I do not go to Garden Grove or any mosque. And you leave out the crucial facts in the government's case. These men were all manufacturing highly sensitive materials. Technology that's banned for export, especially to countries on the watch list."

"Everything's sensitive when you're working for the DoD."

"Toilet seats? Wrenches?"

"You don't make toilet seats."

Sikander has been unnaturally quiet recently. "It wouldn't hurt to be cautious," he now counsels. "In the interest of pragmatism, I'll shave off my beard."

"You'll shave off your beard?" Salma gasps. "You said it's a bigger offense to shave it off than not have one in the first place."

"I can't see that having or not having a beard affects my religious standing. It's not as if I'm giving up praying and fasting."

"We can't let these ignorant people change our behavior," Salma objects. "They'll win. Without firing a shot, without knocking on our door."

Firdaus is quick to seize the opening. "I think Abba has the right idea. Why invite trouble? Girls," she addresses Uzma and Asma, "I think it's time for you to go to your rooms."

Neither of them obeys.

Asma starts playing with Sikander's beard. "Grandpa, are you going to use a big pair of scissors?"

"I don't know."

"Can I watch you?" says Asma. "Can we save the hair?"

"Gross," says Uzma.

"Hair keeps growing after you cut it off," Asma contemplates. "Like a dead person's nails."

"Amma has a point," Tawfiq argues. "We can't run around scared."

"Who's talking of running around scared?" Firdaus says. "These are difficult times. It's war time. We're taking evasive maneuvers."

"The Shi'a always were big on taqiyya," Tawfiq takes a dig at Firdaus's Iranian background. "Dissimulation."

"Blending in can't hurt," Sikander says. "I should stop wearing kurta pajama. No need to scare the shoppers at Ralphs. They're scared enough as it is by what they see on television."

"You're worried about the shoppers at Ralphs?" Salma wonders.

"If I were you," says Sikander, "I wouldn't make such a display of going out on the patio every morning and evening for prayers."

"Prayers, you're after my prayers now?"

"I'm not asking you to stop praying. Just do it inside."

"But the yard is so big. The fence is so high, no one can see."

"If they climb on a ladder, they can see."

"You mean Arlene?"

"Arlene is too busy screwing—oops, sorry girls—enjoying the scenery in the neighborhood to care one way or the other," says Firdaus.

"Arlene!" says Salma. "She's interested in the poet Agha Shahid Ali, who writes in English. I'd never heard of him, but still."

"Agha Shahid Ali is dead," Tawfiq says.

"We've wandered far from the subject," says Firdaus, "which is risk and threat assessment."

"Thank you—spoken like an insurance adjuster," Tawfiq says.

"Fine! You deal with your problems. But I'm not going to shed any tears when they came and handcuff you on a Friday afternoon, and your dear neighbor Arlene is your sole defender in the court of public opinion."

"What do you have against Arlene?" Tawfiq challenges Firdaus.

"If you weren't blind, you'd see."

"While we're at it, do you want me to change my name to Timmy?" Tawfiq grumbles.

"Ooh, Timmy Daddy," says Asma.

"I don't like that." Uzma makes a face

"There's a Timmy in my class," says Asma. "He pees when he's scared."

"What was there to be so scared of in class?" Firdaus wants to know.

"They were talking about Osama bin Laden," says Asma.

"Why were they talking about him in class?" asks Firdaus.

"Uzma's a sixth grader, for God's sake," says Tawfiq.

"We're talking about Asma here," says Firdaus. "Why were they talking about Osama?"

"Miss Harrison showed us a video of famous Los Angeles buildings," says Asma. "She said we used to worry about earthquakes. Now it's man-made disasters."

"They make fun of Asma's name in class," Uzma says.

"You never told me about that," Firdaus says.

"What do they say?" Tawfiq asks.

"They call her Asma-Osama," the older sister reveals.

Asma acts as if she didn't hear. "Wendy Simms said, what if the First Interstate building fell on top of the other towers? Everything toppled like dominoes."

"You talk about these scenarios in class?" says Firdaus.

"They're old enough to grasp the facts of the new world," says Tawfiq.

"What new world?"

"I'm sick of this pointless discussion," Tawfiq says. "I'm going to my room, and I don't want to be bothered."

Salma knows he'll be watching television. Standing outside the door, she's heard the voices of the local news broadcasters for hours on end. Tawfiq is becoming obsessed.

Next day, the *Los Angeles Times* and the *Orange County Register* both carry lead articles on how the South Asian community has maneuvered its way into acquiring control of strategic spare parts production for the DoD in both Southern and Northern California. No charges are made, but it's insinuated that this is something to worry about.

The following week, another Pakistani is arrested and paraded like a cheap criminal, as the family assembles around the television.

"Notice how they no longer care about the Iranians," says Tawfiq.

"For now," says Firdaus.

"If you look for Asians, you'll find them under every rock," Tawfiq says.

"True enough, you must admire their entrepreneurial spirit," Sikander says.

"Sometimes their entrepreneurial spirit gets too zealous," Firdaus says. "The few bad apples make life difficult for all of us."

Firdaus, who spent her teenage years in Beverly Hills, had a father who escaped both the Shah and Khomeini's wrath. He died of a heart attack at an early age, having made a killing in the construction business in Southern California. Salma wonders why Firdaus has always been so reticent about her family. The most she's been able to pick up is that Firdaus derides them as "assimilationists," which makes no sense when she thinks of how Firdaus is raising her own daughters.

"They haven't identified a single bad apple," Tawfiq disagrees.

As frequently as the suspects are picked up, they're also being released. If they were dangerous, wouldn't they be held until charges stuck? The releases are mentioned only as asides in the newspapers, unlike the front-page coverage given to the arrests.

"That doesn't mean there aren't bad guys out there," says Firdaus. "Maybe not the ones they're nabbing, but others with bad intentions."

"Bad intentions?" says Tawfiq. "That takes us back to the dark ages. The rule of law is founded on action, not intent."

"I'm not defending what's going on," says Firdaus.

"But you are."

"Am not." Firdaus sounds petulant like Asma.

Salma has heeded her husband, and stopped praying on the patio. She rarely goes out to play with the children in the yard, and if she can avoid it, skips the trips to Ralphs and other grocery stores. Although Sikander has never asked her to do so, she has switched to less alien-looking dresses, rather than her preferred shalwar kameez. The joy has gone out of life in America. It used to feel so different from India and Pakistan, all that she had known for her first fifty-five years. It's the same here now, the perpetual anxiety about the long arm of the authorities. The old ill ease is so forgotten she can't recall the correct way to respond.

She doesn't know if Arlene still raises a tempest in her garden every morning, but lately she hasn't seen her screeching around the neighborhood in her red sports car. Salma misses the routine of hearing Arlene next door, even if they rarely talked.

The family makes a trip to Lake Tahoe one weekend, and Salma is grateful to get away from the depressing television. It should be shut off altogether. Some of their old spirit returns away from Los Angeles, but relations among Sikander, Firdaus, and Tawfiq remain strained, as the unnameable fear encroaches. Tawfiq never lets Firdaus drive when he's with her, but on this journey he barely notices her hair-raising turns.

Arlene knocks on the door. There's no formal occasion for her to visit.

"Hello, would you like to come in?" says Salma.

"Ah, it's you, Amma. I just wanted to check if everything was all right."

"Everything's fine, just wonderful, why shouldn't it be? Please come in."

Arlene sits morosely in Tawfiq's favorite armchair, and stares at the television screen, which the family now watches without sound, without even the closed-captions.

"Lemonade, please?"

"I'd like a Bloody Mary, but it's too early, and the wrong household for that. Where's everyone anyway?"

"Off to work. And play." Firdaus and the children are at an arts and crafts festival at the Los Angeles Coliseum, and Sikander has started accompanying Tawfiq to work, even if he doesn't do much except hang around the factory floor, where he can't understand what's going on.

"The girls are okay?" Arlene looks worried.

"Uzma and Asma are fine."

"Good, good. You know, it's like I've never been inside this house."

Arlene admires the skylights, the Afghan and Iranian bric-a-brac lining the walls, the Central Asian hookahs that Tawfiq likes to show off to his golf and business friends, and Uzma's water colors of camels, deserts, harsh suns, pomegranates, objects she has no experience of.

"I always thought Uzma had artistic talent," Arlene says. "You can see it in how she talks. You ought to nurture that."

Arlene has been in Florida for a month, taking care of an elderly aunt with a broken hip and early-stage Alzheimer's. Without close relatives, the dreaded nursing home is inevitable for the aunt. Salma and the rest of the family hadn't known Arlene was away for so long.

"I seem to have missed out on a lot of excitement here. The arrests, the harassment, the bullshit going on in the name of security. What has this country come to! Where are people's rights, due process? Where's innocent until proven guilty?"

"Those are wonderful ideals. It's why people still line up outside American embassies all over the world. To have that taste of freedom."

"You know, you're not what I first thought you might be. No offense, but when I saw you praying in your traditional dress, I had a different idea about you. I just came to say, if you ever need someone to talk to in these difficult times, if I can help in any way, please knock on my door. This neighborhood, the school board—a lot of the people are conservative assholes. Excuse my language."

"We will."

"And please give my loving regards to Tawfiq. What a dear, sweet man. A model for his community, a credit to the Pakistani race. Just what we need, a hardworking, innocent man to smash the nasty stereotypes. The media in this country are so one-sided. They're assholes."

After Arlene's visit, Salma worries more about the girls than she has before. She looks at Uzma's naïve paintings in a different light. She wonders if there isn't a guilt-stricken side that she hasn't noticed.

Later that summer, Tawfiq comes home for lunch one day, which he never does. "I got a call from the FBI today," he blurts from the door.

Silence descends. Sikander, who hasn't gone to work because of a cold, assumes a glassy expression. Firdaus chews her nails, a habit Uzma chides her about.

"The FBI," Tawfiq repeats, sitting at the dining table.

The tasty lamb kuftes, Firdaus's specialty, steam in their plates, making Salma nauseous.

"Girls, go to your rooms," Firdaus says.

"No, they need to stay and listen," Tawfiq says.

"Daddy, the FBI only goes after drug dealers," Asma says.

"Be quiet," Uzma silences her little sister.

"So they were nice and polite, the three agents who talked to me one after the other, doing their best to reassure me."

"They've acquired manners," Firdaus says.

"We want to compliment you on the great work you do, and appreciate your strong roots in the community, they said. Community, my foot. I'm at the golf course. Do you see me doing any community work? They said, because of who you are, your work and ethnicity, if you notice anything suspicious, please call this number. This is not racial profiling, we want to assure you, this is just a preventive strategy. We're on your side one hundred percent, and wish to avoid any hint of discrimination, prejudice, etc."

Sikander is relieved. "Arey, that's all? It sounds wonderful. They're going out of their way to put our fears at rest."

Firdaus looks at Sikander with undisguised contempt, and for once Salma wishes she was from a generation who could do the same. She focuses her gaze on the revolting kuftes, wondering why Sikander has gone soft in the head again, after his short burst of pragmatic enthusiasm when he shaved off the beard and switched to Western clothing.

"If they make fun of your name again at school," Uzma tells her younger sister, "you can now go to the FBI. They're on our side." Uzma claps mockingly, then walks out to the patio.

Asma calls after her, "They only care about drug dealers."

"I think it's high time the girls had a dose of their own culture," Firdaus says.

"Culture!" Tawfiq exclaims. "You're the one who's always insisted they should know nothing of the language, the tradition, other than what they pick up in the normal course of things at school."

"Well, they're picking up the wrong kinds of things. They need to know. Their race, where they come from. We carry the genes of a civilization thousands of years old."

"When Europeans were living like barbarians in caves, Persians already had a fine civilization going, with arts and music and theater," Tawfiq says.

"Exactly," says Firdaus.

"Mommy, did the Ayatollah have four wives? One of them nine years old?" Asma takes her place in Firdaus's lap, playing with her fleshy chin.

"Who told you that?" Firdaus says.

"An Iranian boy at school," Asma says. "He's so dumb he was held back a grade."

"How come I don't know about him?" Firdaus says. "Who're his parents?"

"I don't know," Asma cowers.

"So what am I supposed to do now?" Tawfiq says.

Despite the tension, for the first time Salma sees what has made the relationship tick. Firdaus has some inner strength that can't be messed with. Tawfiq is more uneven. When he's down, Firdaus picks him up, in her own strange way. She does it before Tawfiq calls for it, their mutual barbs aside. But Firdaus seems to have retreated to a new distance. She looks older, while Asma, still in her lap, seems to have become infantile.

"I'm sorry, I can't help you with what you have to do," Firdaus says. "No one can. It's a dangerous business you're in. Sensitive technology, DoD, where the big money is. And the big risks."

"They're not shooting at us in the streets," Sikander says. "We're free to come and go as we please. There's nothing to do."

"Why do Sikhs cover their beards with plastic, Mommy?" Asma says.

"I don't know," says Firdaus. "I wish I'd finished my master's degree."

"Then I could have referred the FBI to my educated wife," says Tawfiq. "You could have told them about Kierkegaard and Heidegger. They would have asked you if there's anything anti-American about existentialism."

One of Tawfiq's friends calls that evening to relate a similar call he got from the FBI. When he's through with the conversation, Tawfiq explains, "Bilal has shipped off Mehreen to Pakistan."

"She's only twelve," says Firdaus.

"Uzma's age," says Tawfiq.

"My girls aren't going anywhere."

"Bilal's boy will stay in California."

Salma sees exhaustion come over Firdaus's face. This new fight will linger.

Later, shattering the communal silence, Tawfiq switches from the omnipresent CNN to a Lakers playoff game. He seems to enjoy it, shouting like a madman whenever Kobe and Shaq make easy baskets.

THEY STAND
AND
SERVE TOO

L al Kishan Singh walked on the deck of the ocean liner *Edward*, grateful to make out Alexandria on the coastline. The ship was quiet now, but in less than an hour the early-rising army officers and civil servants would rouse their wives and children to make the most of their first stop along the Mediterranean, as though months or years in India hadn't come near to satisfying their appetite for the new and disturbing. Colonel Abercrombie, Singh's master when he was eighteen and on board the venerable *Victoria*, Singh's first assignment, used to walk three miles on the ship every dawn. This was one of the colonel's habits Singh had picked up. Singh also took care to speak to servants lower on the totem pole than himself with intense respect, and treat the ladies with the delicacy they deserved.

From a distance, all the cities dotting the sea in Asia and Africa looked similarly haphazard, sprung without premeditation. Alexandria was memorable for the profusion of huts made of red-baked clay that lined the steep hill known as Barclays Point. Singh looked forward to the arrival on deck of Hamid, the fried fish vendor. Hamid had told him that to please the British he bought special Italian herbs and spices from a shop in Alexandria, intensifying the normally bland flavor of fish favored by native Egyptians. Before Hamid, it was his father, and before him, his father's father, who carried a special license to cater fish to the British on their ships. In twenty years of serving a bewildering variety of masters aboard British ships, Singh had gotten to know the cast of characters allowed to come on board along various stops to serve the rulers pretty well. At times, he was called on by a lord or lady to interpret some local to their satisfaction, although they could easily have done the job better with their own superior knowledge of other languages.

He could tell that Lady Cameroon, the dowager with a retinue of nephews she had recruited on this journey to look over her late husband's estates near Rangoon with a view to taking them over, would not want to set foot in Alexandria, while they lay at anchor for a day or so. Neither would Lady Simons, who was by far the most attractive woman on board, wooed by everyone from aging majors and colonels retailing grand old war stories to brash young coffee and cotton traders with money on their minds. Lady Cameroon would stay on ship because she was the type who preferred to reign in her own milieu, taking care to carve out an area of influence where no other deity could enter. And Lady Simons would stay because it would be inexcusable for her to spread the glow of her beauty among an unsophisticated audience. He would stay because he wasn't allowed to leave ship at any time, on pain of immediate dismissal.

"Singh, you ruffian, up with the first rays of sun, are you?"

With that greeting, he got a hearty slap on the back. It was William, Lady Cameroon's youngest nephew, the least formal of the lot, taking a leave from Oxford because he couldn't stand the constant drumbeat of war from men who hadn't done a day's hard work in their lives, men who were ready to die as the necessary cost of defending England against the rising German menace. "Once in a century is enough," they used to say about global conflagrations, yet William wanted nothing more than to join the army rather than listen to the blowhards go on and on about honorable patriotism. Lady Cameroon was threatening to cut William off, let alone give him a chance at the Burmese estates, unless he finished out Oxford. William was an honest man, but his backslapping and offers to buy Singh drinks made him uncomfortable. Young William didn't understand the rules; at his age he could get away with it, but soon he would get in trouble— and get an unwitting participant like Singh in greater trouble.

"Sahib, yes, it is a clear morning," Singh said, trying to act deferential. "Does Lady Cameroon wish to go to Alexandria, to see the sights and shop for fabrics? Egyptian cotton, fine, fine cotton."

"The old bird was passed out at four in the morning— the brandy is too strong for her, you know—so I doubt it," said William. "I say, is that a bloody lark? It's the only bird we've seen in days. Well, what say you we go and get some ripping hot coffee and hunt for ancient manuscripts once we reach the city, hey?"

William seemed to be the only one around not to know the rule about Indian servants on ships not being allowed to disembark at ports. Singh found it incomprehensible that William would want to chat him up rather than hang around people of his own class and status. Also, insulting.

"Sahib, please, I must stay on the ship. I am needed in the middle of the morning, the middle of the afternoon, the middle of the night."

"As you wish, old chap, but I must say you're beginning to look a little like that starving lark, for lack of walking around on firm ground, I'd hazard. Terra firma, terra incognita, hey. The great undiscovered lands of the world, at your fingertips, your heels I should say, and you prefer to perambulate this doddering ship at strange hours of the morning and night. Oh well, it takes all kinds, as Lady Cameroon would say, unmercifully, I might add."

Singh felt uneasy even after William was gone. The lone lark, so far out from land, was not a good sign. Over the years, after spending so much time with the British, he had managed to let go of most of his superstitions. If a cat refused food when it looked hungry, he no longer stayed inside the cabin that day except at mealtimes, when his presence was indispensable. But certain myths had stayed with him, despite Englishmen pooh-poohing the Hindoos and Mohammedans for their fear of the new, their anxiety about the future. Lady Cameroon's skin was thick and wrinkled, probably because of all the heavy drinking, but you could still see that she must have been a beautiful young woman. They mocked him for taking cues from animals and insects, but they wanted to forget their own sorrows through drink.

This particular journey to London was one of the rare times he was not assigned to serve a specific master, since there seemed to be an oversupply of personal servants available on short-term contract in Bombay this year. But Captain Fawcett couldn't imagine sailing for England without Singh on board; Singh had been asked to serve for half the normal pay, and he gladly accepted. He didn't like fraternizing with the young pups who seemed to be the outcome of a recruiting frenzy, as if seafaring were suddenly an adventurous man's ticket to happiness. The new guys acted not so much as servants but consorts, daring to look their masters straight in the eye, and laughing at their jokes; this arrogance could have nothing but unfortunate results. Singh wanted no part of it; when the day of reckoning arrived, and the guns went off and blood ran in the streets, he hoped he would be far away from the sight.

Many of the usual masters who sought him out on their journeys back home to England were staying in India this year; as bad as things were in Europe, the situation in India was no less fraught with danger. An explosion was awaited at any moment; the world was on edge. Even sleepy Alexandria, if you looked carefully, now that *Edward* was close to landing, was abuzz with nervousness, a certain speeded-up movement that should scare men of wit and judgment. The number of mangy dogs who sniffed hungrily at visitors' ankles had multiplied many times over since the last visit.

The families were usually the first to disembark, and today was no exception; the single people took their time. Singh took up position at one of the ship's binoculars. From there, he could watch the British valets acting as if they understood every word of Arabic, pretending to find bargains for their lords and ladies. Captain Fawcett was entertaining Lady Diana Dalrymple, nineteen and famished for attention. He had been wrong: both Lady Cameroon and Lady Simons left the ship, and fluttered about in the streets, their spotless white dresses and red parasols standing out, like angels dispensing unwarranted kindness. You felt that their lightest touch on a suffering leper's or consumptive's head might revive the patient.

"Singh, I'd like you to be in attendance on Lady Dalrymple for the rest of the day," Captain Fawcett interrupted his reverie. "My man Lloyd has gone ashore to do some shopping for me. More of his own, I imagine." It was well-known that the British servants smuggled into England all sorts of valuable items that in the normal course of trade would have been difficult to obtain. This was casually accepted by the officer class as a necessary supplement to the servants' income.

"Yes, Captain," Singh said.

"Pretty sight you have of the ladies through these binoculars, hey? You might call it occult skirt chasing."

"At your service, Captain," Singh said, confused.

Before he could attend to Lady Dalrymple, Hamid arrived on board with his two baskets of spicy fish. "It's the last year I'm doing this," Hamid complained.

"Hamid, my friend, you say this every year."

"This year I mean it."

"What will you do instead?"

"I have to bribe the magistrate too much for the license. There are fifty young fish-sellers eager to take my place. They think it would be some bonanza of profits for them, if they could only serve the British on board the ship rather than on land alone. You and I know it's not true."

"Who knows what is true and what is not true."

"What do you mean by that?" Hamid sputtered. "The British are stingy, and they treat you like animals."

"That is false. The British never treated me poorly."

"What world are you living in?"

Singh touched Hamid on the shoulder to calm him down, much as William had surprised him this morning. "Please, not so loud."

"I'll be as loud as I want to be. Things aren't the same anymore, you don't understand that. We want to be free people, independent of the British, the French, the Germans, all the white races. Their time has come and gone. I read the newspapers carefully. The situation in Europe will change everything, you watch. Let them fight and kill each other, and we'll gain from their weakness."

Singh felt exhausted. He wanted no more of these political fantasies. He could see Lady Dalrymple quietly waiting for him twenty feet away. She was giving Singh time to finish his feverish conversation with Hamid. Here she was, being so polite, as if she were the servant and he the master, and Hamid was talking about blood and revolution.

"I must go. The lady is waiting."

He shook hands with Hamid with less than his usual ardor. They said that a library had been burned long ago in Alexandria. He could understand the passion of whoever had done it. The people here were probably too easily inflamed by the wrong books.

"Your ladyship," Singh said, bowing deeply.

Lady Dalrymple turned out to be a chatterbox. "Singh, Captain Fawcett tells me you're a fine judge of character. What do you think of William, Lady Cameroon's young nephew?" Without waiting for Singh's answer, Lady

Dalrymple continued: "I have little hesitation in telling you that I like the young man. My mother actually spotted him at a ball last year, where the Prime Minister was in attendance. I have no desire to be married to some swashbuckling hunter type who makes war with Indian princes and forces me to spend the summers in the Himalayas. I want to be close to home. Can you see how I love England and don't want to spend my life abroad in some godforsaken place? You must love India, must you not?"

Singh said, bowing again, "Your ladyship, I love India very much."

"Then you see my point, of course. William has studiously avoided me, or maybe he's as scared of Lady Cameroon as I am. She'd be totally against the match, you see. We're not exactly in their league. Will you do me a favor and pass along this note to William the next time you see him? I'd be much obliged."

"Yes, your ladyship."

"There's that awful Captain Fawcett ogling me. I daresay he has no respect for his wife and little girl. It's so unprofessional, plying me with drinks early in the day. For heaven's sake, am I some tramp? But Singh, you must do me a favor. Could you fetch me from Sultan Street in the old section of Alexandria some local souvenir, a pipe or hookah, something recovered from the pyramids, for a gift to William? My mother would be upset if I disembarked here. Under no circumstances in Egypt, she'd warned me. India is fine, but not Egypt. You see, she'd had her purse stolen thirty years ago in this very city, and she laments it to this day. I don't think all natives are cunning and inscrutable, but who can change the mind of old people? It's not as if she's omniscient and watching me, but I don't like to disobey once I've given my word."

"Your ladyship, I am not allowed to go ashore."

"Oh, you're not?" Lady Dalrymple thought for a moment. "Because they're afraid you'll run away or something? I can see if they'd put that rule in place for England, but why would an Indian want to escape to Egypt? That makes no sense. I'll talk to Captain Fawcett about it."

"Please, your ladyship, please, you must not talk to anyone about it. This is the way it is."

She looked disconcerted. "Oh well," she sighed, "I guess I'll ask Captain Fawcett to accompany me then. I have no choice. All the other servants, I can't trust them for a moment. They tell tales, I think."

"There is much discretion here," Singh said, not sure what he was referring to.

Singh always tried to stay aware of what was happening on the ship as a whole, rather than attending only to the master or mistress he was serving at the moment. Captain Fawcett had taken up with another lovely thing, but no doubt he would drop her as soon as Lady Dalrymple approached him. He was genuinely sorry he couldn't be of more help to her, but perhaps it was all for the best. It was preferable not to get mixed up in affairs of the heart. He could tell that Hamid was having a miserable selling day. He left ship with almost the full load of fish he came with.

Later in the day, before the sun set, Singh observed a commotion on the wharf. A young British sailor—one of those who ended up on a luxury ship like *Edward* through some fortuitous turn, rather than sailing on a decrepit ship meant for his kind—had insulted a fortune-telling dervish for committing fraud. The sailor seized the dervish's earnings for the day, and it took a threatening mob to end his drunken speech on behalf of the integrity of the British shopkeeper, who knew how to earn his money by the sweat of his brow instead of pretending to be in touch with oracles and gods.

Singh was troubled that things might never be the same again. A violent bloody sun, reddening the sky with its lust and hunger, unusual for these parts, at last put an end to the day. Passingly, he hoped that Lady Cameroon would force young William to be the one to take up the Burmese estates; then he thought of the way William fondly touched him on the back and withdrew his ill wish.

THEY STAND AND SERVE TOO

Anis Shivani

ACKNOWLEDGMENTS

Thanks to the editors of the following journals in which the stories in this book were first published:

- "The Abscess of the World," *Other Voices*
- "The Censor," *Nimrod: International Journal of Poetry and Prose*
- "Dowry," *Phoebe: Journal of Feminist Scholarship, Theory, and Aesthetics*
- "The Fifth Lash," *Asia Literary Review*
- "Growing Up Blind, in a Hotly Contested State," *Flyway: A Literary Review*
- "The House on Bahadur Shah Zafar Road," *Crazyhorse*
- "In the Shade of the Wavering Palms," *Weber Studies*
- "Jealousy," *Confrontation*
- "Love in a Time of Communication," *Xavier Review*
- "The Rug Seller's Daughter," *Nassau Review*
- "They Stand and Serve Too," *The Dalhousie Review*
- "What It's Like to Be a Stranger in Your Own Home," *turnrow*

My thanks to Gina Frangello, Francine Rhingold, Chris Wood, Tim Cribb, Steve Pett, Mark Powell, Brad L. Roghaar, Martin Tucker, Richard Collins, Paul Doyle, Robert M. Martin, and Bill Ryan for publishing these stories in their original form. My gratitude also goes to Eric Miles Williamson, Richard Burgin, Jay Parini, Gary Heidt, Kevin Prufer, and George Braziller for their support in the early years of my career. A special thanks to Ali Eteraz for all his help. For their support of this book, special gratitude to Murzban Shroff, George Singleton, Gina Ochsner, Ron Rash, Aamer Hussein, and Ali Sethi. Thanks above all to Chad Prevost, Ryan G. Van Cleave, and Jamie Iredell for believing in this book. My lovely wife Mehnaaz stood with me as full partner during the years of pain and anxiety—but also innocence and infinity—when these stories were written. I couldn't have done it without her.

Anis Shivani's debut book, *Anatolia and Other Stories*, was long-listed for the 2010 Frank O'Connor Short Story Award, and included a Pushcart Special Mention story. A debut book of criticism, *Against the Workshop: Provocations, Polemics, and Controversies*, was published in 2011 by Texas Review Press, and a debut book of poetry, *My Tranquil War and Other Poems*, was published by New York Quarterly Books in 2012. Anis's fiction, poetry, criticism, and interviews are regularly published in the *Georgia Review*, *Southwest Review*, *Iowa Review*, *Boston Review*, *Threepenny Review*, *Antioch Review*, *Michigan Quarterly Review*, *Agni*, *Denver Quarterly*, *Fence*, *Subtropics*, *Times Literary Supplement*, *London Magazine*, *Meanjin*, *Cambridge Quarterly*, and others. A member of the National Book Critics Circle, and the winner of a 2012 Pushcart Prize, he publishes criticism in many newspapers and magazines. Anis's recently finished novel is called *Karachi Raj*, and he is at work on a new novel called *Abruzzi, 1936*. He lives in Houston, and studied at Harvard College.